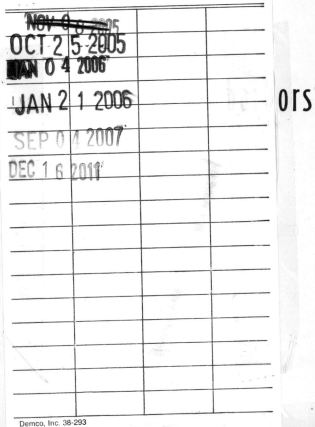

DATE DUE

~~NOV 0 8 2005~~		
OCT 2 5 2005		
JAN 0 4 2006		
JAN 2 1 2006		
SEP 0 4 2007		
DEC 1 6 2011		

Demco, Inc. 38-293

ors

kate benson

two harbors

a harvest original
harcourt, inc.

orlando   austin   new york   san diego   toronto   london www.HarcourtBooks.com

Excerpt from "How to Sleep" from *Collected Poems* by Phillip Larkin. Copyright © 1988, 2003 by the Estate of Phillip Larkin. Reprinted by permission of Farrar, Straus and Giroux, LLC, and Faber and Faber Ltd.

Library of Congress Cataloging-in-Publication Data
Benson, Kate.
Two Harbors/Kate Benson. — 1st ed.
p.   cm.
"A Harvest Original."
1. Minnesota — Fiction. 2. Loss (Psychology) — Fiction.
3. Abandoned children — Fiction. 4. Maternal deprivation — Fiction.
5. Mothers and daughters — Fiction. 6. Hollywood (Los Angeles, Calif.) — Fiction.   I. Title.
PS3602.E695T88   2005   2005002406
ISBN-13: 978-0156-03124-0   ISBN-10: 0-15-603124-8

Text set in Electra
Designed by Linda Lockowitz

Printed in the United States of America
First edition
K J I H G F E D C B A

For my family

Child in the womb,
Or saint on a tomb—
Which way shall I lie
To fall asleep?

—PHILLIP LARKIN,
"How to Sleep"

part one

dream of the fall

A mother takes her daughter's hand and leads her underwater.

Blue. Cold, and shimmering through the dark. In reality, just the high school gym—but with the lights dimmed to a wintry sparkle, poster-board seaweed reaching up the walls, it's easy to pretend you've fallen into something magical. Today is the end of Winter Frolic, the annual Two Harbors fair. The theme this year, "Beneath the Ice," has sunk the town past the solid surface of Lake Superior to an arctic, exotic underworld, and the daughter looks around with a ten-year-old's appreciative awe: silver balloons in bubbly bursts, wispy blue streamers across the windows. The icy facade of those watery lights. Hand-cut paper snowflakes defy the laws of physics and shed their twinkling glitter across the hardwood bed of the lake. And in the middle of the basketball court, rising up like the Atlantis of the north shore, a gigantic white float waits for the coronation of the Winter Royalty, its red thrones like sunken hearts all in a row.

It's the last and most important event before the all-town chili dinner; the daughter savors every breath and detail of this, her first and last year as a member of the court. They move through the crowds, past bleachers packed with students, parents, grandparents, neighbors, the whole town awaiting the selection of those girls who will become, briefly yet brightly, minor celebrities in their respective schools.

"When I was crowned," the mother whispers in her ear, "they put my picture in the paper. Front page. There were boys from all over calling the editors for my number—Silver Bay, Beaver Bay. These twin brothers in Duluth."

"Dad, too?"

"Relentlessly. Endlessly." She sighs. "Endlessly. That's when they were saying I should take my chances in Hollywood."

The mother was the Winter Queen in her senior year of high school. She still has the crown; some of the fake diamonds are missing now. The daughter is not allowed to wear it, though she sneaks into her mother's closet sometimes and becomes, in secret, a captive princess, waiting for someone to find her and rescue her and fall tragically in love.

"Just remember not to cry if they crown someone else princess," the mother whispers. "The odds are against you, so don't get your hopes up."

Pretend you are a princess inside, secretly. I'm the only one who knows.

The daughter nods, heart swollen with love or fear or the familiar knot of both. She squeezes her mother's hand, adjusts her shimmering dress nervously as they approach the rest of the "10 and under" court waiting near the float.

"Blue as your eyes," observes Mrs. Simmons from nearby, pulling a little too hard on the sleeve of her dress. The daughter looks down modestly. "Just look at you. Seems like yesterday your mama was up there and *her* mama was watching. What do they call it—succession?"

"The royal family," someone says.

The mother pulls her hand away from an ever-tightening grip. "Let's not count our chickens."

"Boy, does she look like you, Lila. Just the spitting image." Mrs. Simmons shows her teeth, gapped and grayish and sharp if you're looking up at them. There are murmurs of agreement from the crowd.

"Really," the mother says, "she takes after her father's side."

The women slip away while the daughter eyes her competition: Missy Norris, plump and shy, but with the advantages of dimples and naturally curly hair; Anna Krumm, those long dark tangles and pink glasses, no chance in hell; Ellie, to whom she sidles up, although today there is a strain here, a competitiveness they've never felt before as best friends. And looking down upon them all, the tallest girl in the fourth-grade class: Stacie Simmons, the undisputed favorite for the crown.

"We got my dress at the Mall of America," she is telling a gaggle of idolizing third-graders. "It's only been open a year, but I've been there thirteen times already."

"Thirteen times," murmurs an admirer.

"Maybe twelve."

"After this," Ellie whispers, oblivious to the other girls, "we can sneak to the sledding hill. My sister told me the middle school boys go there after Winter Frolic. Like, without their parents."

"My mom won't let me," the daughter whispers.

"So don't tell."

She shrugs, distracted, the buzz of the wait wearing her down. She is watching her mother flutter nervously to and from various groups of neighbors and parents; she is watching a change come over her, but not as it usually does. Usually the mother slips into a new role like a negligee: one smooth, easy motion over the head, arms stretched up and out and reaching as a calmness slides over her face, her body, all of her floating away into something soft. But today, she wanders, chatters loud and ungracefully, pats her hair and widens her eyes and laughs without meaning it. It's as if her role of the moment is one of the high school girls clustered across the gym, fawning over each other and looking anxiously beautiful. Sometimes the daughter sees her mother looking at those girls with a face like a damp sponge, wilted and old and sagging in the corners.

"What are you staring at?" Ellie whispers, annoyed. Ellie is thinking of a first kiss at the edge of the sledding hill, a boy's pink lips blooming out of the snow—frightening, thrilling. She wants company in the fantasy.

"Nothing," says the daughter quickly. "How do I look?" She turns for her friend, who turns for her, and both praise the other, selflessly but secretly crossing fingers, as the most deserving of the coveted crown.

Like a princess, says her mother's voice, a tickle in the ear—a smile. *Like the most beautiful princess in the world,* though she's still halfway across the gym with the high school girls; harder to pretend, now, that she's really saying the words.

"Ladies and Gentlemen, may I have your attention..."

They form lines like lacy soldiers, barricaded in tulle. The women observe, proud commanders, as each watches her ticket to PTA fame march past. Last one in the line, the daughter snags her mother's eye. But it skitters away like a wounded bird, and before she can catch it again they are clustered in a blinding blue spotlight, the high school girls gliding in behind them.

She can't see the crowds now. She can't see anything except the squinting brightness, like falling into a cavern of light. Lonely.

Just pretend, the daughter hears then, *that you're a movie star.* She closes her eyes. *The Academy Awards. Red carpet, wide smile. Don't let your teeth stick.* A fluttery feeling rising up in her chest as the lights and the eyes and the cameras soak in—*a beautiful actress, just like your mom,* and the change comes over her, finally. She is another person now, a person who knows what to do in a light this bright, *there you go, you got it,* the rhythm of applause quivering up through her feet, and with her eyes closed it's easy to imagine her mother nearby, whispering so quietly that only she can hear it:

Look at all the people who love you....

And something else is changing. The world coming into focus, everyone's eyes swinging into hers; she looks back fearlessly but blankly, and it takes the handshake of the mayor, the icicle glint of the crown in her face, the astonished expression of Stacie Simmons twisting up beside her for the daughter to realize it's her own name they have called—that she has, for the first time in her life, become her mother.

And here's the crucial moment. A chance, a brief chance, that the dream will turn out differently this time. That they will place it on her head, a year's worth of popularity, and she will ascend the winding stairs of that float (*the tallest*, bragged the mayor, *in Winter Frolic history*), and when she takes the throne beside a newly crowned queen (king and prince as well, but who cares about the boys at this point), she will look down and find her mother in the crowd and see it in her smile and it will be the happy ending she's always wanted: *I'm so proud of you.*

Except that's not how it goes, not this time or ever. As she nears those stairs and the moment of ascension, her mother's voice rises above the applause—"Oh God, oh God, please, *no!*" And she feels the embrace from behind before she understands it, loving and wrenching all at once: "Not again, not *you*," yanking her back from the float, the collapse of her body as the crown flies off, away into the light and then—

Stillness. A sudden and painful calm as they lie there together on the gymnasium floor. The town stares, the mother cries. She reaches for her daughter, grabs her, pulls her close: "I knew," she sobs, the words like frenzied hiccups. "I'm sorry, baby, but I knew, could see it, I could *see* it—the float falling in and everything piling up on top of you and I knew it, baby, knew what was going to happen—" And she holds her tighter, both of them on their knees now, and all of the eyes, and the waiting.

The squeezing, the silence, runs pins and needles through the daughter, but she doesn't really mind. She hasn't felt this alive for as long as she can remember, this safe and unafraid.

She is thinking, simply, quietly, pulling in the fairy-tale thrill of it: *I've been rescued.*

"I'm so sorry," the mother whispers, "so sorry. I didn't mean to see it," and the daughter holds her face in those small, cool hands, wipes the mother's tears away with slow, careful strokes. She doesn't understand, and she doesn't care. She doesn't hear the whispers of the town surging around her and pressing in—*jealous…nervous…crazy, do you think?*—doesn't even notice when Stacie Simmons surreptitiously picks the crown up off the floor and hides it underneath her dress. She is aware only of her mother's eyes, the way they're looking at her right now: about to look away and down, ashamed, humiliated and forever dethroned, but not yet. Right now they're like twin pools to crash into and beneath—their frantic blue, the deep-sea sink of finally, finally being seen.

Like drowning. Hopelessly, beautifully. It's what I feel every time I wake up: that unfathomable weight, the pressure of memory, down and down and down beneath the darker leagues of love.

basements

The other story starts here, nine years later, in the cool gray corners of our basement. The right place for a mystery to start: one dirt-crusted window, filmy slice of sunlight filling the corner, a milky afterglow and the packed-away smell of dust. Silence. In the dark, objects are undefined, edges blurred, the way the world looks in the periphery of vision — one shadow blending into the next until you're not sure where things end and begin.

A ghost story. It has the right feeling.

I come down here one last time before I leave. I don't really know why; I haven't been down since she's been gone, kind of an unspoken agreement between Dad and me. But walking through the kitchen this morning, it hit me suddenly, sharply, what was waiting beneath my feet as I moved across the linoleum. The emptiness I took for granted all this time, blindly believing that someday she would come back to fill it, never thinking I'd be leaving home before it happened — and the uncomfortable thought, then, that I've forgotten something, a missed clue, a familiar quickening like maybe I'm letting a memory slip past—

They hit me like that sometimes. Those panicky last-chance moments.

So I sneak down after I've packed my bags, tentative on the soft wooden steps and their telltale creaks, and I stand in the patch of yellow light and breathe it in deep, that thick and warmish mustiness of a childhood packed away. I listen to my father's footsteps groan heavily across the ceiling and remember: this is just the way it used to be. My father above like distant thunder and the two of us here in this corner of the basement, back when the shadows weren't so fuzzy, soft-ened and staled with time like bread. I can close my eyes and picture, briefly, images as stuttered as photographs or stills from a movie:

Her face. Turning inward, turning away, slice of my own but deepened with the fringe of wrinkles and something sadly beautiful, the face they said could make it big and never did.

Her hair. Long for a mother, and gold, and glistening. How it brushed my neck once in a love scene, eyes so close to mine I could see my body floating, doubled, inside: *This is when we would kiss, if you were the actor.*

Her hands, soft white fingers clawing dramatically at the air as we practiced drowning—the art, she said, of visualiza-tion, and the hardest thing to visualize is death—until my own hand slipped into hers, squeezed, and we bowed to an imaginary applause. The empty room whatever we made of it: that was the magic she taught me.

You can be anything. You can be anyone.

I used to think of these moments often, after she'd left and the shock had worn off and it was just me and Dad. By then the two of us made sense. That is, it wasn't just me and Dad and this weird in-between time, waiting, like she was going to come breezing back from the store any moment, *Sorry I took so long*, and it would be the three of us again— after that mostly wore off, I used to remember these moments and think maybe I had dreamt them. They had that sugary glaze like good dreams do, that gauzy time-stop that's all you can catch as you wake up. But standing here in this lemony light, my eyes adjusting and the long-dead room slowly brightening, it feels real enough—as if I've stepped into the movie of my own life and everything is starting to flush with color, things are only now beginning to make sense—lights, camera, and action—

Outside, honking. Probably the cab; I listen for the yell of my father, but it doesn't come. So for a moment, desperate to feel something other than numbness, than nothing, I open my mouth and my eyes and my lungs, breathe in this filtered, summery light as if to taste it, hold it on my tongue and swallow and bring it, somehow, with me. Just in case. And when I hear him calling—"*Casey? Your cab*"—I turn and something is different, something has come alive in this room: years of dust uplifted by my movement and hazing the space in front of me. The sun bleaches the air a trembling, translucent white, and for a moment, I don't move, don't breathe. I wait for it to fall back into place. But it just hangs there, a minor chord before the resolution, and when I reach the stairs and look back, it's still suspended, without release: a held breath, a sigh that doesn't come.

———

We don't go down there anymore.

It was late. One of our first dates, just a few months ago now, spring still struggling to break through crusts of ice. We'd been out dancing, drinking, enough for me to feel the buzz like a fallen wire, hot and dangerous and coiling with energy as we stumbled through my front door. Laughing, *shhh, my dad,* the flush of the night in our faces and our mouths, warm soft kisses and Dex's hands, *shhh,* rough hands from working on the docks, but they felt so nice. And the way his eyes stammered into mine and away, like they were afraid but not really, his big arms around me—when suddenly he reached for the doorknob and it took me a minute to realize that was my whole hidden past he was peering down into.

"No, wait—" And the slam of the basement door louder than I meant it.

"Why?" Dex whispered. A pause, uncertain, then his breath against my neck, smiling: "Don't you want to go someplace quiet?"

I felt the words running together in my mind, the slurring of distractions against my skin; I leaned my head back. "We don't go down there anymore."

"How come?"

"It's late."

"Buried treasure? Evil stepmother?"

Laughing, low, quiet: "Dead bodies."

"Kinky."

And I laughed louder, pushed him away. "Just a mess," I said. "You should go home anyway."

But he didn't leave for a long time. He just kissed me there against that door, patient kisses like he was waiting for me to change my mind. No idea that I'd already escaped the danger of his lips and his voice and his wide, warm hands, crawled into myself and let the right role take over: *You are cool, calm. You are on the ground. You are not the kind of girl who falls for someone without looking*, and eventually, he gave up for the night and just held me close.

"Skeletons," he whispered against my hair, "in the closet. Skeletons in the basement. What have you got buried in that head of yours?"

"Why doesn't Daddy ever come down here?"

I asked her once and she didn't answer, not until I asked again and she said, "Because he's jealous. Because he doesn't like our plays."

"He liked them before."

"No. He never liked them." She looked down at the costume she was mending, bright glints of sequins on faded black cotton. "He never wanted me to be an actress." Her voice deeper now, softer, but I couldn't tell if she was angry or sad. Then she looked back up, hair falling away from her face, and smiled as if I'd said something surprising. "Should we see if we can get him down here?"

"How?"

"We'll be hostages. You pretend someone's got a gun to your head. How do you feel, what are you going to do?"

She poked the needle into the fabric and leaned forward. I just looked at her and tried to put it into my face, the sick feeling in my stomach that was partly from imagining a gun, but mostly from her smile that wouldn't go away, the way she wasn't quite meeting my eyes. She was imagining the gun, too, I figured, only she wasn't afraid. She looked, for a moment, hopeful. She looked up the stairs at the closed door.

Then she opened her mouth and her scream blew out of it like a siren, so loud I put my hands over my ears, and she grabbed my shoulders and screamed into my face until I started screaming too and we screamed like that together until our voices began to fray at the ends. But he didn't come down. And when we went up to lunch, dizzy and thirsty, there he was at the kitchen table: didn't say anything, just gave her this look. The sort of tired and helpless look he's giving me now, so many years later, from the top of the stairs, my suitcase in his hand and that same sadness in his eyes. Like *Why are you doing this to me?*

"Your cab's here," he says quietly, and I start climbing. I reach the top step and wait for him to move out of the way, but he just clears his throat and shifts his feet awkwardly. "I said you'd be a few minutes."

"Fine."

"I was thinking we might have a quick talk." His voice is careful, measured, light on the words but heavier behind them, and I can tell the fight last night shifted something between us. Knocked it out of place so now we're balancing against each other without knowing for certain where the other is standing.

"So talk," I tell him, wincing inside at my own words— *Just remember it's easier this way, remember he deserves this . . .*

He looks past my shoulder, nods at the gaping darkness behind me. "Did you find anything?"

I don't answer.

"I packed away some of her stuff down there. Thought you might be looking."

Just stare at him and try not to notice the hurt in his face, the sting of my silence.

"Honey," he says, and stops. He looks down at me, tired, beaten. "I promise that's the whole story, Casey. It's everything."

I tell him, "Yes, it is."

"I did my best."

"We already talked about this," I mumble, reaching to take the suitcase. He pulls back a bit and we freeze like that, both our hands on the fake-leather handle.

"I'm sorry," he says. "I am. But I can only say it so many times."

And I feel my resolve start to slip inside me, softening and collapsing into itself until I look away and tell him quietly, "You can at least tell me what you're sorry for."

"What?"

"You can tell me *why* you're sorry." My voice growing louder, strong, merciless against the midday quiet of the house. "Are you sorry for yesterday, Dad? Or are you sorry for the last eight years? How many *sorry*'s are we talking about?"

That muscle in his jawbone hardening into stone; the tightness of his mouth as he looks past me. "Case—"

"Are you sorry about Dex? Are you sorry for giving me a hangover? Are you sorry for lying to me, for telling me the truth—"

"Casey, stop it!"

Stop, enough. Why is it coming out this way, sort of exploding all at once? I suppose I'm trying to shock him enough to make him let go, and it works—he gives up, I pull on my suitcase, it comes free from his hand and I'm loose, I'm free—but as soon as he lets me go, I catch myself wishing he wouldn't. He could ground me, or at least he could try; no matter that I'm nineteen, it might still work. He could send me upstairs and tell me no dinner and then later, without knocking, he could leave the cold meat loaf outside my door. He could pull on the handle and pull me closer and put his arm around me the way he would have not so long ago.

But that's not the way it goes. He just stares at me until I push past him and move clumsily out of the door frame. "So," he says, hesitating. His wide face and heavy shoulders slump toward defeat, and for a moment he seems smaller, almost as small as I am. But he shakes it off, or at least pretends to, and tries a smile. "So call me when you get there, huh?"

He has forgotten my words already, everything forgiven from his end, which makes me feel even worse. "Sure," I tell him quietly.

"You've got my phone card?"

I nod, and I can feel something hot collecting in my chest, know I have to go now to avoid a messy good-bye. "I'll call," I tell him again, the only emotionless thing I can think to say, and I swing my bag quickly through the living room. The green-and-white taxi idles in the driveway, the blacktop beyond it quivering with mid-July heat. When I get that far, I think, this part will be over; if I can just get that far, then maybe I'll feel ready to make this trip alone. But I can feel him behind me, hovering close and persistent as a shadow, a third ghost ready to follow me to L.A., and I can't help the words bursting out of my throat—"*What?* What is it, Dad?"

"I just—wanted to tell you—" His arm reaching up to mine uncertainly, unexpectedly, before he stops and pulls away. "Well," he says. "You'll be back for your class on Monday."

It doesn't sound like a question, but I know it is, and I can't look him in the eye when I nod this time. Can't tell him, don't want to let on, that it's an open-ended ticket sticking out the side of my bag and that I've packed enough underwear for several Mondays. "Just be safe and all that, you know?" he says. "Hollywood's not Duluth. What I hear, anyway."

The cabbie honks loud, long, and we both jump. "Sure, Dad."

He pushes open the screen door, holds it for me and nods toward the taxi, and I know then that this is how I'll remember him: his arm stretched out like a ticket collector, *last theater to your left, enjoy the show.* "Hollywood," he says again, shaking his head. "Small world, huh. If you run into your mother, say hi for me."

It's about presence, she used to tell me, though I realized later that's not always true.

It's about being in the moment. Which wasn't right, either.

It's about becoming. About forgetting. It's shedding everything you are to put on someone else's skin and pretend you can own your own life.

But try understanding what that means before you learn long division.

Then it's just about acting, Casey. Sighing, running her hands through the sunlight of her hair. *That's all. It is a game of make-believe on a respectable level.*

It was only after she was gone that I figured out she was

wrong. That all this talk about presence was more about absence, a way to fill a space inside you, beside you, with someone imagined, someone not yourself, until you could feel it rising and churning and brimming over the edges: Ah, yes. This is who I will be today.

I will be Stacie, queen of the class, cool and untouchable.

I will be a French exchange student. Not a word of English, just glamorous silence all day long.

I will be an orphan. Stoic ward of the principal.

I will be my mother.

And always, always I will be filling that space, re-creating her presence beside me.

Pretend, she used to tell me, *that you are strong*, and I did, and I do. "Duluth airport," I remind the driver in a calm voice, clear, strong. But I can't resist a look back, twisting around in my seat to watch the slow-shrinking image of my father as we move away, his face squinted up in the late-morning light. It makes my eyes water to look back at him like that, as if we've both just emerged from the darkness to find ourselves, startled, in the middle of something unforgiving. He stands there at the end of our driveway and watches the cab move slowly away; just stands there, hands in his pockets, even after we turn off Second Avenue and I can see him for only a second more, fading and flickering through other people's trees.

Then he's gone and I look forward again. We make our way through town and toward the highway, heading south along the shore with a creaking catch in my stomach, like the soft-wood sink of a broken stair.

when i missed my chance

Dex asked about her once, only once, the day I took him to the lighthouses at Canal Park. He bought us popcorn near the breakwater, held me tight from behind as we fed seagulls in far-flung handfuls and watched them cluster frantic and hungry, a squawking gray surge of bobbing heads. Out along the shore, beyond the newly broken lake, spring was just beginning to thicken on the branches. It was one of those days when the sunlight isn't wintry anymore, blue and gold where there used to be white, and your breath doesn't fog as you're laughing; the kind of day that feels like beginnings, that you forget has to end until he pulls you close and says into the top of your hair, "Casey. Where's your mother?"

Just like that. What he was always hinting at, getting close to, but never asked. It made everything stop, the whole world still and listening; even those pecking seagulls at our feet seemed to be holding their collective beady-eyed breath. I turned myself out of his arms and leaned against the railing, looked down into the water where a cool silver reflection of myself wavered back.

I told him, and she told me, there in the water, "Guess."

"That's your answer?"

"Why not?"

"That's not an answer."

"Maybe your guess is as good as mine." My voice was small enough to pull him close and double the bodies in the water: that shivering surface like something unstable, breaking continually apart. "Go ahead," I said. "Give it a shot. Really."

"A guess?"

I nodded. He looked up and out across the lake as if considering the possibilities. "My guess"—he stopped, leaned deeply into the railing, and glanced up at me with a straight face—"my guess is she ran off with her best friend in a blue convertible."

I stared at him and felt the smile building in spite of myself.

"You know. Fugitive road trip. Off to Mexico. That kind of story."

"I've never known a guy who liked *Thelma and Louise*," I told him.

"Damn. Too easy, wasn't it?" He shook his head, looked out at the water to hide a smile, and something relaxed in my chest. The falseness of fantasy, of film, like a kind of relief.

"Try again."

"How about…" He paused, turning back to me. "Surfer girl?"

"Too general."

"Bank robber, then."

"Surfer-girl bank robber?"

"In California."

I blinked and looked away: too close. "*Point Break*, right? Or was it *Break Point*?"

"Something like that." He wasn't smiling now either. We weren't looking at each other when he said, "My guess is you didn't see it coming."

"See what?"

"That she was leaving."

I kept my face blank, mind blank. "That could be a lot of stories."

"Okay." A pause. "My guess is she OD'd on painkillers the week before your nineteenth birthday. Maybe on purpose. Maybe not."

Shaking my head. "I don't know that one."

"I do."

And I could hear in his tone that he did. I couldn't look at him. We'd only been dating a month now: long enough to know there was baggage, but not long enough to have carried each other's.

"See? I know what it's like, okay?"

I didn't answer.

"How about this," he said after a while. He took our hands and prayed them together, our fingers dissolving into meaningless tangles, and gave me a look so deep I thought he might be seeing something I didn't want him to see. "My guess is maybe you don't want to tell me where she is."

I looked away.

"Maybe you don't want me to know that much. Is that it?"

The pulse of wind against our faces, the push and stop of a faltering breeze, like the echo of what my mind wouldn't stop whispering: *She left me. She left me. She left me.* And this is where it could have happened, some sort of connection if I'd let it. *Where's your mother?* And I could have told him the truth, let it slide out of my mouth in a smooth, easy stream — *Hollywood, believe it or not, she always wanted to be a movie star, more than she wanted to be a mom, I guess, and I bet that explains a lot* — and who knows what might have happened. The sweet release of something let go, or an impromptu trip out west, or time, finally, to cry about it and let someone see. Or maybe, better yet, he would've just held me there along the railing and not given a damn about the whole thing. The sun around us and the truth between us and somehow this would have changed the next day, which would have changed the next, and the next, changed what would happen in those coming months, stretched out invisibly and inevitably before us — what if I had let him into the story, let their stories come together, *what would things be like now* —

"You don't know," he said. "Do you?"

Something disappointed in his voice, like giving in to a lie he knew was a lie. I looked up. And I felt it all so strong right then — the silence and the pressure, the sun against his face, all curving glows and shadows and those eyes, blue beneath green like something bloomed against the sky — all of it built up so high that I laughed, loud and long and sudden. It scared the seagulls. It scared me. "No," I told him, and I was crying a little, too, all of it mixed together into something so confused. "I don't know." And he pulled me in and held his hand against my hair and didn't say anything for a long time, and it was the perfect thing. To have someone not knowing it with me.

"My guess," he whispered into my ear, "is that's the hardest part."

I breathed against his jacket, reached up to wipe my eyes. "What is?"

But he didn't answer. He just pulled away and wiped my eyes for me and never asked about her again, though I could sense him wondering sometimes. Who she was. Who I was. And maybe, most of all, who *we* were as we walked back along the pier, *where* we were, through the gulls rising up in a throb of beating wings, higher and higher before coming back down again —

a week ago

The plane crash was on every channel.

Which made sense except there was nothing to see, just the blank gray stretch of ocean where it had gone down: a vast, empty space they kept showing over and over as if something were going to pop up, which it never did. We couldn't get away from the nothingness of it. Yet we couldn't stop watching, waiting.

"Survivor guilt," my dad repeated, shaking his head. The news was cutting back to a tearful couple who had missed the late-night flight out of L.A. and seemed frantically upset about their good luck. "I don't get it," Dad said, "I just don't."

I handed him his coffee and put the toast down in the toaster. "I don't get what you don't get."

"Survivor *guilt*," he said. "Who the hell feels guilty about living?"

"Come on, give 'em a break." I sat down at the table across from him and stole a sip of his coffee. "When was the last time *you* almost died?"

He shook his head again. "Crazy. Why am I watching

this, anyway? Why are we watching this? I gotta get to the plant." But he turned the volume up and stayed.

He was nervous, I could tell. I could tell we were both waiting for names.

"I'll be late at school today," I told him, trying to find something, anything else to talk about. "I've got a film exam Friday."

He glanced away from the TV. "It's just summer school."

"It still involves studying."

"You study here."

"I study here, I study there. I study everywhere." He smiled, which made me feel a little better about lying. I didn't have an exam, but I didn't want to be home this afternoon, didn't want to be around when Dex called. It had been close to a week since Independence Day, when I'd last seen him; I knew he'd break down and apologize soon, and I wanted a few absences before I talked to him, a few *I wonder where she's been*'s on his mind before I let him think he'd gotten to me. Which he had.

"Red-eye flight." He leaned back and rubbed the top of his dark hair, silvered at the temples. The toast popped up, but neither of us rose to get it. "Kind of crowded for a red-eye, huh?"

"I guess. Not that it means anything."

"Obviously. Anyway, she wouldn't fly at night."

"Right."

"Not that she's—"

"Right."

He glanced at me, but we both turned back to the screen before our eyes could disagree. It was our game, our way to deal, and the rules meant never admitting she was gone for good.

Because it was her birthday today. Her fortieth, the one she'd always said she was afraid of. It was a flight from *there* back to *here*. She'd been a believer in the significance of co-incidences, and it had rubbed off on both of us, jump-started that small but shared hope that one day she'd find her way back home....

"I bet she's still asleep," he said. "Bet she doesn't even know yet."

And I wondered if I knew it yet, really. When things would stop feeling like a dream.

"I bet she won't know for a while."

A mechanical malfunction, they said. Engine stopped, hopeless as a heart, and then that smooth glide into the Pacific on takeoff. The angle of a terrible yet graceful dive: a hundred and eighty bodies destined for Minnesota, lost somewhere forever beneath the blue.

Three days later. My hands flat against the door, the flat varnished wood, the dull glassy eye of the peephole from the wrong side: I wanted to look in. I wanted to know if he was in there, looking back—we hadn't spoken since our fight on the Fourth, more than a week now, and as much as the space had cooled my nervousness about him, the cooling-off time was starting to make me nervous in a different way. It made me start thinking, start listening. His arguments in my head, over and over, like a broken record I couldn't stop spinning: *Because this could be something good*, he kept saying, *me and you. The you underneath all of it, whatever it is…*

Looking away. I couldn't see his face, and it made me nervous.

It's going somewhere, he said. *That's what you're really afraid of.*

I closed my eyes.

"C'mon, Dex"—knocking softly, over and over, a slowing pulse—"open up, please?"

The same thing he used to ask me. I tried to picture him on the other side of this door, so close, yet without the feeling of closeness. I pressed my palms against it, pressed myself against the wood, my eyes still closed. I could imagine him doing the same, could almost feel him on the other side.

I was still standing like that when the police came down the hall.

Dex lived in the Agate Bay Apartments, near the railroad tracks and just a block away from the ore docks. He said he loved that, being able to roll out of bed and into his new job. *Before,* he said, *I used to drive hours to work. You can't imagine how nice it is to look out the window and see where you're supposed to be.*

Where?

Here.

No, where were you before?

Oh. Nowhere. Looking away now. *Small town. You know. Nowhereville, USA.*

You can tell me.

I could. Smiling. *But then I'd have to kill you.*

He liked holding back sometimes. I didn't mind. We let each other keep our secrets.

But I never liked that he lived in those apartments.

Part of it had to do with the landlady, Mrs. Larson, an old Swedish woman who used to be my high school librarian and remembered, I suppose, catching me with various boys in the reference section. Her apartment was practically next door to Dex's, opposite ends of a gold-papered hallway with bad lighting and a damp, brownish smell. Sometimes, when I'd leave late at night or early in the morning, I'd catch her peering out at me from her barely cracked door with a disapproving sneer, mouth pursed tight and white as something dried up. And I'd smile, wave, an outwardly innocent recognition, though we both knew I was just flipping her off politely. It always startled her and she never waved back, just nodded as if I'd confirmed her worst suspicions and clicked her door pointedly shut.

Aw, come on, she's not that bad.

You didn't know her before. She hates me, I can tell. I'm waiting for her to hang a big cross in the hallway.

Why would she hate you?

Some people get—I don't know. Judgmental sometimes. About me.

Why?

Just because.

But her accent is so great....

Coming from Nowhereville and its clichéd perception of Minnesota, Dex expected everyone in Two Harbors to have Swedish accents, and he fell mindlessly in love with people who actually did.

Which was another thing I hated about his place—it was so awkwardly and artificially Minnesotan. He haunted the local gift shops on weekends, bought all the knick-knacky, north-shore junk he could find, and made it the theme of his decor: fake arrowheads, cedar boxes with state maps varnished to the top, miniature loons and polished agates and dozens of postcards taped to the wall. He said he loved feeling like he'd come a long way, like this was *home*, and of course I smiled and didn't say anything, dutifully admiring the giant posters of the suspension bridge and Gooseberry Falls. But it was just another acting job to hide what I was thinking—that his place looked like a museum for tourists, a Hollywood set from an outsider's perspective, far from any real home I'd ever seen and something I couldn't imagine living in.

Why not? When you go back to school in the fall, I mean… it's just as close to Duluth, you're here all the time anyway, so why not?

No way. You'd get sick of me. Trying to make it lighter, laugh it away: *You don't know the ugly sides yet.*

I could learn.

I like my space.

Me, too. We could learn together.

Dex—

Turn ourselves into a pair of grown-ups.

Dex, stop, okay? I can't just leave my dad alone like that.

Because one of these days—a deepness in his voice when I mentioned my father, a curiosity mixed with fear, the way boys get about fathers sometimes—*we both have to grow up. Leave stuff behind, move on. Stop putting family first, you know? Out on our own…*

I know.

Even though I didn't. He moved closer, wouldn't look away: *Let me learn the ugly sides. Let me inside you.*

But I didn't know then that it would happen so soon, or how.

There were two of them: one tall and thin with silvery hair and a hard-looking chest beneath his dark blue uniform, the other a little shorter, wide and soft, with a tan face like this teddy bear I used to have when I was little. I thought I recognized that one. Friends with my dad, maybe; high school or hunting buddies. They'd come out of the landlady's apartment, Swedish nastiness behind them, stopped and stared with obvious surprise when they saw me standing there. "Miss?" called the thinner, older one. "Could we have a word with you?"

I guess I knew then that door wasn't going to open at my back, no escape from the news coming inevitably this way. I knew if I could just keep them talking, whatever was wrong didn't have to exist for a while longer, and as those twin silver badges bore down on me, bright as a pair of wide white eyes, I tried to think of something, anything, to say. But my mind had stuttered, stopped. My body seemed stuck to the door. I could only watch and wait, the way you can't cry out in a dream, even when you know you're done for.

"Hello," said the tan cop, wide face smiling politely. The other one nodded wordlessly. Mrs. Larson just stared with her beady gray eyes, fingered a gold cross resting against the jut of her collarbone, and hovered near the wood-paneled wall. "Maywood, right?"

I nodded.

"Katie?"

"Casey."

"That's right, that's right, I'm sorry. Haven't seen you in

a while; maybe you don't remember either. I went to school with your dad."

"Yeah, I know."

"Mom, too."

He paused to see how this registered. I kept my gaze on his, didn't blink or look away, though I hated his obvious curiosity—*Yes, it's true, okay? I'm right here, all that's left of the Hollywood legend.* "No kidding," I said, spontaneously faking fragility this time, my voice as wounded as he expected based on everything he thought he knew. For a moment, it seemed to work; he looked down uncomfortably, logged an unnecessarily long note on the pad, and I felt the ball in my stomach unknotting a little. "You must have been pretty close to my dad," I added.

He didn't look up, hand still moving in slow, cursive strokes. "Why do you say?"

"Most people remember her. They don't remember my dad first."

"Well." Eyes back up, but not landing on mine for very long. "I, uh...I did know him better."

The tall one finally swooped in for his partner, clenching his hands behind his back and wiping the thought of a smile from my mind. "You're Mr. Stone's girlfriend?"

Sort of. I think so. You tell me.

"You could say that."

Mrs. Larson raised her eyebrows, mumbled something about mothers and daughters under her breath; I stared at her until she looked away. "Actually," I added, "it's something I'd like to ask him about."

"Oh." A pause. "Well, I don't think that's going to be—"

"Because we haven't really talked about it," I said quickly. "We still need to have that talk. I haven't talked to him in a while, actually, and if you give me a little time to find him, I can let you know, you know, where he is—let him know you want to talk to him, too—"

But the way they all looked at me then, with the same silence and condescending pity, I couldn't pretend for long.

It felt kind of like stepping into Lake Superior, which never rises above forty or fifty degrees. How only a very small part of you is steeped in this, but you feel the numbness everywhere: the sudden shock, a slow, cold burn rising up through your body, then fading away to a duller ache.

I said quietly, "What happened?"

A clearing of throats, shifting of eyes: *You gonna tell her? You want to?*

"I'm assuming," the tall one mumbled, "you heard about flight 308?"

I remembered the flat stretch of empty blue, flat glass of the television: the flight that ended in nothingness. My father's relief when he told me the next day that all families had been contacted, no news for us, and no noose is good noose, right? We'd started laughing at the same time, the same loud and half-embarrassed laughter—*so stupid, who are we kidding? No coincidence could be that cruel.* Then we'd stopped, looked away and wondered, privately, how we could laugh about this in the first place.

I nodded. I'd heard.

"I'm afraid Mr. Stone was on that flight."

I almost smiled—it was so silly, so unlikely—but I couldn't smile against the sea of images in my head: blank face of the ocean, Dex's face, and my mother's, the one I'd pictured, going down and into darkness. "That's impossible," I told him. "That flight was out of L.A."

"Yes, that's right. And headed for Minneapolis."

"But Dex lives here."

"Yes. It was headed here."

"No," I said, my voice growing louder, "he *lives* here. He wouldn't have been in L.A. in the first place, I'd just seen him, I'd seen him—"

The week before. Six whole days.

How many flights between L.A. and Minneapolis in six days?

"Miss," said the other one, the one who knew my father better, "were you aware Mr. Stone was in Los Angeles the week before the flight?"

It was like a math problem. *If Dick and Jane fight on Friday, and there are five flights away from Jane per day, what is the probability that Dick leaves Jane in time to die six days later?*

"Yes," I said. "I mean, no. No, I didn't know he was in L.A."

"But you knew he used to live there. In Hollywood. Right?"

I blinked. I didn't answer, everything fading a little in clarity. They exchanged a look, then looked back to me: "Well, you should know we don't have the whole story. The airlines are mainly handling this one. But our best guess is Mr. Stone was in L.A. visiting family or what have you, and 308 was his flight back."

"We figured he told you."

They looked at me blankly. Waited for me to fill in that

blank, but my mind was too empty to fill it with anything, my body too empty. Like a fist in the stomach, all the air punched out. "Told me what?"

"You know." A pause. A shrug. "Where he was from," said one. "Where he was going," said the other, and I can hear a voice like a whisper at my back, crowded with echoes: *Nowhereville, USA.*

You can tell me.

Tell me you love me.

I could. But then I'd have to kill you.

"Are you sure?" My own voice was flat, staticky, something broadcast from far away. "I mean, the news said they couldn't find all the bodies, right?"

"Miss," one of them murmured, "we know. They know. His brother called us to find you, to let *you* know."

"His brother." And I felt it sinking in then, the horrible duality of it, the numb nothingness of everything I didn't, couldn't, would never know: because how could I understand he was dead if I didn't know the person who had died? "I'm a little confused," I said quietly. "I thought he was an only child."

"One younger brother, as far as we know. Out in L.A."

But he would have mentioned a brother. At some point. Right?

"If it makes you feel better, he knew about you. Said Dex had talked about a girlfriend; only remembered the last name, though. Not that there's so many Maywoods around." He cleared his throat nervously. "Your house was our next stop, after Mrs. Larson."

She gave a grimace vague enough to be misread as a sympathetic smile.

"Anyway," said one of them, clearly ready to get out of this hallway, "we'll give your contact info to the brother, if that's okay. If we have your permission, I mean."

They stared at me. They were waiting for an answer, I think, but I didn't know which one had spoken; things were losing focus, distinction, the comfort of sharp edges blurring as if through water. I nodded vaguely. I listened to their voices start up again, but it was like listening to someone else's conversation through a wall.

"Did you leave anything in his apartment? That you'll be needing, I mean?"

"Because it's probably a good idea for you to clean your stuff out."

"Right. Take what you need."

"Mrs. Larson can let you in, I'm sure."

Mrs. Larson looked away, fingers on the cross around her neck and pinched lips moving silently. But she nodded sharply when the men looked over at her.

That waiting. That thick, tingly, frozen feeling.

And I realized numbness was better than the alternative. At least for now.

"Thank you," I told them, voice empty, mind empty, everything forced out and emptied, "for letting me know." I nodded as if giving them some final permission to leave, and already they were backing down the hall: *We're so sorry — Do you need a ride somewhere? — I've got your dad's number — If we hear anything else, new information — But you shouldn't get your hopes up —*

Which sounded familiar.

I closed my eyes.

When I opened them, Mrs. Larson was walking back to her own apartment. She moved slowly down the long hall-way, longer now than I had ever noticed. At the end of it, the cops were halfway out the door: one last glance back, mur-murs of requisite concern. And then it was quiet. Just the humming gold of the lights, questions I knew not to ask my-self, and the empty stretch of the hall after they had gone, strong and sharp as a feeling in my chest. The whole world pressing inward—I leaned against the wood, sank down, and waited. I knew she'd never come out unless I knocked, hard, to ask for the key, and it was all I could think to do. I waited for her not to open that door.

That was how it happened the second time

how it happened the first time

The morning I found the note, we sat at the kitchen table with the cereal box and warming milk, two empty bowls, and the head shot between us. We didn't look at each other. We looked, as if in mutual understanding or confusion, at the photograph of my mother, cut out in the shape of a heart and signed across the bottom: *Love Mom*. She'd signed it in red before leaving it on my dresser sometime, secretly, in the dark middle of the night—lipstick-red across her breasts in an almost illegible scrawl, a feigned messiness that wasn't at all like her normal neat and bubbly handwriting. Maybe it was supposed to look frantic, out of time and on the run, the way a real star would sign an autograph. But it seemed more as if she hadn't signed it, as if someone else had.

Love Mom. No comma, like a reminder.

My father put the picture, facing him, across the empty space where my mother's bowl usually sat, and besides the fact that she wouldn't stop smiling and was laid out flat and wore too much eyeliner for breakfast, she didn't look quite right to me. An uneven familiarity, a counterfeit. It must have been my perspective, looking at her upside down: the sagging smile, nose jutting awkwardly and too high, twin black holes of her nostrils suddenly prominent, and I couldn't stop staring at this strange image of my not-quite mother — could easily pretend, from this angle, that it wasn't her, like the signature. Which is why I couldn't look away.

My father, though, was seeing something right side up and very clear before him. I know that now. I know it must have hurt to look at something so beautiful, something he'd lost, what so many men, until the breakdown last year, had tried to take away from him and what fate — or maybe just my mother's understanding of fate — finally had. What I don't know is how he must have seen me, suddenly all his own: a burden? A prize? Some miniature way to keep her alive, an eleven-year-old game of pretend? Because in those surreal days after she left, the following weeks unfolding into months and years without her, he knew what not to talk about, how to keep it far away from both of us: the guilt, the self-interrogations, those questions you can't stop asking yourself. *Was it me, my fault? Did I chase her away?* He knew how to take on a role with the best of them, and until yesterday, this was something we could act out together. It started that morning at the breakfast table when he reached over and pulled a paper napkin over her photograph. He closed his eyes and rubbed his beard, then rested his chin against a balled-up fist and looked at me across the table and did not look down at the napkin.

"So. Did you do your homework?" I don't remember if I answered or not, but he nodded approvingly as if I had. "Okay. I'll be late tonight. Don't forget."

I nodded, too, and we both nodded together for a moment

until we both realized we were still nodding. We stopped and looked at each other.

"You sure that's okay?" he said.

"Sure."

"I've got a delivery in Anoka, so I'll be on the road all day. Till your bedtime."

I said, "It's okay," though there seemed to be two parts to me now, quickly diverging: the part that accepted this, obedient and calm, and the part that had shrunk back into a corner of my mind, closed a door, and refused to come out.

My father started to say something else and stopped. He moved the spoon around in his empty bowl, its ceramic staccato like chattering teeth; he cleared his throat. He let the spoon drop into the bowl and pushed back his chair. "Hell," he said and didn't even flinch, the way he usually did when he forgot himself and swore in front of me. "How about this instead. You don't have to go to school today."

The way he said it, it wasn't a statement, or a reward, or a surprise. It sounded more like a question to which he expected a validation: *Yes. That is exactly what you are supposed to say at a time like this.* I twisted my napkin down to paper crumbs and waited for more. "Because that's not good for you. To come home alone." He paused. "Anyway, I'm thinking I'd like some company on my ride, you know? It's a long way down."

And something about this suggestion—skipping school with my father, an oddly allowable broken rule—made everything seem so wrong, so make-believe, it became somehow safe. I felt myself coming out of that corner and peeking through a keyhole to glimpse the Wonderland before Alice wakes up. Frightening, but harmlessly surreal, unreal.

"Okay," I said. I knew, somehow, to ride out this feeling as long as I could. "Will I get in trouble?"

"Nah. I'm your father. I can make a call; I know what's best for you. What are they going to say?" He stood up. He sat back down, then stood up again. He went to put the milk away, and I didn't say anything even though I felt my hunger coming back, suddenly and surprisingly gnawing through the numbness I'd felt since giving him the photograph and seeing his face and knowing what all of it meant. "So," he said, "I'll go do that, then. Tell them you won't be in today. I'll go do that myself. Okay?" I nodded. I smiled, and it caught him off guard; he blinked, then smiled back, then left me alone in the kitchen with an empty bowl and the silence settling in, sun slow to burn the darkness from the corners.

Of course, it wasn't long before I had to pull the napkin away from her face. Then cover it up, then uncover it again: forget, remember, forget, remember, like a peekaboo game I've been playing ever since.

Sometimes when I wake up early, before the fog thins out and the kitchen still has that dazed, purple feeling in the air, I'll sit in my chair and stare at that same spot until the world pulls back to cinematic objectivity. I'm still sitting there, staring, even now—a smaller me, third-person as a dream, and that photograph, third-person as fiction. Zoom in on those flattened upside-down eyes as they take on new meaning: at times they are my mother's, staring back without recognition. Other times they are my grandmother's, who died the year before—ghostly, chilling, until they become my own eyes, like looking into the mirror of an older me, of what I'm meant to be. I'm watching them, I think, for some sort of cue, something that means *This is what you do next.* You put the cornflakes in the bowl and eat them dry. Rinse the dish, wait for your father to come downstairs. In a moment, he will walk in with your coat; he will seem a little more tired and a little less confused. He will leave the screen door unlocked and tell you to sit in the front seat, and you'll feel strange up there where you're not used to sitting: both too old and too young for this wider view. Like suddenly you're expected to know so many things at once, and at the same time, not enough.

Why did she leave?

But for now, just listen to the silence of the house, wonder if it always sounded so quiet and watch the thickening shafts of morning light stretch themselves across the floor. Hypnotizing: it feels good to fall into them, a welcome mindlessness, and you can almost pretend it's yesterday, it's the day before and every day before that and your mother is crossing the kitchen in her red robe, hair limp but gleaming—*The bus is coming, better hurry up* as her bare feet glide through those puddles of sunlight, a fluid gold rising up her ankles—then back to sudden shadow as she steps away, as it swims into your vision, this valentine-shaped prank that means only thinking and thinking and never knowing.

Because there are things this photograph will tell you— and I want to convey this to my younger self, the smaller seed of what I will become, the girl who can't look away— there are things to learn here, but *why* is not one of them. Not yet.

vital statistics

Two Harbors got its name from the land, from the shape of the shore where it meets up with Lake Superior: two large bites taken out of the coastline, making twin ports for the ore boats to come into. A simple enough name. But one that doesn't feel quite right if you're standing at the edge of the water, only one harbor visible at a time. The duality gets lost somewhere, between the curve of coast and the length of land, or maybe in the angle of someone standing there, alone, looking off into the distance. This used to bother me when I was younger, the lie of the name: how in theory there are two. But in thought, in the way it feels, fused by that distortion of distance and perception, there might as well be one.

The lesson: places don't always live up to their names. Take Hollywood, which comes from Holy Wood. They used to call it Hollywoodland, like an amusement park, but at some point, they took out the land and the holy. Who knows why, but my guess is people were disappointed.

My name, Casey, means "brave, vigilant," although I was named Casey only because it's my mother's maiden name. My father's name is Frank. I used to know what it means, but I don't remember anymore. My mother's name is Lila, which can mean a lot of things, depending on where you are in the world: sometimes "lilacs," sometimes "brave protector," sometimes "whimsical dance of God." It's not a movie-star name, or at least not one I've ever seen blaze across the opening credits of a movie. And I've been watching.

And then there's Maywood, our last name. I don't know where it comes from, but it seems like the right name, the perfect fit for a family prone to fantasy. A name that is hopeful, yet conditional: *may, would, might, could*. In a way, then, here is my excuse, my legacy to uphold—I come from a family of dreamers. Who better to make this kind of trip?

Of course, if places don't live up to their names, maybe people don't have to either.

The name Dex must be short for something, but I haven't figured out what.

My life in categories, my own small history broken down. That's the way it's starting to feel, anyway, here in the dusty backseat of the cab. Like if I hold the pieces far enough away from myself, really *look* at them with open eyes, maybe I'll figure out what to do. How to direct this story.

"So where are you going?" says the driver, and I glance up, a little startled.

"The airport," I tell him quickly. "Duluth."

"Yeah, I know. I mean, where are you going?" He glances over his shoulder, and I realize he's younger than I thought at first—only slightly older than Dex, late-twenties, aimless, probably the type that likes to call himself *free-spirited*. He adjusts the mirror so it frames his eyes, aims them at mine; his are coffee-dark and squinty from the sun or from smiling, and the softness in them makes me feel, momentarily, a little calmer.

"Minneapolis to L.A.," I tell him. "Then Hollywood," and I see his heavy eyebrows lift a little.

"Oh, boy. Don't tell me you wanna be an actress or something," he says. "Please. I hear these stories more often than you know, drive more down than you can guess. Small-town girls. No idea. They're lucky to end up in a porno." He glances up from the road, narrows his eyes in the mirror, and I can tell for certain he's smiling now. "Not that *I'd* know."

I smile back, but I don't answer. I can tell he's flirting with me, and usually I'd like that, usually that's my excuse to become the girl I'd like them all to see: a fusion of sweet-yet-coy, sideways glance, curve of the lip and the hip, all confidence. But not today.

"So what's the real story?" he says. "Why Hollywood?"

A fake funeral.

What?

Bet you haven't heard that one before.

"Vacation," I tell him.

He nods. He looks disappointed in a way—not the story he wants to tell on another ride, to another girl, and it almost makes me tell him the truth. "Guess that means you're not an actress," he says.

"Not exactly."

"A model?"

"Nope."

"So what are you, then?"

I look into the mirror, hold his gaze. I open my mouth and wait to hear what comes out. But nothing happens. Nothing there but empty air.

When I open my eyes again, there is only green, blurs and streaks, the steady and uninterrupted length of it past my window—no way to tell where we are, just that we're between two towns, lost somewhere in the shaggy wilderness. I look up at the driver, but he's not looking back anymore. Irrationally, a strange uneasiness in my stomach, I wonder if I've imagined this conversation, and I blink, hard, try to find something to feel.

So what are you, then?

The echo of it still in my head. Hovering in the air and waiting for an answer—I watch the familiar becoming unfamiliar on the other side of the glass and think back to what's brought me this far.

the lullaby boys

My first memory of her. It comes back to me, sometimes, riding the wake of dreams, this memory of falling asleep to the drowsy lullaby in her hands: slowly, gently, she bends my head backwards into the sink and combs my hair into the stream of water. My scalp prickles, winces away—"Too cold, Mom"—and she sighs, turns the tap until it warms a little.

"It's better for your hair," she says. "The cold makes it smoother. That's what Grandma told me when she did *my* hair." She glances up at her own reflection. "That's what it takes to look your best." Her face, looming large and smooth-skinned above mine, makes me think of movie stars seen from the front row. Painted bright, smiling, perfect, but stretched so wide across the screen, I can't see enough at once. My neck hurts to look.

So I close my eyes, and then it's only warmth. The sweet smell of shampoo, the water through my hair, and her fingers through my hair, smooth as water. The whispery sound of her voice as she sings a song from her high school musical, the one that first made her a star, that got them talking:

"*Gleaming like gold in the starry-eyed spotlight…better not let her out of your sight.* It closes the cuticles," and suddenly the water is cold again. "Makes it shiny. Don't you want pretty, shiny hair?"

"Like yours?"

"Beautiful, shiny blonde hair," she says, "just like mine," and against my closed lids, I picture how it must have been to be my mother onstage, all those years ago, the whole audience thinking to themselves, murmuring to each other: *Isn't she beautiful?* Not knowing how sometimes that means being cold.

"I'll be beautiful like you. Won't I, Mom?"

"You'll be a heartbreaker," she tells me. "You'll break all the boys' hearts," and even as young as I am, I understand this is a good thing. It fades back, then, the memory, as I'm fading drowsily beneath the rhythm of her fingers, and I'm left with this peaceful still of almost-sleep, of knowing she's still there and knowing someday I will be beautiful, I will be a heartbreaker.

I find, sometimes, a boy who does it right. There are prerequisites: gentle hands to navigate. A certain way of slipping smoothly through without a tangle. His face looking down, his body curved over mine, the kind of boy who likes to be above me—this is the most basic prerequisite. It assumes a certain type: big-muscled and protective, they think they're making the decisions. The *I love you* type, who says it first and maybe even means it, who makes you feel small and safe—that kind of lullaby.

Dex was one of them, but only one of them, and not the first. A boy named Travis was the first. It was a brief first, lasting exactly the length of a high school hockey game, plus the time it took him to walk me home and kiss me behind the oak tree my father planted when I was born. I was thirteen; I was just starting not to miss my mother; he was drunk and somewhere in the middle grades of high school, probably not going to make it to the end. But there was something about him in the ice arena, this slow-smiling way he wandered up to my group of friends and looked at *me*, only at *me*, came closer than anyone had come before. His wide white smile, "You cold? Hey, *I'll* warm you up," and Ellie, with a wink, shoving me from behind into his chest so he had to steady me—the thickness of his arms and cool-skinned hands. The way he pulled on my ponytail and, later, pulled out the rubber band slowly, so slowly, *this must be what sexy means*, and let my hair fall down around my face—and his smile in the silvered light of a weak moon, the naked shadows of late-fall oak branches scattered across his face as he leaned into me and put his hands deep into my hair. I closed my eyes and tilted my face up, feeling in his tenseness how he liked that. I did it again. "There's something about you," Travis said, leaning harder against my chest (for closeness or for balance, it didn't matter), "something about you that feels…familiar." And in his older-boy kisses that tasted sweeter than anything I'd ever tasted, like bubble gum and warm beer and the empty words that were all I needed to hear, I thought I knew what he meant. *Something about you that feels familiar*, and that's when I figured it out, the *point* to everything. Figured if you tried it enough times, maybe you could piece them all together and find, finally, what you're missing.

He never asked me what my name was, though maybe he knew it, secretly, the way I knew his. He never tried to go farther than my lips and the tangles in my hair, which had come undone in his wide, warm hands. He never called, I never talked to him again, but it didn't matter. It was the first time I believed it, thought someone could someday fall in love with me, and that was all I needed then.

"Pretend you just found out your husband's having an affair," she said, and I did: tight clench of the mouth against tears and words, faraway eyes and a folding up toward my chest, everything curled inward and afraid, like a lost child.

She'd shown me how, once. It was one of her favorite roles.

"Now pretend you're the other woman."

And I pulled my shoulders back, smooth and slow. Thrust the flatness of my chest forward, sly glance from the side: *A mouth like Mona Lisa,* she called it. *No one's ever going to know for sure.* I looked up at her through my lashes, gauged the reaction; "Not bad," she said, and I glowed with it despite the funny look she was giving me, like she was the one curling inward. Then a low voice, a glance upstairs: "Which one feels better, Case?"

I didn't answer. She nodded.

"Remember that," she said.

If Travis was the first, then Jeremy Gale was the second: one of those boys teachers didn't pay much attention to, this quiet, invisible way about him so you might not even notice he was there unless you were looking. The calm of him, the desk in the back, a blank-faced detachment—I couldn't resist. At fourteen, I was hooked to the lack of emotion, that jaded cool.

That's not what cool is, Ellie tried to remind me. *It's just weird.* And she would give me the kind of condescending look only best friends can give, point out the tall debate guy who by her standards was too nerdy, but who was popular and seemed to have a crush on me, so why not go for that one, or else that linebacker who hit on you last week, or both? *You can double with me and Bob, then, it'll be great....*

Yeah, right. Last time we doubled, you ditched your date for mine.

But you didn't like him. Isn't that what best friends are for?

Maybe it was Jeremy's story that kept me interested, the fact that I alone knew why he was two years older than the rest of our grade and twice as quiet. The generally held belief—that he'd been held back twice in kindergarten—didn't fit with his cynicism, the too-smart-for-this flicker in his eyes if you could hold them long enough. I'd found a better explanation down in the paper archives of the public library, his name in smudged print beneath a heartlessly terse headline from four years before: *Local businesswoman Joanna Gale drowns in Superior.*

And I knew these ropes.

I'd been on this circuit: those awkward, attempted talks with my father, that brief-but-embarrassing trip to a psychologist in Duluth, sitting in the windowless lobby reading bridal magazines and glancing, in quick-flickered skims of the eye, at the other people waiting quietly in their chairs. Wondering what was wrong with them, wondering what they thought was wrong with me, wondering if they were right—the whole mess takes *time,* and I figured I knew where Jeremy Gale's two years had gone, or been lost.

Something about you that feels familiar…

So I followed him home. Rather, I figured out his path home so I could time it with mine, make it look coincidental. It involved going three blocks out of the way, not to mention sprinting out of last-period gym to get the head start necessary for timing, which meant more than a few murmuring stares at my back. I didn't care; on the third try I timed it right and there he was, walking stony-faced and alone on the other side of the street. I slowed my steps, paced him stride for stride without looking. It was October; the leaves were piling up in the gutters, crunching on the same beats as we walked, and the air was filled with cool yellow light like the afterglow of something warmer.

It wasn't long before he crossed the street to walk beside me: staring at his feet, still silent, but close enough for me to understand we were walking together now.

"I saw you following me," he said finally.

"When?"

"Now."

I let a mildly indignant pause deepen before smiling, meeting his eyes with a flirtatiously raised eyebrow. "This is my way home, you know. Maybe *you're* following *me*."

He raised an eyebrow back. "Maybe I am."

Silent then, eyes down but flicking occasionally to the side, same subtle tilt to the head like a mirror sizing up its own reflection; we walked until we reached my street and hesitated at the corner. "So we split here," he said.

"Guess so." The autumn light caught in his hair, streaks of red, slow-smoldering flames glinting out of the dark. I felt the rise of it in my chest, press of a sun-tinged breeze against my face, the whole world full of color and heat.

"Admit it," he said finally, coming closer.

I leaned in the way she taught me. "Want to follow me home?"

"Admit it first." The challenge in his voice. And I knew then what we both wanted: the assurance that, coming out of this, we weren't on the line, we weren't walking behind. Neither of us wanted to be the one who cared.

I told him, low and quiet, before I even thought consciously of saying it, "I know about your mom."

He didn't answer. He cocked his head and thrust his blue gray stare into mine — there was that kind of aggression in it, and defensiveness, too, shot through with an interest he didn't try to hide. I could see myself reflected there, face warped against the curved blue, but momentarily just as confident and that same aggression, the same interest.

Then he said, "Well, I know about yours. Loony Lila, isn't it?" Stepping closer still: "Or *wasn't* it?" and I felt something drop a little inside me. Wanted to but couldn't look away because that would be following, that would be slipping, falling, couldn't do anything but hold my own by holding his eyes. It must have worked; he looked away first and when his eyes came back, they had softened to something less familiar, but just as nice.

"Hey," he said quietly, a little awkward, "I didn't really mean that."

"Yeah, me neither." I took a step forward, held his gaze. "But I'm not admitting anything."

"Me neither," and he reached up, hesitant, to brush something away from my face even though nothing was there. His hand lingered on the way down. And after that we both knew where things were headed.

So maybe it was only because we shared something lost. So what. When you're looking for love a second time, it's all about filling an emptiness anyway.

He didn't last, of course. Neither did the tall debate guy, the linebacker, half of the hockey lineup. The star pitcher fell in love too fast, the shortstop seemed suspiciously interested in the star pitcher, and Bob (whom Ellie happily passed on to me) followed me in his car for two months after I stopped returning his calls.

My father used to say he was a rock collector when he was young. "Everyone needs a hobby," he'd tell me, "everyone needs a way to organize their life," and that was his: the classification, the assessment and evaluation—even love?—of rocks.

My hobby, it seemed, was broken hearts.

"Just remember there are things to learn," she told me, "before you think you know what you're doing." The blankets pushed up around my neck, that cozy comforter cocoon, and my mother perched at the end of it. She found my foot beneath its sheath of covers and squeezed hard, smiling. "For example—don't always believe them when they tell you you're beautiful. Sometimes that's just a line."

I wiggled my toes. "Okay."

Though you are beautiful, of course.

The heavy warmth of those imagined words, spreading up through my quilted body; I could almost feel them. *I know,* I told her in my head, and I believed it then.

She turned and looked out the window, through the open shade and glossy black of nighttime, her sharp-edged profile softened by the dark and the blonde hair floating out behind her into waves. I wondered how many people in her life had been in love with her. I wondered if I could learn it, whatever she knew, the secrets of pulling people to you and watching them, one by one, fall.

"There are other things you shouldn't believe," she said quietly. "Other lines. But I'll tell you about them when you're older."

"Tell me now, Mom," I pleaded. I knew from her tone she was talking about sex—something I understood only through hard-to-believe rumors and a children's book on babies, and about which I was relentlessly curious—but she just shook her head and yawned. It was late; Dad hated it when she kept me up like this, and I knew to expect a cranky silence tomorrow at breakfast. But then again, maybe he wouldn't find out, might be working the overnight shift or off on what my mother called a "late-night *rendezvous*." I never asked what she meant by that word and she never wanted to talk about it, not even those times I caught her crying, or the night I found her tearing through his dresser drawers, flung-aside undershirts and lonely socks drooping at odd angles from the bureau mirror—even then, I didn't push. I'd learned by now that too many questions would make her angry, would sometimes send her down to the basement, locking the door from the inside and leaving me behind, upstairs, alone. I remember, even now, the hard, smooth feel of the sanded wood; I remember leaning against it, waiting.

I knew not to push.

"But you might as well know this," she said, there at the end of my bed. "It's okay to pretend you love them," and I nodded vigorously against my pillow. I'd heard this before, I'd been taught this lesson; I'd been part of her audience down past that basement door, part of the crowd looking up at her admiringly. I remember streamers along the wood-paneled walls, a tight circle of girls in pajamas and too much makeup: my third-grade birthday, a basement slumber party, one of the last years before Winter Frolic and back when parents still let their children come to our house. I remember the focused attention in the dim-lit room, everyone's eyes on my mother sitting cross-legged and silk-clad among us like a goddess. "Men like it when they think you love them," she whispered, lowering her words dramatically from my father upstairs. "Or at least they like it when you pretend you need them, even if you don't."

"How do you pretend?" someone asked. I think it was Ellie, who, like me, was a dedicated pupil of everything related to love: its masks, its empty husks, its ways to fool.

My mother tilted her head. "It should come natural. You're women, aren't you? Just lean into them, look up at them, the way they do in the movies—the old movies, the classics. Back when men made all the movies." She fell suddenly prone in front of one of the quieter girls, looked up at her with serious, heavy-lidded lust that sent us all, especially the quiet girl, into nervous giggles. "Rule number one," she murmured. "No falling in love. And if you remember that, nothing's holding you back. You can be anything."

"You can be anyone," I added, remembering my lines—she smiled at me, sat up again.

"Just remember you're *actresses*," she said. "Remember who you are; remember *you* can play them, too." Her smile widening and the light of it in her eyes, or the light of something else reflected: it flashed in the dark like the glitter of a lighthouse lamp, forever spinning in the same circle. Something turned *on*, bright and dazzling, that way she'd get whenever we had company—you'd never believe she'd have anything to cry about—or walking down the street dragging the glances of shy, silent men in her wake. I could feel them, and I could feel all of us, falling endlessly in love with her. "You give them the lines they want to hear." She looked at me. "Simple. If they think they know you, if they think they're the ones playing you—" She pinched my toe in its sleeping-bag sheath, I jumped and giggled, so proud right then, *this is my mother, mine, look how jealous they are. This is my mother who loves me.*

And she leaned into me and looked at me the way they do in the movies. "It'll give you that much more power," she said. "When they figure out it's *you* who played *them*."

The way I met Dex was not the way I met the others.

Since high school, the others meant putting up with that familiar game, a kind of ritual they all, somehow, knew how to play out: vague interest to feigned lack of interest to casual approach, when you know all they're thinking about is how long it'll be before they have your clothes off. The others meant two-for-one Coronas and Top 40 mixes at cheap Duluth bars and maybe a first date, another night, at Blackwoods or Grandma's. The others meant backseats and parking lots and, in exchange, a body to hold: warmth, distractions, easy promises.

Nevertheless, the others were getting old. Until Dex happened.

I met him at work, the movie theater in town, taking

tickets for an indie film festival in March. Usually my job involved running the film projector and doing paperwork no one else got around to doing, the closest part-time job I could find to directing—what I was actually majoring in at school. I never collected tickets, a task so mindless they saved it for kids who couldn't remember enough to take orders at the Dairy Queen. But we were short-staffed that weekend, everyone collectively focused on getting away from the "artsy films," and my job, as fate would have it, was to stand inside the empty lobby and wait for someone to show up.

And then he did. Tall, tan, early or middle twenties; messy blond hair, dirty-gold stubble long enough to feel (I imagined) soft against your skin. He wore a brown leather jacket and jeans that seemed like they'd been through a war, which probably meant expensive. And the way he looked at me: a double take as he walked inside, unmistakable interest he didn't try to hide, a strange recognition in both our eyes slipping loose and fast through my body, and down. He moved slowly across the old red carpet with his ticket in hand and something close to a smile, but not quite. Like he wasn't so sure, anymore, what he was here for.

"Two Harbors," he said, coming up from the side. He brushed against the red velvet rope between us. "Hope I'm not late."

I just stared at him. His height, his smoldering foreignness, his anywhere-but-here mystery. It took me a moment to remember that *Two Harbors* was the name of one of the just-released indie films we were showing, and I took his ticket, ripped slowly.

"You're right on time," I told him. "Second door down the hall." I held out his stub, but he didn't take it.

"You look familiar." Leaning back a little, like he needed distance to tell, and I mirrored his lips: measured, modest, flirtatious.

"I've heard that line a few times."

"Bet you have."

"You're new here."

"And I've heard that one."

I shrugged. "It's true," I said. "I pay attention," and I did; I knew he must be a tourist, or else (oh please, please) new in town. Not someone who could escape my notice for very long.

"Have you seen it?" he asked, nodding at the door to the theater.

"Twice."

He raised his eyebrows. "Guess that's a good sign."

"You'll have to let me know." Actually, I'd seen it three times already, but I didn't want him to think I was a complete loser. The film was about a woman sleeping with a director to get a part in a movie about a woman sleeping with a director to get a part in a movie—a breakdown of the lines between fiction and reality, or at least that was my best interpretive guess. I didn't think it was very good, and neither did anyone else I talked to; my boss had ordered it based solely on the title (proud, I think, that our little town was a buzzword in Hollywood, even if the buzz had nothing to do with our town). But I kept watching it anyway. I liked the wannabe actress, fantasized myself into her place, her role, her control over a man and her ability never to let anything touch her too deep. I tried to hold my body, now, the way she held hers in front of the director: confident, but turned a little away, same curve of the hip and angle of chin and curtain of blonde hair. I wondered, when this man watched the sex scenes he was about to see, if maybe he'd think of me.

He moved closer then. Green eyes, I noticed, or blue, or both, and flecked with gold like sun on water; I thought I could smell his cologne and something else. Hot, maybe cinnamon gum. A taste. I held my breath, waited for him to ask for my number or tell me his name or do whatever he'd moved closer to do.

But he just took the ticket stub out of my hand, slow slide of the paper mysteriously sensuous, turned around and walked down the hall. He paused in front of the theater door, rubbed the side of his neck as if reconsidering something, and glanced back: "Did you like the ending?"

She'd left the director, I remembered, though it was never clear why—just that she'd gotten the best of him. "I can't spoil it."

"You won't. It's like dessert first. I like to know if the ending's worth my time."

I shook my head casually, but I knew he could see it in my face—the thrill of him, and the fear and the hope and all of it, I noticed, written across his own face like a reflection.

"You're late." I nodded at the theater. "Have to wait and see."

He hesitated. "You'll be here when it's over?"

"I'll be here." And our reflections smiled, turned, pulled away without looking away until the door sighed closed. That energy still between us, a charge in the air. I felt it jazzing through my body, a broken current waiting to reconnect.

You're late—
Wait and see—
You'll be here when it's over…

Later that night, in the darkness of the locked movie theater, we watched it again. His hand over mine. His hand in mine. Shadows, sideways glances. Skin soaked with blue light, wavering, flickering with the changing screen, the developing story: I watched his eyes watching her and pretended she was me. And he turned.

I didn't expect this, he whispered. *I didn't mean to find this—*

Shhh… and I kissed his mouth silent, though I knew what he meant. This feeling like sinking, submerged in each other—

I don't even know who you are
You know enough

And onscreen there it was, the end of the movie, or the lack of an ending: the actress is leaving the director, gone without warning, and all he can do is come up with reasons and never know which ones are true—because she couldn't play the role she wanted? Or because she wanted another life, a new start? Or because she didn't love him enough, or because she did, too much, or some other unknown reason entirely, and these are the questions that will stay with him, that will follow him like ghosts across the harbors of Los Angeles as the image fades to black, the only certainty that she's gone and he doesn't know why—she's gone but he's here with me—

The credits rolled. I took a deep breath. Pulled away from him but he hung on, so I pulled into myself instead and closed my eyes against his neck.

So close. Be careful. Be careful with this one.

"Did you like the ending?"

I opened my eyes. "Honestly?"

"Why not? We've known each other long enough to drop the pretenses."

I laughed and shook my head. "You don't find out what happens. She just walks away. There *isn't* an ending."

"But don't you get the sense of it? Like, of what's going to happen? He's looking for her, he wants to find her. It's kind of…"

Considering.

"Hopeful," he said.

"You must be a romantic."

"I've been called worse." He pulled my chin up, cut the darkened space between us so the light surged full and deep into his face: *Be careful.* "He's learned how to love," he said.

"Maybe." I leaned in. "But she isn't going to love him back."

A challenge, a gamble—he heard it and smiled. "You're a tough one, aren't you?"

"I'm a realist," I told him, and closed my eyes.

And his fingers against my face, my hair, the darkened screen, the lightness rising inside me. "We'll see," he said, and in that way he was different. He made me wonder, imagine a different ending, and in that empty theater we began another story. In those half-truths of skin, of closed eyes, the pulse of what we didn't know was coming, we made each other ache for conclusions.

There are only a few I remember her singing: "Rockabye Baby" and "Toora, Loora, Loora" and the one about swinging low and coming home. Their strange, lonely and longing stories, a deeper voice, thicker than the way she talked and soft, like dark velvet against my ear—too beautiful to put me to sleep.

I told her, "Your songs are too sad, Mom, when you sing me a lullaby."

She said, "The good ones don't always have happy endings."

Eventually, of course, he wanted to know why.

Why I stopped his hands from going too far down.

Why I had that untimely tendency to fall asleep, or at least fake it as he brushed my hair out with his fingers late at night.

Why, in essence, I wouldn't let him do what the others did. "Because you seem like you've done it before," he said.

"That's a nice observation, Dex. Thank you."

"I didn't mean it like that." Face half-buried in the pillow, quiet, serious, and I knew he'd never mean it like that, in any bad way. I pushed the blanket aside, pushed my hair to one side, pulled back into a position that mirrored his so our bodies faced each other. He lay there, very still, and watched. "I know you're scared," he said quietly, "but I don't know what you're scared of. I don't know if it's me."

And maybe I should have told him then. That it *was* him, but not in the way he meant it—that there was something about him, different, deeper, scarier than any boy I'd ever dated. Because he was right; I had done it before. I'd done it a lot, I had it down, had learned by now the secret of sex, its mysterious and illogical appeal, its perfectness. I'd figured out the whole mess: that everything you've hoped for is wrapped up in that moment just after he's forgetting you, looking up into the air, those broken noises he's making, that look on his face like he's far, far away and then the part where he comes apart from you even as he's deepest inside — in that moment after, when he falls back to earth and remembers suddenly you're there, *thank you thank you thank you* in his eyes and something that's as close to love as I've ever seen — in that moment, for that moment, every time they return to me, skin against skin, and I get to hold that moment close, I know: *This is the point, this is what you've been waiting for.*

I ran my fingers up and down his chest, light, steady, as if movement and body might save me from words. It was late, almost early; I could see the corners of the room beginning to flush with color, thin lines of morning stacked up in the spaces between his blinds. I felt his hands beneath the sheets and thought of what it would be like if I let him — daylight bursting through the cracks of me, an explosion from the inside, nothing left to hold the rest together —

Until the phone rang, sudden and shrill, to save me from myself. I stopped and waited; it rang again. He didn't move. "Don't you want to get that?"

"This is important," he said quietly.

"But it's, like, five in the morning. You should get up and get it."

"Stop changing the subject."

"What if it's an emergency?"

Another ring, and another. He pulled me close, let me lie in that hollow space between his heart and his throat. He waited for the phone to stop before he took a deep breath, and by then something had cooled inside me, quiet and safe. "I don't want to pressure you."

I sighed. "So don't."

"Because I'm afraid, too. Of what might happen, of getting—"

He stopped, a long beat of hesitation. I listened to the pulse beneath his skin, its steadiness, its deeply buried rhythm.

"Do you think she loved him?" he asked.

"Who?"

"The woman in the movie. The *actress*," he added, and his tone was so pointed, I almost pushed away, but didn't.

"No," I said. "The actress left him at the end."

"But why?" Arms tightening around my shoulders, like he was afraid of losing me in this half-dream break of dawn. "Because she didn't love the guy? Or because she did?"

"What are you really asking me?"

"I just want to know how you think."

"If you think she loved him," I said into the dark, "then I think she was a good actress." He looked down at me, and I had to look away.

"I think you're wrong."

I put my hand over his mouth. Closed my eyes. "Let's just go to sleep," I whispered. "Can't we just go to sleep?" And he ran his hands slow and soothing through the tangles, humming a song I didn't know, and we lay for a long time on the precipice of morning, both of us waiting for the other to nod off first. His breath in my hair. My hair in his hands. Sun burning in thin parallels through the blinds and rippling tenuously across our bodies: those delicate fingers of light on the surface, and so much darkness between them.

the other end of it

"Of course there will be times," she said, her face turned away, "when you will hurt someone. There might even be times when someone will hurt you. It might be an accident, and it might not be. It probably won't be."

An edge to her voice, an ache, and even as young as I was, I could understand the fear behind it. "What do you do then?" I asked her, and she shook her head. She shrugged. She looked, for a moment, unsure, not like my mother with her calm eyes, calm smile, her sharp-shouldered way of staring the world down.

Tell me what to do. Tell me what to do when they hurt you, and as if reading my mind, she came suddenly to life.

"I suppose it's acting again," she said, "but secretly. That's when you give *yourself* the lines, Case. That's when you tell yourself a story. If you can pretend it went another way, sometimes—" A pause. "Sometimes it works to forget."

I smiled, already forgetting the fear in her eyes. She

leaned over to kiss me, and I knew then all that mattered was holding on to this feeling, the warmth of her mouth on my forehead, too perfect to be real.

"And sometimes," her voice so quiet against my skin, "they break your heart anyway."

how i learned the truth

Heading north, things got darker. Not just the sky, though night had already bruised the horizon purple by the time we crossed the border into Canada. But other things, too: the flat faces of cliffs along the side of the road, their familiar brown deepening into rough-edged, redder shades, and the trees seeming denser, deeper up here, as if cut from a heavier green. "It's funny," said my father, his hands steady on the wheel, "to *know* you're in another country, to understand it, when it feels the same. It looks exactly the same as home."

"I know what you mean," I told him, though that's not what I was thinking. Actually, I was thinking I'd never seen Canada look quite so foreign, as if we really had crossed a line here, or were about to as we drove deeper into Thunder Bay. *The world's largest trading post,* my father had billed it, *or at least fur-trading post. They built a monument to it, I think,* like he needed claims to fame as titillating as this to convince me to come along. *And I know you're busy packing, I know you're leaving tomorrow and it's a long drive for dinner, but I'd like to take you out, you know, hit up some of the bars together; you're old enough to drink if we're up there* (as if I didn't know that by now, as if I hadn't gone straight to Canada the weekend I'd turned nineteen). *It'll be like we're grown-ups on the town—what do you say?*

And what could I say to such a strange request, such an out-of-character and sudden interest in seeing me grown up, except yes? It almost felt like things were back the way they were right after my mother left—just me and Dad playing pretend—and I wonder now if that's what he was trying to recapture by putting me in the front seat and taking a drive.

Anyway, it kept my mind off Dex. Off what I would be flying into tomorrow.

"So here we are," he said. He pulled into an empty parking space in front of a small, kitschy-looking restaurant called The Lodge and made a grand gesture at the log-cabin facade. The building was patched over and run-down and showing through, in one corner, to the dull gray cinder blocks beneath the wooden frame. But my father sighed nostalgically. "My hangout once. Back when I used to go camping up by Grand Portage. I even took your mother here before you were born. We used to do things like that. Before." He glanced at me uncomfortably, cut the engine. "They've gone under a few times, I think, and part of it burned down a few years back. It didn't used to look so…"

"Unstable?" I offered.

I didn't mean it as an insult, but he seemed to take it as one. "*Empty* is more what I meant," he said. "Sorry."

"Hey," I told him quickly, apologetically, "it looks great. And I'm starved. And you're always saying how great the food is up here."

"They do have good fried chicken," he admitted.

"Though your mother used to go for the walleye. Your call."
He bounded suddenly out of his door and around to my
own, chivalrous as a first date. He said through the window,
voice muffled, strangely nervous, "You ready?"

When I was young, there were simple ways to make it easier. Like taking her things in secret, things I somehow
thought my father wouldn't miss: her rarely kept journal, discovered beneath the now-unused side of their mattress; a set
of real pearls from a dead aunt I'd never met; that red satin-
and-lace robe with the dragon embroidered on the back,
the one that made her look like a movie star. This last treasure, of course, was my favorite. The cool, slippery feel of it
against me, like sliding into a borrowed skin, one that meant
beauty and exotic foreignness and sexiness and, mostly,
being *her.* I used to wear it only in secret until the day my
father walked into my room and discovered the scene: my
hair twisted back, the way she used to wear hers, bobby pins
needling into my scalp and the red robe knotted tight over
my pajamas. Turning away from my mirror to meet his eyes,
I could see the startled look in them fading slowly to a
wounded confusion. "That's your mother's robe," he ob-
served quietly.

I said, quickly, guiltily, "I'm borrowing it. Until she gets
back." Balling up my hands beneath the cover of the too-
long sleeves, pressing my nails into my palms—I felt a
possessive resolve come over me, tempered only by that still-
pained look in his face. "She'd want me to wear it." Though
of course this probably wasn't true.

"She would not," he said, calling my bluff. "It's too old
for you."

"She let me wear it before," and I don't even remember now if I was lying or remembering or wishing, wistfully. "It's special. It's from Japan, from a soldier she knew." I paused, gauged his reaction—unreadable. I tried again. "She wouldn't want it to go to waste. It's good for dress-up. She wouldn't mind if I was careful." And, sensing his continuing disapproval, a last-ditch effort: "It makes me feel better, Dad."

Of course, that did it. He leaned his head sideways against the door frame, his eyes lingering on the red reminder wrapped around me before looking, finally, away. I saw something tighten in his face, harden in the clench of his jaw. He nodded, looking down. Then he said, "It's not from Japan. Just so you know. She bought it at the Wal-Mart in Cloquet." Turning to leave, and closing my door on his own words: "Try not to give too much value, Case, to things that don't deserve it."

After he left, I sat on my bed for a while and stared out the window: sunny and cold, the world aching for snow to cover up its ugliness, its mangled branches and dried-out lawns. I imagined how warm it must be in California, how green and gold. Then I locked my door and examined my hoard, which had grown slowly but steadily over the past few months. I put on the pearls, put on the dark lipstick I'd taken from a bathroom drawer before he cleaned them out—Passion Plum, a color like dying roses. Eyes closed, I traced my fingers over the pages of her journal, not wanting to break her trust by reading the words (which, I discovered later, were only movie plots rewritten as if she'd lived them). I stroked the texture of the paper from behind: the ballpoint braille of her handwriting, such intimacy in this raised surface, and I held my breath and tried to memorize this feeling. How it might have been to live inside her.

Would she miss these things herself? Probably. But if she missed them, she would have to know they were gone, and to know they were gone, she would have to come back. It was kind of like a bribe, running my fingers over those pearls and those words and wearing the robe so often it became pilled and worn thin on the seat and elbows. *Come back to claim them, come back to claim me.*

Inside The Lodge, we got menus shaped like wagon wheels and a table in the corner. My father sat with his back to the room, leaving me to face the almost-empty span of it: dark wood paneling on the walls and a single ceiling fan whirring indifferently against the heat. The still, unmoving air smelled stale but strangely welcoming, like wood smoke and sweet lemon cleanser, and I wondered what it was like twenty years ago. Wondered where my mother sat and what she thought of the giant moose head coming out of the wall, wondered if she sat here in this seat and looked across the table at my father minus twenty years. And I found myself wondering further into the past and into her mind—what she thought of him then, what were they like before I came along and made them three.

A *crowd*, he used to call it, or was it my mother who'd say that? *Two's company, two to tango, but three…*

We ordered drinks first: an awkward moment, since I wasn't sure what to say in front of my father. Everything I could think of seemed to admit to the fact I'd been drunk before. To match his own order (Jack and Coke) seemed too hard-edged; to order a Guinness, what I actually like best, seemed too informed about the differences of beers; to order wine was trying too hard. In the end, he decided for me— "And a Bud Light for my daughter," he told the waitress, who nodded her silvery head and trailed a stale cigarette smell as she moved away from our table. "Have you had it before?" he asked me quietly, conspiratorially, after she left.

I looked at him uncertainly. "No?"

"I didn't think so. It's pretty light," he said. "If you don't like it, you don't have to finish it."

Hard not to smile at his innocence, his ironic perception of me as a little girl even on this, our pseudo-grown-up date. "I'm sure it'll be fine."

"It goes well with the walleye, if that's what you're look-ing at." He looked up at me. "That what you're looking at?"

I cleared my throat and glanced at the menu. "I kind of feel like a grilled cheese."

He smiled vaguely and nodded, looked down at the menu and stroked his beard and looked back up, and all of a sudden it was like I was eleven again—so aware of the empty chair beside me, so aware that something was missing and there were certain things we couldn't say to each other, didn't have to say and shouldn't say because that would make it real.

"Honey?" he said suddenly. "You okay?"

"Sure. I'm fine." I fumbled with the folds of my menu. "Just thinking."

"About your trip?"

"Just—a lot of things."

My father cocked his head thoughtfully and hesitated. "You know," he said, and stopped again. "You know, I always thought when this time came, I'd know what to say. But I don't."

I looked at him, confused. "What time?"

"I guess I just...well, anyway. Just be careful, okay? Don't get your hopes up too high. If you can't find her, I mean, and even if you do—"

"Dad, what are you talking about?" And it took the echo of my own words, the contrast of the silence after them, to realize how loudly I'd spoken; I lowered my voice. "This trip isn't about me, and it isn't about Mom. I'm going to a funeral—I told you that."

"No, I know," he said quickly, running his hands through his thinning hair. "I know that."

"And anyway, what makes you think I'd be able to find her? It's not like I can just go knock on doors across L.A. and ask around."

"I just figured—I mean, why would you go all the way out there, unless—"

He stopped, looked up with confusion and dismay at the smoky waitress who had drifted back to our table. She looked back at him, then at me, set our glasses down between us, and nudged the menus toward my father. "I'll be back," she whispered.

He nodded, then sighed as she hurried away. "I just thought that it was funny you were going so far for a funeral when you didn't seem to know him that long."

I started to interrupt, but he could see it coming, a whole new argument—*What does it matter how long I've known him, you have no idea what I feel, what it is, what it means*—and he blocked it with his hand. "I know you miss her," he said quietly. "Okay? That's all. And I know you wonder sometimes, still. I just don't want you to get your hopes up. You know, in case she's..." He frowned. "Changed."

I stared into the bright golden eye of my beer, wide, glowing, blinked, and shook my head. "It's been — a weird time, I guess. Sorry, I shouldn't throw that back at you."

"It's okay." He looked awkwardly away. After a moment, he took another drink; I joined him this time, and he nodded at my glass as I set it down. "Like it?"

"It's great," I said quickly, quietly craving a heavier drink, substantial enough to calm the jittery anxiety spreading through me. Despite our apparent resolution, something still wasn't sitting well in my stomach. "Hey, Dad?" I started, but the waitress had returned (perceiving a truce in the battle, I figured, from across the room), and as we placed our orders, I felt the unsettled thing slipping from my mind like an unfinished thought, something I could press down and maybe, if I were lucky, not think about later.

"Yeah, honey?" he said as the waitress walked away. He smiled. He looked, for a moment, the way I like him best: calm and confident and forward-leaning, all of his attention focused patiently on me. I hesitated. Then I smiled back and held up my glass for a toast.

"Thanks for the drink," I said, and he clinked his glass with mine.

"To growing up," he said. "Here goes."

The first time we had dinner together, just the two of us: his eyes looking straight into mine, clear and cool like the lake on a calm day, no one to interrupt them or pull them away, and I found myself secretly liking that.

The first time I brought home a test with a perfect score: his eyes like the lake in the sun, that bursting sparkle. It was something she had never cared about. It was pride, I guess, revealing itself in the way he looked at me, and that's when I started getting straight As.

The first time I brought home a boy: his eyes like the lake after a dry summer, low and tired and cold. The same sad, almost-jealous look he used to give my mother and me from the top of the basement stairs. After that, I still got As; I still sat in the front seat like a sidekick, still played the converted role of Daddy's-Girl-ex-Momma's-Girl. But I had found the thing, finally, to drive us apart: the third person, that extra variable, coming in between us like a wedge. A splinter, a lump in the throat.

Three's a crowd, and it was again. And in so many ways, some of which I have only just learned, it has been ever since.

By the end of the meal, those last cold, crusty french fries sprawling loose across my plate and the buzz of a second beer swirling in my head, I remembered what it was that didn't sit well, and he noticed.

"You got something to say," he said, chattering his ice cubes and finishing his drink. "I can tell."

I looked down into a third beer I didn't want. "Can I ask you something?" He didn't answer, which I took as an expectant *yes*; I pushed my glass away and looked up. "What did you mean when you said maybe she's changed?" And when I saw the response in his face, down-turned eyes that wouldn't look back at mine, I knew there was a story here, a bad one, waiting to be told. "You don't, like...*know* something, do you?"

"Not exactly." He hesitated.

"What then?"

No answer. He sipped from his glass as if forgetting it was empty, wiped his mouth and his face with the paper napkin beneath his silverware. Pulled on his beard and I realized I hated it when he did that—it was his way of stalling, seeming to choose thoughtfully between his words when he was actually avoiding them.

"It was in one of her letters," he said finally. "Way back, you know, when she still wrote sometimes. She sent her address. Said she sent it to you, too."

I nodded. I'd written there twice without telling him, long letters asking about auditions and the ocean. She never answered either of them.

"Thing was," he said carefully, "that address wasn't hers. She said so. And the way she made it sound, it made me wonder...."

He reached across the table for my hand. A strange gesture, one that seemed more appropriate for a lover than a father, but I let him take it, cool and lifeless, and wrap it up into his own. "Case," he said quietly, looking down at my plate. "You should know something by now," and I could tell from his tone it wasn't something I was going to like. I tried to catch the waitress's eye—*check, please—please, just get me out before I can hear any more—*

"I think," he said quietly, "your mother might be married."

I laughed then, relieved, and looked back to my father who was looking down. "I don't think so, Dad."

"Remarried, I mean."

"I know. But you can't get remarried without a divorce."

And he finally looked up. The air changing with that look, a strange buzzing, something building—not exactly the buzzing of the beer. More like the sound of a car on wet pavement as it gets close to you, louder and louder...

"Don't say that," I whispered.

He nodded, and *whoosh*—the force as it passes you by— tumble of your heart, wake pulling at your body, the reced- ing, eerie silence of afterward as you watch the taillights blink away into the black. Leaving you stranded.

"I'm sorry, honey, I should have told you."

"How long ago?" I asked him.

"Almost four years." An answer so surprising, it didn't even surprise me.

"And you never said anything."

"I didn't want—"

"And you let me think—all this time, you let me *believe*—"

I stopped; my breath stopped; everything stopped. He stared at me helplessly. The waiters were listening now, I could tell, filling and refilling the saltshakers with focused concentration. "Okay," I said quietly, leaning in. "Okay. Tell me."

"Tell you?"

"What happened. The story, whatever. *Why.*"

My father sighed. "It's not that simple, Case. A lot of things go into it you didn't know. Fights we used to have, certain things about her health. Her mental health."

He glanced up, but I didn't look away, my mind calm, steady, even. The buzzing had succumbed already to an empty clarity, that numbness again, as if I'd waded a little far- ther into the icy depths of the lake—no more pricking, no more pain, just a lifeless detachment, as if a part of me wasn't there at all.

"I guess it started when you were nine or ten," he said. "She got pretty depressed one winter, the winter Grandma got sick, and she never really came out of it like usual. The Winter Frolic winter—you know."

I stared at him. "Everyone knows."

"Right." He cleared his throat, ignored my tone. "It was around then she stopped sleeping. Stayed up all night when I had the graveyard shift, you remember? How she'd keep you up with her? So sure I was lying to her all the time, so suspicious. And somehow she got it in her head I was having an affair." He rattled his ice cubes like a drink might appear there; I slid him my glass and he took a long, grateful pull on the beer. "I thought it was going to pass," he said. "This crazy paranoia, but not crazy enough to really be *crazy*, you know? I was used to her moods by then. She got like that when she was pregnant with you, and I figured it would just go away like before. But it didn't go away. And then it got worse when Grandma died, that whole year before she left for Hollywood—crazy-paranoid, hiding in the basement and picking fights with me and still not sleeping. Wouldn't take her pills once we got her some pills. And acting. It was always, every day, all the time, about *acting*." He sighed. "I tried to understand it. I really did, tried to give her grieving time and all that. One of the doctors said it was like an escape, that it was probably how she used to deal with Grandma's drinking and she'd snap out of it when she came to terms with everything. But she didn't. She *wouldn't*—like she was a kid again, this long game of make-believe. It got to the point I couldn't tell what was real anymore, when it was really her and when it was this obsession with pretending, mind games all the time and lying all the time and calling it

a performance until it built into this thing that was too big—
for us, for anyone."

He stopped, took a deep breath, and looked up from our
hands. The yellowish light above his head made him look
very old or very tired, deep shadows in the caverns of his
eyes. "Listen," he said quietly, "it wasn't that we didn't love
each other once. And I wanted her to come back, I did. But
when it's everything building up over so long, over years, and
then she just leaves it like that, all built up and ready to
fall—" He shrugged helplessly. "Something had to break
eventually."

"But that's not why she left," I said. He frowned as if he
didn't understand. "She didn't leave because of you. She left
to be an actress. It was like…" I looked down, realized how
naïve it sounded now. "Her destiny."

"Not exactly, Case." Looking down, too, when I looked
up. "I think—I think she left because she thought I was seeing someone else."

"But you weren't."

"No, I wasn't." A pause. "Not then."

And that numbness now, the most aching kind of emptiness, spreading through my whole body. Spreading out from
my hand, up my arm and into my chest and my lungs which,
suddenly, wouldn't take in enough air when I breathed—I
pulled away.

"It wasn't a big deal, Case. Years ago, and it didn't last—"

"Stop—"

"You gotta understand," he cut in. "It's like—" He flung
his gaze around the room as if confused: the empty tables,
the waiters moving quickly away as if caught. "It's like carry-

ing a tray of dishes, and someone's standing there telling you you're going to drop it. And while they're telling you this, they're adding on plates, stacking everything up against you. It's like eventually you start to believe it, you can't escape it—you're going to drop it, period. It starts feeling like you *want* to drop it, just to finally get it over with. To finally deal with something."

I looked away. I wasn't seeing him anyway. I was seeing women assembled in rows, a police lineup of suspects: our young, widowed neighbor, looking up from her begonias to cast heavy-lidded glances across our lawn. My seventh-grade English teacher, who requested extra parent-teacher conferences under the pretense of troubling personal narratives. The college girl who taught me piano, or some secretary from the plant, or the pediatrician with my mother's hands. I wanted to ask, but more than that, I wanted not to know.

Just pretend it's someone else. A story. This is not your father, not you. This is not your life like his goddamn plates.

"She'd been in California for years at that point," he said. "She was already writing me about a divorce. She was seeing someone else before I even thought of seeing anyone. I was almost sure."

I nodded.

"You understand?"

"Sure." Smiling, though I don't know what it looked like; he didn't smile back. "You're telling me it's *her* fault," I added calmly. "I completely understand."

"Casey—"

"No," I said, not smiling anymore. "No, Dad, it's one thing to tell me the truth—it's one thing to tell me my whole life I've been lied to and here's the truth, finally, have fun at your funeral, *that's* one thing—but don't blame her for it, don't try to tell me—"

"Hey, listen, please. I'm not *blaming* her, okay?"

I stopped then and sat back and tried to digest this as he folded his hands beside his empty plate. I felt everything burning hot and ready to burst inside my chest, hated this feeling, too close to crazy. I craved something logical, the neatness of cause and effect: *She's not here because she was right. Even if she didn't know it, she was right about him in the end. She left because of him.*

She did not leave because of you.

If I could just hate him, everything would be so easy. But looking across the table and into his eyes, silvery and shining and waiting for me to say something, anything to break this silence, I realized I could never hate anyone who still loved me back.

I said, my voice not so cool anymore, "She told me she was coming home. In the letters. That she'd be back some-day." He nodded. "I believed that," I said. "I thought you be-lieved that," and he reached for my hand again. His palm wide and waiting to be filled; I stared at its openness, its emptiness, the suddenly unreadable map of his life. "An actress."

"She always was." He tried a commiserating smile, but I didn't smile back. I felt so sad for him right then, his blind belief that things could ever be the same now.

"She lied to me," I said.

"Yes." He wasn't smiling anymore.

"You lied to me, too."

Hesitating: "Yes."

"It was nice, in a way. Letting me pretend for so long. That she might come back."

"Case—"

"The thing is," and I felt my voice getting thicker, the racing heart of holding back tears, "if she didn't leave because of me—if she loved me like she said—"

Then why didn't she take me with her?

Then why did she lie to me?

He shook his head. "I don't know," he said helplessly, and that's when I started to cry, felt it come over me like a wave and succumbed to it, easy as falling backward and letting it drift you away. It became something deeper than myself, the crying, and it felt wonderful, though I think it scared my father. He moved to the chair beside me, tried to wrap his arms around mine, and pulled me half into his potbelly, half into the edge of the table. "Let her go," he kept saying, "I had to let her go," and after a while I stopped listening. I watched the window, my quivering reflection, and beyond that, the stifling clouds rolling over the stars. *Watch for the ones to wish on*, Dex used to say, *the stars that shoot forward are the ones with good luck.* And my mother's voice behind his: *That's your life mapped up there, that's fate in the sky. No way to change where fate's meant to lead you.* But I knew, I still know, they were both wrong. All I could see, all those stars really showed me, was old, dead light, cool and false in its brightness: something long since past yet somehow present, the only thing to find in it a kind of resurrected beauty.

After a moment like that, he pulled away, as if sensing the awkwardness of this embrace. He handed me an extra napkin and I blew my nose, closed my eyes and tried to clear my swollen head. "Please understand," he said, "I never wanted to tell you like this. I mean, right before you have to leave, go to this funeral, everything. But I didn't want you to go there without knowing the truth. If you found her. If she told you another story, made it sound like—" And he put his hands together one last time, put them together on top of mine, and leaned so close I could smell the brownish hint of whisky beneath his words. "Maybe it's selfish. But I didn't want you to find her, to be there, hating me back here."

And I'd known it before, but I felt it then: that I would never hate him, that I couldn't.

But I didn't tell him anything.

what love means

She's seen it a dozen times by now. She keeps it a secret, afraid it could be construed as a kind of obsession, a cinematic ritual: same movie, same theater, same seat in the middle of the sparse crowd as if she is the heart, the warm center of this room where fiction meets reality. Usually she goes alone. She's trying to figure it out, why the idea of a role about a role, of fiction inside another fiction, feels achingly familiar.

Onscreen, the director hands the actress a script: The scene is a callback, the actress's second audition. I love you, *he reads aloud, and she blushes, though maybe she doesn't mean to; already the lines they read are not just the lines they read.* I love you, *he says again, and keeps his eyes down. His jaw tightens against something not printed on the page.*

Liar, *she whispers.*

You would know.

Not me. I can't lie about what I don't know about. *She clears her throat. The rustle of a turning page.* And I don't.

Don't what?

Know. What love means.

I do.

See? That's what makes you a liar. *Glancing up from the script, mouth tightening with resolution — but whose mouth, whose role? The actress, or the actress playing the actress? No way to tell, no way to interpret where the lines break down, blur and blend two stories into one.*

She'll watch it a dozen times, she could watch it a dozen more — same lines, same lies and silences, same walking away without resolution or explanation — and still she'd wonder why she can't stop seeing her own life in the story. Why it feels so right, somehow: not having an ending. Not knowing what love means.

Why she can't stop trying to figure it out anyway.

connection

From the plane, I can see the changes as we make our way across the country: first those flat green farms in patchwork patterns, like quilts across the quiet Midwest. Pulled up, then, into fractured mountains, pulled back to expose the red-brown nakedness of canyons, their wide and craving mouths. Then, briefly, green in the hills like something waking up—and down to flat brown—and up again toward green with white patches of snow, taller and brighter—

So many states I've never seen. I start thinking, can't help it, of the places Dex might have taken me, phantom stops on a ghost ride through the country.

We could have driven along the lake sometime, straight up through Canada with the anchor of water on my side to guide us. A ribbon of stony shoreline to follow, up and up until we reached the top of the map, everything else below us and far away.

Ladies and gentlemen, we're beginning our final descent into Los Angeles....

We could have driven westward to retake the trip she must have taken—by bus, I'm guessing, or in other people's cars—passed farmhouses, supermarkets, train stations, seen what she must have seen, and I might have told him everything this way.

What are you doing? Where do you think you're going? There could be someone sitting beside me.

Who is it you're looking for? And with a squawk of rubber, sudden surge of gravity, the wheels touch ground, we're here, we've landed, and I think: we could have gone anywhere. We could have driven home and been somehow different for it, the kind of trip that comes full circle for a reason, that doesn't shoot straight across the country into nothingness.

It was the night after I spoke to the police—four nights ago, now—that I answered the phone and heard Dex on the line.

At least I thought it was Dex. It sounded just like him, his husky *hello*, his way of saying my name: *Casey?* An upward tilt at the end, waiting for confirmation, and I felt the blood sliding down beneath my skin, my head empty, thrown full into a white-spotted spin—I fumbled for a chair.

"Dex?" I whispered. Waiting for confirmation...

That didn't come. His voice again, but not saying the words I wanted to hear: "No, sorry, this is Kevin. Kevin Stone. I'm Dex's brother."

"Oh." I sank down, stared at the reflection of myself in the kitchen window, hunched and ghostly in the square of black glass. The voice was still rattling nervously against my ear, and I tried to focus on it, this dull reflection, this proximity to something gone: "...hope I didn't upset you. The police gave me your number, and I thought I should let you know they made the official declaration…" (I could hear, now, a slight difference in their voices. This one spoke a little too fast and a little too high, too young, a clipped nervousness that didn't match Dex's lilting, lazy tone. Like he didn't know, couldn't know, what he was talking about.) "…thought you should know we're having a memorial for him this weekend. In L.A. I know it's short notice, but my dad figured you might want to come out here. He's arranged a ticket for you if you're interested. We'd really like to meet you." A pause, still nervous. "I'd like to meet you."

"Why?" I asked. The word dropped from my lips and tumbled awkwardly into the phone, rude and heavy and hard to answer. "I mean—oh, God, I don't know. I really appreciate that. The offer, I mean."

"They say it's for closure."

"Yeah, I've heard that."

"So you'll come, then?"

I hesitated. I tried to imagine how it would go: the black-clad family with puffy eyes, gnarled hands clutching at each other, and the bass chords of weeping filling a half-empty church. Not the kind of closure I was looking for, and I shook my head to clear the image.

The voice said suddenly, "He talked to me, you know. About you."

And that stopped me. I held my breath. "What did he say?"

"That…I don't know. That he loved you, I guess." Sighing lightly, but loud enough for me to hear it. "Probably the last thing you want to hear."

Strange how nice it sounded now that I couldn't say it back.

"It's okay," I told him, and I could hear the thickness coming into my own voice, closed my eyes and swallowed some of it down. "I like hearing it."

"He said you're the reason he was meant to leave L.A."

I couldn't help but smile at that, at how much it sounded like something he would say. I realized if I let myself fall into the darkness behind my eyes, just fill my sight and my ears and my chest, all my senses, with the echo of this voice on the phone, it was almost enough for me to imagine him there, telling me himself, on the other end. Some colossal joke, some crazy, balls-out, cruelly romantic way of making me see we were meant to be together—*Gotta admit it now, don't you? You love me, don't you?* and I could hear him breathing in my ear, pressed it closer, slid down in the chair and felt the blood coming back into my face.

"It would mean a lot to me," he said. "If you'd come."

I said, "When's the flight?"

There is no one to meet me at the airport.

Which is what I expected—I have clear instructions to give a cabdriver, directions to a hotel where someone I don't know has arranged a room for me—but it still hurts like being stood up, an empty mailbox on Valentine's Day. It's stupid, but I almost expected him to be here, waiting for me, dressed in the guise of his brother, or maybe his brother dressed in the guise of him, a fantasy, someone, anyone, ready to put me in a car and drive.

"Excuse me, miss?" A deep voice, rugged and rough underneath, and I turn with a dreamlike, illogical hope in my chest—"You're holding up the line," says a pale-faced security guard, frowning at the clot of travelers behind me. "Step out of the way, please."

"Sure," I mumble, moving quickly to the side where I stare at the masses as they heave by. I've been to airports before—Minneapolis, Chicago, one long-ago trip to Florida—but it's never been so hectic, so crowded with faces and sounds and bright, bursting colors. A freckled boy darts past me, slams my legs with a red backpack as he runs, his tired-looking but laughing mother following in pursuit; then a group of dark-haired, dark-skinned businessmen chattering loudly in a language I don't understand; behind them a Hispanic couple, arguing I think, voices rising like sirens as they move past me, past a sign beside an American flag: *Los Angeles Remembers Flight 308*, and I turn quickly away. Feel myself moving backwards toward a convenience store, out of the way of a beeping golf cart with a fat old lady hanging off the back and right into a rack of postcards that spills sideways before I can stop it, Disneyland and the Hollywood sign spitting themselves endlessly across the floor—"Oh, shit, sorry," I tell the clerk, kneeling to help her clean up until she shoos me away impatiently, trills something sharp in Spanish I don't understand and I back up, back out, nowhere to go but into the crowd and this surge of faces moving blindly past—

I close my eyes. Pull myself into myself and let it flow around me, a rock in this current of other people's lives.

When I open them again, it seems a little calmer, though that's probably just me. I turn and wheel my bag toward that safe-looking sign in the distance, GROUND TRANSPORTATION, because that's what I want: I want to be grounded, stable, steady as I move. I don't want to make my way through this alone, my bag dragging behind me like dead weight—

(sudden flash to a man leaning against the wall, longish blond stubble like Dex, the same build, same everything…)

If only you were here with me, you could lead the way. And I could tell you I love you, whisper it from behind into your ear, just once, just to make sure you know. Maybe that's what I'm still dragging with me, and if I could just find you to tell you—

(another one in a brown leather jacket, hat covering the face, starting to turn)

Just say it once to test it out, hear it back…

"May I help you?" And I pull my hand away from the delicate shoulder it's resting on—the woman who's distracted me from all the men who might be Dex. She has turned around, face quizzical, only slightly irritated. She's younger than I thought, not much older than I am, but the way she looked from behind—the burnt-sugar hair like mine, gold and gleaming, and that sharp-edged grace to her shoulders, that jump in my stomach—

Mom?

"I'm sorry," I mumble. "I thought…you were someone else…"

And stumble away. I feel drunk, alien, an impostor, no place for me here. I see signs for taxis and move numbly toward the line of cars, all the same yellow in the afternoon sun.

"Yeah, this is Kevin. Casey?"

"Yeah," I say, too loudly. "I mean, hi."

"Well, hi."

"I just wanted to let you know I made it. To the hotel."

"Okay." A pause, as if he's waiting for me to say more, neither of us sure whose turn it is; I feel a mutual awkwardness, that first-date kind of awkwardness, twisting painfully through the phone line. "I gave you directions to the church, right?" he says at last.

"Yes."

"And you can catch a cab there on your own? Like I said, my dad will cover the travel costs, so don't worry—"

"No, no, it's fine, really," I hear myself saying, though I realize as I'm saying it how little money I actually have with me. I clear my throat. "Or we can talk about it later, whatever. I'm sure you're pretty busy—"

"So I'll see you tomorrow then," he says quickly, and I finally catch it, something cool in his voice, something that says I *have better things to do right now than talk to you.* Not the tone I remember from my kitchen phone, the warm intimacy of his voice in my ear. Had I imagined it then?

I tell him, "Sure, see you tomorrow," and hear the airy sound of the open line contract to static.

Which means I'm alone tonight. Nothing to do but examine the facts, start piecing it together, finally. I hold this in my mind and weigh it for a moment. Then I hang up the phone. I lock the door and open the curtains and unzip my suitcase before I lose my nerve. Take an inventory of what I've gathered, like pieces of a puzzle before I know what the picture will be...

First, a pile of letters, files. Some of them my own, worn and creased with time and handling; others, my father's attempt at a peace offering, slipped under my door last night. The envelopes are frayed along their seams from careless, eager ripping. The file folders, from a stuffy psychologist's office in Duluth, are crisp and clean as a lab coat. They still hold all the possibilities, explanations that might be good ones and might not be. Which is why I haven't read them yet.

I put the papers on the bed, and they seem so small against the wide, floral expanse of the comforter. Then I put these things beside them:

A red satin robe that's starting to unravel in one corner.

That heart-shaped head shot, folded down the middle; those blank, smiling eyes. *Love Mom.*

A tattered postcard.

And the map of Los Angeles I found abandoned on a bench in the airport. A souvenir, an artifact from someone else's life; they were visiting Dodger Stadium, which is circled in ballpoint. A neat black path curves out of the circle like a balloon string, winds backward up the freeway, and stops at Paramount Studios, downtown Hollywood, just a quarter inch away from my invisible hotel.

So that is where I am. I am at the frayed end of a balloon string.

I don't mean to think it. I don't know what it means. But I know how it feels, and that's how this feels. The let-go end of something that's forever floating away.

I lie down and look up at the blank white page of the ceiling. I say "Balloon" out loud just to hear my voice, which doesn't sound like mine. "Balloon, balloon," until it doesn't make sense anymore. The air conditioner grunts loudly in response. I think it must be broken; there is occasionally the gurgle of water, the sound of breaking ice like a death rattle, and I think I should either call the front desk or turn off the air. But I don't want to move.

So instead, I close my eyes. I put my arms out and feel it surrounding me, the papers and the satin and the creased heart, all of it. I will lie in this. I will sleep in this and wake up hours from now to find it scattered, randomized, waiting to be ordered, and then I will pick it up, then I will put it in order, and maybe in the process of this I will start to understand what happened to her and why.

I feel it folding together against my fingers. The paper crackles — the sound of his smile. I wonder, for the first time, how they'll bury someone who isn't there.

survivor guilt

When she was six, my mother killed her father.

At least that was the story as I understood it—but then, I was young at the time, and my grandmother, the teller of the tale, was drinking. It was summer, and the air was juicy and sweet with the heat, like overripe fruit—even that smell to it, and dampness, the feel of breath on the back of my neck and sweat drooling down my half-full glass of Coke. We sat at my grandmother's kitchen table with our drinks, looking out at the way the air wavered on the blacktop, both of us watching the driveway and waiting for my mother's car to pull in and take me home.

"Like ghosts," said my grandmother, slurring a little. She nodded at the heat-blasted pavement: air that seemed somehow liquid, the vibrato quiver of stepping into a puddle. "Think your grandpa's out there?"

I turned, confused, to the loose pink folds of her tired face. I was seven or eight: old enough to understand that my grandfather, whom I'd never met, had been dead for a long time, and young enough to think if he was out in the drive-way, maybe it wasn't a good thing.

"Your mama wasn't much younger than you are," my grandmother added, breath like a cellar as she moved her face closer. "When her daddy died. Did you know that?"

"No." A twinge of excitement, the shock of those words and the underlying shock of thinking my mother was ever my age. "What happened?" I asked.

She paused, turned her watery gaze back to the window. Mouth poised and pursed over the rim of her glass and eyes blurring with distance—"I could tell you a story," she said. "But you can't tell your mother you know what she did." And I promised (though I knew I was lying, of course, would never hide anything from my mother), and this is what she told me. Or at least this is the image I created, directed in my own mind—the film clip of my mother's early life, fil-tered through alcohol, memory, time, and all that's hap-pened since—

As she walks home from school, sleet. It's the silvery October kind that cuts against your face like pins, the kind you wish would just relax into snow, but this is not a forgiving after-noon. My mother takes small-legged strides into the wind, head bent, gusts of the coming storm strong enough to knock her off balance. She is how old—in kindergarten? First grade? Old enough to walk alone to an empty house; young enough to walk without the assurance of gravity's hold on her.

And fade in to the warm silence of the living room. Her fa-ther works until dinner in Industrial Park, making the sides of other people's homes. Her mother isn't home, is rarely home

*this time of day, so for a moment, once she's changed her socks
and pulled the melting ice chunks from her hair, she forgets
about her chores and sits beside the window, that eerie blue
afternoon light against her face as she watches the sleet fade,
gradually, to white. It's hypnotic, it must be, the way slow-
building afternoon storms are. The sun going down, the pelt-
ing ice slowing as it fattens into flakes, and suddenly the
swirling depth of it across the neighborhood, sharper white
against softer white—she has to blink her eyes and look away
to steady herself. Or maybe she doesn't, maybe she keeps her
eyes open and something strange is running through her,
thickening into swirling, white rising up and dark coming in
behind it . . .*

Something is going to happen today.

*The sidewalks, dark and wet, the snow-laced grass, the
bright-lit sign of the funeral home down the street flickering
out in sync with the light in the kitchen—she shivers in the
sudden dark, grateful to glimpse the slow-moving headlights of
her mother's crusted car. They curve into the driveway, hesitate for a moment before blinking out, and the daughter can
see her mother adjusting her hair in the rearview mirror. She
smooths the swoop of blonde above her eye, tucks in a stray
curl. She has a standing appointment every Monday afternoon at a salon in Duluth, likes him to come home to a hot
dinner and a beautiful wife, thinks it's safer that way. Satisfied, she balances two grocery bags in her arms and steps
effortlessly from the car, hurries past the window without
noticing the hungry eyes watching her. An afterimage lingers
in her wake, graceful and tenuous as a ghost: pressed green
dress, stylish brown coat, the hair as polished and perfect as a
magazine model's. It is a presentation for him, of course, not*

for her; already, the daughter understands that this is how things are supposed to go.

After a moment, she hears the grinding sound of a key and her mother's voice calling, without hesitation, Have you heard from your father?

And maybe the light is fading faster now, maybe she can't look away, falling deeper into the trance of it—is she afraid of what she knows? Could she want it in some way she won't admit? Does she think about it before she says, quietly, to her own reflection: Daddy's dead, Mom.

A pause. There has to be. Then the rustle of grocery bags settling on the counter, distracted hands digging around in their depths. A cleared throat. Did you have a good day at school?

Fine.

Why are you sitting here in the dark, baby?

The lights went out.

Outside, the storm deepens, distant houses fading into white. She listens to the futile flicking of a light switch behind her, a pause—then the angry crumple of crushed paper bags, sudden and sharp enough to make her jump, glance toward her mother. Dammit! Well, that's beautiful. That's just god-damn beautiful. Your father...*Looking over at her daughter as if expecting her to finish the thought. Her face, once beautiful itself (at least allegedly—hard for me to picture this), twists now into something like accusation.* And how am I supposed to cook dinner?

The daughter sinks back against the couch cushion, turning away, finally, from the fast-fading light. It's not your fault, Mom.

He's not going to like this, he's not— *She closes her eyes, shakes her head, and opens them again.* Why did you say that?

Say what?

Daddy's dead. My grandmother balls up the grocery bags with quick movements, tries to stuff them in the trash can where they overflow like burnt popovers. Daddy's dead, she mimics, mystifyingly angry, why? Why would you say something horrible like that?

There is a burning feeling behind her cheeks, a confused shame. Why did she say it, except that it seemed true, this thing that doesn't seem true anymore? I don't know, *she mumbles.*

Do you think he's going to like hearing you said that?

No.

Do you *want* that?

No, *and maybe by now she's starting to cry. Because what else is there to do in a dark room filled with yelling and guilt and this strange moment creeping away like a bad dream, nothing left behind except that feeling of something wrong and the frustration of not remembering what it was you dreamt?*

Of course that's when my grandfather walks through the door: the unexpected twist, the anticlimax to prove my mother wrong. He is tall and quiet, the kind of man who looks down in photographs and smiles like a grimace. He glances around: an angry wife, a tear-streaked daughter, a storm coming in and no lights on. You see? *my grandmother says sharply.* Your father's not dead, is he?

And what would he say to this, how to cast the starring role? He seems, from my mother's closely guarded and rarely revealed memories of him, like the kind of man who would not say anything, who would grimace and walk slowly upstairs to a hidden bottle, the broad expanse of his back like a blank face, unanswering.

But that doesn't make a good scene. Instead, I imagine he moves quickly to my mother and smooths back her hair: What's wrong, Lila? *Because in my movie he is the hero, the one to face off against the beautiful, evil villain smoldering across the room. I see him in an appropriate black-and-white, like a cowboy in an old western; I've only ever seen him in black-and-white pictures, and it's hard to bloom this image into color.* Don't cry, *he tells her, and his voice is soft, effeminate, soothing in her ear.*

I'm so sorry, *my mother whispers, looking up for forgiveness: the most penitent of survivors, guilt tinged with the luck of a second chance.* I didn't mean to see it. *She chokes a little on the confession and he pulls her close, his grayness coming over and around her colors as if he's already dead, fading away.*

Tell him, Lila, *my grandmother orders. A residue of frustration in her face, but also something close to fear (a fear my mother could recall, but difficult for me to imagine: Who would be intimidated by this gentle John Wayne, this older version of my own father?).* Go ahead, *she insists, cannot let this go, this thing that will, she believes, deflect his impending anger away from herself—* Tell him what you told me.

And maybe she knows it isn't fair to blame her daughter, knows it in the years to come when she continues to blame her for the outcome of this night. Knows, as her beauty fades over double shifts and sudden bills, a lack of insurance and a shortage of eligible men, that the blame for her life is her own to take on, the inevitable upshot of dependence upon one man. But maybe this is her lie, her escape route, her game of pretend; maybe this is how my mother learns it, how to find relief by changing her story. Tell him, Lila, but through her tears, my mother can't answer. She is pulling into herself now, shrinking the world down to nothing; and as she closes them off, she feels for the first time that lovely and lonely escape of the mind.

I could pull her out. Here behind the camera, I could have her look up into his forgiving eyes, ask him to stay, to put her to bed with a happy ending and sit at her feet until she falls asleep. I could change her life, change all of their lives, a director's cut of memory. At the very least, I could let her tell him good-bye when he leaves that night.

But she doesn't, and I won't. Because when does it ever happen like that? Instead, my grandfather closes the door against the dark house, his wife's voice, and the still-throbbing undertone of my mother's sobs. Can you see him there, looking out into the frantic white? Amid the lonely silence of falling snow, nighttime hovering behind a purple sky, he recalls those words when he walked inside: You see? Your father's not dead, is he? Turning that over and around in his mind, wondering what it means as he walks slowly to his car, he slams the door and spreads his calloused hands against the wheel.

Or maybe he isn't thinking this at all, is thinking only of his next drink as he turns the ignition.

What I do know is this: there was a premonition, a tap into destiny. There was a storm—nineteen inches overnight, a record for the date. There was a bar, a drink, a next drink and, sometime during the quiet white of that evening, a crash on

Highway 61 involving my grandfather, a telephone pole, and no one else.

"Almost perfect, the cops told me. Almost perfectly head-on," as she took another swallow. "Couldn't have aimed it any better if he tried."

She didn't sound so sure.

I asked her quietly, "Was it the snow, Grandma?"

She sniffed a little and looked out at the driveway. "It wasn't the snow, dear." But she didn't say what it was, what had caused it, and as I watched her thin lips tighten when our car came into view, I found myself wondering if she thought, somehow, it might have been my mother.

I imagine my mother wondered the same thing.

I'm starting to understand how she felt.

the wrong reasons

It was sometime in the middle of that hazy space between the police and the plane ride, those strange few days when time seemed both to stop and speed up, blurring days together into one long day of waiting, waiting, endless waiting, that I ran into Ellie. I didn't mean to. Usually I went out of my way to avoid Fourth Street (she worked there, a clerk at the pharmacy), anything to prevent dealing with the awkwardness that accompanies running into someone from whom you've grown apart—especially when she used to be your best friend. But remembering anything seemed harder than usual during that week; I'd forget to brush my teeth, feed the fish, buy groceries when I went out for groceries, and it was the day I forgot to walk on Third Street instead of Fourth that I saw her unmistakable gleam of dark red hair down the sidewalk and realized my mistake.

She was standing outside the pharmacy, smoking a cigarette in the glaring sunshine, arms crossed against her chest and looking just the way she'd always looked, just the way I'd always wanted to be: calm, cool, a little angry at the world, but in a way she could control. A puff of smoke, an arched eyebrow, impatient gaze trained at the distance as if waiting for her real life to come along, or at least for a boy to distract her from this one. It was the same cool stare I saw looking back at me that day on the sidewalk, and I knew it was too late, couldn't turn around no matter how tired my brain was from rolling Dex around its empty caverns. I kept walking and she watched me, waited for me to come to her.

"Long time, Case," she said as I got closer.

I nodded. I stopped in front of her and looked her straight in the eye, the same way she was looking at me. "Too long," I said quietly, and that was all. I was too tired to fake it, pretend everything was the same between us and fall predictably into the small talk she expected; she blinked and shrugged and dropped her cigarette to the ground. When she looked up at me, her face seemed softer. She smiled.

"You look like hell," she said.

Which was just like her, and it made me smile back.

"I'm on my break," Ellie told me. "Not busy today anyway. Want to walk?"

And I nodded, and we turned together toward the water without having to suggest a destination. Past the drugstore, past Barber John's and the duck lady's house with its shit-strewn yard and patient mallards waiting for their next feeding. Down the hill past First Avenue (a tempting glance down the heat-trembling length of it: Dex's apartment, don't look don't look), along the tracks until we slowed instinctively, nearing the familiar shadows of the docks. As if she knew without asking I was headed there anyway, and it made me so illogically grateful, so nostalgic for those days we seemed to know each other inside out, that I wanted to cry.

"How's school?" she asked after we'd gone for a while in silence. I hesitated, not sure how to answer; it had always felt weird, this difference between us, my leaving the previous fall and her staying in Two Harbors to work at the pharmacy. Not that my leaving was all that different than her staying—I still lived at home, still borrowed my father's rattling Oldsmobile and commuted daily to the theater building at UMD, a half hour away. But it felt different, like my world had grown a little while hers had stayed the same, and maybe that was the beginning of it, the split that Dex would widen.

I forced a smile and shrugged. "Not as fun cutting class without you."

"Get out. You never cut class and you know it."

I laughed, but it came out awkward, loose and heavy as a flat note. I watched her out of the corner of my eye. The way she swung her arms on the same beats as mine, or maybe the way I did. She'd gained weight, I noticed, but in an attractive way, an older way, reshaped with the kind of cheekbones and hips and breasts that clashed with my own frame of sharps and angles; she looked good, but she also looked wrong. And I wondered with every difference I noticed—the neat white blouse, sleeveless but buttoned high, the responsible shoes and lack of makeup, this stranger I'd known my whole life—if maybe she saw something in me that scared her the same way.

"Hey, El?" I said, both our eyes squinting against the sun on water. "I haven't changed, you know."

She smiled. She nudged me a little with her shoulder, or maybe she just stumbled; it didn't matter. "We never do," she said.

And down to the lake. We sat on the grass at the periphery of the shade, beside the long, dark docks waiting boatless and empty for something to come in. It was where we used to go after school to smoke cigarettes and watch the dock men load ore into the boats, and Ellie automatically offered me her pack of Camel Lights. I took one and lit it off her match, smoked it the way I had back then, pulling the smoke only as far as the back of my mouth and letting it trickle out in a thin, airy stream. Wondering if I still looked as glamorous, as hard-edged and ready for a bigger life, as I thought I did then.

"I heard about Dex," she said suddenly. She rubbed the damp end of her cigarette with a jittery thumb, looked sideways at me and blew smoke in the other direction. It was inevitable in a town this small—probably everyone knew by now—but it still took me by surprise, and I found myself looking hastily away. I felt the heat of the day creeping up along my back; the ugly part of July was nearing, and summer had started to sink into itself in the worst way. That rotting feeling, sticky and languid and wasting away without promise or direction, thick, humid days the lake breeze couldn't cool—it flooded into my face, seethed behind my skin, and I rubbed the heel of my hand against my damp forehead.

"Must be rough," Ellie said quietly. She sounded concerned, more tender than I ever remembered hearing her; she'd always been my tough friend, my love-you-with-teeth-and-nails friend, and this Ellie seemed suddenly like a sympathetic impostor. "We don't have to talk about it," she added.

"No," I said after an awkward pause. "Maybe I *should* talk about it."

Maybe that's what I need to do to make this go away.

"You miss him?" She exhaled, gray ghost of a breath, and I considered. Remembered: the deepness of his eyes, his kisses, like there was so much I had left to discover. How I could fall asleep against him; how I'd never been able to do that before with anyone. The way he made me laugh. The way he made me forget.

When I looked at her, I didn't have to say it. She seemed surprised. "It's funny," she said, and stopped to exhale. "Don't take this the wrong way, but it doesn't feel right. To see you this way about a guy."

I waited, watched her watching me. "What way?"

"Like—I don't know, like how you are. So *down*. And how you were before. The last few months, I mean, so wrapped up in all of it. Him and only him." She paused, and I felt the flush creeping up again, the built-up guilt at letting a friendship slide for anything—*But especially*, I could imagine her saying, thinking over all those months, *for a guy*. "I just didn't see that one coming," she said. "That you'd ever be so sure about someone, *any*one. That someone could ever…" She shook her head, seemed to be struggling for the right words. "You were always a wanderer. Like me, huh? Guy to guy, like a drug."

"From the addict herself."

She smiled. "But that's what I *mean*. We're always the same, Case. Things change and people change and God knows guys change. But this—" She shook her head again. "It's *you*, you know?"

I looked away and moved this observation around in my head, tumbled it over and upon itself, wearing down the edges. I looked at the tall, impossibly heavy dock rising up against our field of vision, blocking out part of the cloudless sky, and I wondered if I was wrong not to forget about him by now. I wondered if the men I saw walking along the bank and the beams, waiting for the next boat to come in, all the men who'd known him and worked with him, had already moved on.

"Listen," Ellie said, "I know it's been a while since we talked. And I know there's stuff we never really talk about— but can I ask you something?"

I let my gaze fall back to her face and nodded.

"You remember that year my stepdad died, the year your mom left? How it felt then?"

I nodded again, sucking so hard on my cigarette I almost inhaled. I'd forgotten how that had happened to both of us in the same year, but I hadn't forgotten the unspoken rule that we never mentioned either of them to each other.

"It's dumb," she said. "I don't know why I'm thinking it now, but I always kind of wondered what would have happened without that year. If the chemo had worked, or if your mom had come back—what would have happened to us." I watched her anxious fingers pulling grass blades out of the dirt one at a time, her knees rising up and folding into her body. "If we'd still be friends, for one. But also, if we'd be different in those ways we've been the same. The wandering ways." She looked up from the grass and seemed genuinely concerned, or curious, or both. "Do you think we'd be different?"

I told her truthfully, "I don't know."

"Because there was this one time—back in junior year, I think—I was dating this guy, Judd Bergstrom. He went to Silver Bay; I don't know if you remember. I didn't tell you this then, I didn't tell anyone, but he reminded me, in all these little ways, of my stepdad. Stupid ways. Like his handwriting, and the way he parted his hair, and how he pronounced things like *hallway*—they were both from New Jersey, they'd say *hole-way*." Ellie laughed and repeated it: *hole-way, whole-way,* until I couldn't tell what she was saying anymore. "And his hands," she added. "Or how he'd call me Elizabeth, how Dad used to. I couldn't help it; I loved it. He almost reformed me," and she smiled a little into her own smoke. "I could have been a one-man woman, too."

I smiled back, but I shook my head. "I don't remember him."

"Guess not." She leaned over and rested her hands on her knees, her chin on her hands. "We didn't date that long. After a while, it got so great, I broke up with him."

The breeze picked up a little, blew back the red tendrils curling along her face. "I don't get it," I told her quietly, and she sighed.

"I don't know if I get it, either. But I think what I'm trying to say is I almost fell in love. I could have loved him, if I let myself, for all the wrong reasons." She looked at me, a long and unwavering sideways glance. "All I'm saying is, don't fall in love with this guy for the wrong reasons."

"Like what?"

"Like that he left you first." She paused. "Or that he isn't coming back."

I stubbed out my cigarette against a half-buried stone. "Rule number one," I reminded her coolly. "No falling in love."

Ellie smiled a sad kind of smile and fiddled with her matches. "Sounds familiar."

"We only dated a few months."

"Okay."

"It's not like—" I paused, searching the empty horizon, hard and white and glittering like ice, for words that weren't there. I said finally, "He's dead, Ellie. It takes a while. You should know."

She nodded. "I know." She looked at me for a long time, and it seemed I knew so much of her right then—the way she always tilted her head slightly away, that dimple of seriousness in her left cheek—and I felt it sink deep and sudden, the comforting familiarity of her presence. The sameness of us.

"So what now?" she said, and I shook my head; no words to say. I wanted to cry, but there weren't any tears. No right response, no response at all. So instead of talking, we sat there and waited for a boat to come in, waited to watch them load the hull the way we used to watch when we were younger, calling out to the dock men—*Fill her up, baby, fill me up, baby*—laughing the same smoky smile and flicking away the memory of anything happier than this. We waited until the afternoon sank to shadows, until the evening light, pinkish sky and gold on the water, made me remember she must be hours late for work, and still she waited with me even after I asked if she needed to leave.

It's the way she used to be, ready to cut everything for me, for us, and I was grateful.

But there weren't any boats that day. Nothing to take away from shore, and as darkness stained, strained into night, we both must have realized this, and yet we both kept waiting. For their low moans across the water, their constant returning just to leave again. Their ceaseless second chances. We waited, side by side, for that same old light on the horizon.

paperwork

Sept. 15, 1995

Dear Casey,

~~I hope you~~ ~~Just wanted to~~

With love from <u>Hollywood!!</u> Am safe and happy here, Please don't be angry.

Just wanted you to know

My agent (!!) says any day now is my big break——so watch for me at Cinema 8, hopefully I'll see you there soon!! The picture on the front is the Hollywood sign. I saw it yesterday. Its bigger than you'd think.

Will write soon, please understand——no room left——
love mom

p.s. Remember what I told you by the water. Sometimes these are the right goodbyes.

June 20, 1996

Dear Casey,

I'm sorry its been so long, things are just so busy. Everything in fast forward——not like home or even the cities, although sometimes walking around these buildings its like when we went to the state fair, everything just so <u>sprawled</u> and so many people. You can forget who you are so easily, where you've been, and just be anyone you want. It's like that, always. We'd have fun here. No one knows you here...I don't know, I guess I've been remembering things lately and thinking of MN and you, but things will pick up here soon I'm sure. I'm sure my big break's coming, so cross your fingers for me——

Been meeting so many interesting people though!! I'll tell you about them when I come home, maybe Christmas but maybe not if I get something big. ~~I'm staying at~~ This woman named Olivia is my best friend now, she's kind of an actress too. Maybe next summer but not this one. I have things lined up. How is your father. Are you still going to be in the plays someday at THHS, a big star like your mom? And will you send me pictures? 1117 Sunset, Hollywood CA, 90038. Though don't feel you have to write back, I understand.

If Mrs. Heinzel is still directing at the high school give her my regards, though she is probably dead or retired by now.

So I guess I'm stalling——really ~~wrote to say wrote to~~ wanted to tell you I ~~hope you will~~ hope everything is good at home. ~~I miss you.~~ I really do. And you'll see me again, don't worry, maybe next summer but dad needs you more right now and besides, Hollywood is not a good place for you to grow up so please understand. I won't write again. But I do love you so please don't forget me. It might not seem like it yet, but this was meant to be, I know fate's watching out for you like it watched out for me, its my <u>destiny</u> here somewhere and I know it brought me here for a reason, you'll see——

love always mom

BRADFORD COUNSELING CENTER
REPORT OF PSYCHOLOGICAL EVALUATION

NAME: Casey Lynn Maywood
SEX: Female
DOB: Dec. 9, 1983
ADDRESS: 128 Second Avenue, Two Harbors, MN 55616
PHONE: 218-555-3719
EXAM DATE: May 5, 1999
EVALUATOR: Gerald Spivy, Ph.D.
OTHER INFORMATION: Parent contact, Frank Maywood

REASON FOR REFERRAL: Patient (15 yrs.) was brought in by father for psychological evaluation pertaining to mother's abandonment three and a half years ago. Seeking possible referral if evaluator determines a need for therapy exists.

BACKGROUND INFORMATION: Father described patient as "a real smart girl, but real quiet." He feels he does not know how to adequately address her lack of outward response to maternal abandonment, nor how to address what he deemed "her dating thing," i.e., an apparent and recently manifested tendency toward promiscuity. Father claims he and patient became close following incidence of abandonment but have "grown apart" over the past year. He also expressed concern that patient may be at risk for hereditary bipolar condition. Note that patient's mother, Lila Maywood, left family to pursue acting career, Sept. 1995. SEE PATIENT FILE "MAYWOOD, LILA."

BEHAVIORAL OBSERVATIONS: Patient was polite but not

effusive; an overall sense of reservation in the presence of evaluator. Body language suggests heightened self-awareness and lack of self-esteem, though father claims patient has "got her head on straight" and "doesn't care what people think, usually." Self-consciousness may be a manifestation of the clinical situation. Direct prompts to discuss mother were accepted outwardly but answered with detachment and apparent lack of emotion; indirect prompts were a better indicator of maternal sentiments (see below). Interview was scheduled for fifty minutes but was terminated at forty minutes at the request of patient.

TESTS ADMINISTERED: None.

RESULTS: See below.

IMPRESSIONS AND RECOMMENDATIONS: Patient appears to be in moderate emotional denial about maternal abandonment, although she claims to consciously understand the term "abandonment" and its personal implications. The course of the interview suggested an idealized perception of mother, or a moderate lack of individuation, or both; patient likens attributes of mother to those described as ideal personal attributes with specific references to acting/actresses/cinema. Professed career aspiration of filmmaking may suggest a desire to control cinematic world with which patient associates her mother. The evaluator found no indication that patient may be at risk for a bipolar disorder other than genetic factors; onset of adolescence has likely brought issues of concern to the attention of father, as both he and patient seem uncertain of their appropriate relationship without the context of maternal involvement. Individual therapy is recommended but not mandatory. Family therapy is strongly encouraged.

Jan. 3, 1996

Dear Frank,

I hope Casey is okay. Please take care of her the best you can, I'm sure you figured most of it out by now. You need to make sure she leaves for school by 7:40, and its not good for her to be alone so much in the afternoon, so maybe you can find it in your heart to not stay at work so late in the evening——

Now I am not missing. Okay? Don't try to find me or call the police or anything. I am not missing, I know where I am. I've got myself back now, no thanks to you, and I know who I am for once. If you need to write, here is an address but its not mine and you wouldn't like who you found here so don't do anything stupid: 1117 Sunset, Hollywood CA, 90038. I'm sending it to Casey but make sure she doesn't try to call somehow. Also she likes if you tape the soaps for her, The Young and the Restless is her favorite.

That's all. Don't try and find me, I know you want to but don't. You lost me, but I've got myself back, I need to do this, its not something you'll understand but I hope you'll forgive me someday especially since I've forgiven you——

   Lila

Dec. 2, 1999

Dear Casey,

Remembered last night your sweet sixteen——had to
write, I hope you understand!! Also had to tell you things
are good here in case you were wondering after all this
time, things are changing so fast for me its like I have
a whole new life now but you came to me in a dream
last night anyway——we were at Owen Park and I kept
losing you in the crowd, it was summer and I was on the
stage. I hope your father gave you something nice, I got
pearls on my sweet sixteen from Aunt Susie. Sorry you
haven't seen me so far on screen, its a long story but
things are picking up for me here!! Will you also tell
your father he needs to answer my last letter, thanks.
And I have to tell you about the psychic cats!! I was
walking on the promenade in Santa Monica and there
is the man who has psychic cats who pull your ~~four~~
~~fortune~~ fourtune out of this bag with their paws and
then you get this card with a cat and a future on it. Some
of mine said <u>To your change the cat bows</u> and <u>Destiny</u>
<u>sends you a cross</u> (like <u>across</u> the country, get it) so I just
wanted to tell you this is for the best and I must be doing
something right, fate's got its eye on me like always. No way
to change it and things are happening so fast I hope you
understand why sometimes it has to be like this——Anyway
maybe I will show you hollywood someday but maybe not,
its really not that nice here and things are changing for
the better

love Lila
p.s. and Happy Birthday!!

BRADFORD COUNSELING CENTER
REPORT OF PSYCHOLOGICAL EVALUATION

NAME: Lila Casey Maywood
SEX: Female
DOB: July 10, 1963
ADDRESS: 128 Second Avenue, Two Harbors, MN 55616
PHONE: 218-555-3719
EXAM DATE: April 28, 1994
EVALUATOR: Rita Pratt, M.D.
OTHER INFORMATION: Husband Frank Maywood, daughter
Casey (10 yrs.)

REASON FOR REFERRAL: Lila came voluntarily to clinic,
albeit at strong urging of husband, complaining of
occasional depression. Private interview with husband
indicated that Lila may also suffer from paranoia,
insomnia, post-neglect trauma, and/or manic depression.
Public incident of hysteria in Feb. 1994. Husband seeks
recommendation on course of counseling and/or
medication; Lila initially indicated a strong aversion to
both counseling and (particularly) medication.

BACKGROUND INFORMATION: Background information
supplied by husband indicates a history of maternal and
paternal alcoholism. Husband describes persistently
"rocky" relationship between Lila and her mother,
moderately estranged since Lila "graduated, stopped her
acting thing, and married me." Mother currently in late
stages of liver failure. Father deceased since Lila was six

(drunk driving). Husband claims his relationship with Lila (together since high school, married 1983) has grown strained in recent months due to Lila's lack of emotional stability, recently manifested in prolonged periods of detachment and overt distrust of his fidelity. Husband claims that no particular incident was the catalyst for distrust, and that detachment has been developing gradually for as long as two or three years. Only recently has emotional instability manifested itself in severe depression and occasional hysteria. Husband cites history of similar emotional instability during Lila's pregnancy with daughter, although he was told at the time that incidences of hysteria and/or depression were hormonal in nature and completely normal. Lila's relationship with daughter is reported to be possessive, but at times "not really loving."

BEHAVIORAL OBSERVATIONS: Evaluation was composed of a one-hour interview and thirty minutes of test administration. Lila did not exhibit external symptoms of physiological depression; she seemed eager and open with the evaluator, animated, extremely talkative, and willing to cooperate with testing. The course of interview and test administration suggested a significantly heightened and/or narcissistic sense of self as well as a lack of attentiveness and concentration. Distraction increased as a response to inquires about mother, particularly mother's recent hospitalization, though Lila seemed to enjoy reminiscing about their relationship, which she described as "pretty close" (note significant inconsistencies in Lila's and husband's assessment of this relationship). Inquiries about marriage were met with uncertain and/or contradictory attitude. At times, Lila described her husband as overbearing and smothering; at times, as neglectful and unappreciative. She denied suspicions of husband's infidelity. Discussed at length her inability to sleep through the night and requested strategies she might take to remedy situation (see "Recommendations"). Did not discuss relationship with daughter in depth.

TESTS ADMINISTERED: CES-D; Rosenberg Self-Esteem Scale.

RESULTS: CES-D score of 15 indicates some symptoms of depression with significantly high somatic symptom and depressive affect subscores. Results of Rosenberg Self-Esteem Scale indicated extremely high self-value.

IMPRESSIONS AND RECOMMENDATIONS: Lila's interview and test scores are strongly indicative of a manic-depressive disorder. Background information suggesting manic depression was corroborated by both behavioral observation and personal testimony; moreover, manifestations of the condition seem to be negatively affecting Lila's marriage and possibly her family life. Clinical treatment and counseling recommended immediately; medication for both insomnia and manic depression prescribed (note: lithium 300mg one cap tid; flurazepam 15mg one cap hs prn). Family counseling also recommended, particularly in response to terminal diagnosis of Lila's mother; referral offered.

Oct. 30, 1999

Frank,

Someone by now should have served you with the
papers. I don't know how it works, he helped me do it from
here, but I expect this will be easier if it doesn't have to get
messy. I am not coming back, I mean it so don't make this
into some way to get me back there. Things are good for me
here, ~~I am getting better.~~ I am getting my life back together.
If you ever loved me you would let things be good for me.
I've moved on. You might even be proud.

Don't ignore me.

Lila

conversations with myself

All of it is bright and wrong. The white church, red roof glowing in the sun, fluorescent flowers in the windows and grass bursting with emerald green. At the top of the stairs, a tall brown door is flung open and waiting; someone, some-where, is playing salsa music, ecstatic chords twisting up to a racing pulse and behind all of it the hot, burning blue of sky. Everything so dazzled with light, flushed with color — so horribly *happy*. I look how I think I'm supposed to feel: In my dark shoes and dark skirt, thin sweater damp and clinging in the heat, I'm black enough for a funeral. But as I watch a stream of brightly dressed mourners file into the church, chatting among themselves with such normality, even animation, I start to wonder if maybe I'm the wrong one, the obviously foreign one, the stain that doesn't match this glittering pattern.

And I've started to talk to myself.

Who knows how long it's been going on; I don't realize it until I'm standing in front of the church willing my legs to walk up those pink-carpeted stairs, through the door and into whatever's waiting on the inside. That's what I'm think-ing: One foot in front of the other, you've come this far and this is *why* you've come isn't it, so why are you standing here, go finish this, go find your ending, and I'm ready to do it until I realize I've said something out loud—the echo too real to be inside my head and I look around, face burning, a frantic train of thought speeding, rushing by, *get it together, what's wrong with you, you're not crazy, am I going crazy?*...

I take a deep breath. I remember watching our movie that first day we met, you sitting beside me in the dark of the theater, and up in that safer black-and-white world, the ac-tress leaving her director behind. Cool, calm, she turns away and does not look back, and that's how I will play this: I'll slip my hand out from underneath yours, I'll walk purpose-fully out of this theater without looking back, without a sec-ond thought. And I hold it in my head, up the steps before I lose my nerve—*I'm coming in to leave. Listen: I'm coming in to end it.*

I take a seat in the last pew, alone. It's mostly because I'm late—the pastor has already started to speak, a thin drone that's easy to ignore—but I prefer this peripheral feeling, as far as possible from the front of the church, where a picture of you is smiling teasingly at the congregation. I try not to look, try not to meet your eyes. Mine are gliding over every-one else, this sea of bobbing heads spreading out in front of me, bleached-blond buoys around the island of altar. Same hair, same thin, fragile bodies and dull, empty expressions.

Like mannequins, I think. Realize I'm hearing it as a whisper, you, beside me, in my ear; I smile, close my eyes. *Here is the church, here is the steeple.*

Open the doors—
Where's all the people?

I feel laughter building up like bubbles—bite my cheeks from the inside, hard, and look around. Maybe I expected the dark heaviness of gothic arches, stern gazes of saints staring out from the corners, candles and crosses and sad, sagging music appropriate to the occasion. And somehow all this would force me to feel sad, too, dark and despairing, feel *something*, and I would cry and pray and let you go, do the things I'm supposed to do. But it's not like that. No one here is crying, and there aren't any saints, aren't even any crosses, and everything's still pulsing with that neon Hollywood sunshine streaming through the windows: no shadows to hide in here.

It makes me remember my grandmother's funeral, the only one I've ever been to, the only thing to compare this to and think: *It's not supposed to be like this.* That time it was in a small church with small windows and appropriately bad lighting. There was a tape recording of somber organ music that someone kept missing the cue to play, and I remember long, awkward silences in the middle of the service while the pastor looked helplessly around the room. It was summer then, too, but hot, airless; no casket, just a small blue jar of all that was left, yet I worried (with a ten-year-old's imagination and horror) if we waited long enough in the humidity, we might start to smell her, could only think of getting out of there, getting home to the coolness of our basement, when I realized my mother was walking toward the altar in the middle of the sermon. I felt my father, on the other side of me and too far from the aisle to hold her back, stiffen in his seat, and we sat there together in mutual dread as she started to talk to the little blue jar.

"I sold all your china," she said. Her voice was quiet, almost a whisper, and the entire congregation seemed to lean forward, straining to hear; finally, something worth paying attention to. "It didn't get me much."

The pastor hesitated and glanced pointedly at my father before turning back to his notes. "And as scripture tells us—"

"I thought there'd be more. But you didn't leave me anything."

"—though we will all someday face that valley—"

"What do I do with nothing, Mom?"

He cleared his throat, she lowered her head, and the congregation began stirring behind me; I could hear some of their whispers in the sudden hum of voices.

("Oh, you remember, I told you last winter...")

("—who broke down at Winter Frolic, that's right—")

"Mrs. Heinzel said empty yourself out before you take on a role."

"—we should not fear it, we should not fear—should not fear that valley, for the *shelter* and *love* of our Lord will be with us—"

("That's not what I heard. I heard he committed her.")

"Something from nothing, I did that once..."

"—*inside* us, someone *greater* than us *loving* and *protecting* us, and will someone in the congregation please help Mrs. Maywood?"

Which quieted all of them, even my mother, and created a silence that both prompted the organ music and jump-started my father, finally, into action. He squeezed past me and hurried to put his arm around her shoulders, slumped and wilting in their wrinkled black linen. I saw her lean into him, heavily and with defeat, and they stood there for a long time, tangled up in each other and looking down at whatever they could see from that angle. Everyone watched. The sound track droned on. Then my father turned them carefully around and they walked down the aisle to the sluggish tune of those heavy chords, heads down, feet falling in time to the music and each other's steps.

Looking back, it's almost funny. Almost. Like a slow-motion wedding reception, irony I could sense even before I understood irony.

Except I remember, right now, their faces as they moved past—blank, without emotion, not looking at each other and not looking at me even as I reached out to touch her empty hand. I remember no one's eyes meeting mine. And I remember the feeling of aloneness once I heard the back door slam, turning my head forward again and watching the mouth of the pastor move over soundless words, a rushing in my ears as I stared at the faces around me and found each one as unfamiliar as the next.

The feeling of being wrong, alien. The extra piece to someone's puzzle, the one that doesn't fit; and back in this bright California church, I look up these rows and rows of people, each one of them somehow anchored to your life, and all I can think about is how I don't recognize a single person. How I still don't know, will never know, so much of who you were. I feel it pressing in, what must have been pressing in on her as she stood there and felt my father against her side—*How do I make an end with nothing?*—and I stand and wait in that last pew for a long, lingering moment. I wait for someone to turn around and notice me, for the pastor to glance up and falter, to wonder what I'm doing here. I wait for someone to come to my side, someone I can walk away from. But no one looks back. No one sees. It's just you and me staring each other down across this church: two ghosts without presence, without body, without answers. Without the ending I came to find.

I walk to the back of the church. I walk through the door and into the rest of the bright, blinding world, close my eyes against the white wash of sun and picture myself in front of the stage lights, ready and resolute in a red dress. But when I open them up and look down those pink-carpeted stairs, nothing has changed. The world looks exactly the same. And I'm right back where I started.

"Do you need a ride?"

He's tall, dressed in navy blue, keys in his hand and waiting for an answer—waiting, I realize suddenly, for me to answer, and I look up at his face from my seat on the church steps. The sun surges around him, a hot and unforgiving halo; I make a shadow with my hand, pick out the similarities. He looks, beneath the tight skin across his cheekbones, the stubborn sadness in his eyes, and the lag of a few years, like Dex.

I tell him, "I need a way back."

"Don't we all."

"I took a cab."

He nods. He's looking past me, up the stairs at the cluster of people swarming out of the church. I can't help staring at the smooth, tanned angle of skin where his jaw meets his neck, clenched and strong and so manlike for someone not much older than I am. "A waste," he says, shaking his head. "All of it."

"I know," I tell him awkwardly, not sure what else to say. "I can't imagine…how hard it must be for you.…"

"No," he says, "I mean this. The crowd and the church, the whole show—for what?" He sighs; he sounds tired. "The whole damn production. He would've hated it."

"Hollywood," I shrug. I'm not sure what I mean, but it gets him to look down finally, meet my eyes and let me crash into his—that familiar, dive-deep blue.

"It's over," he says. "You know that, right? No one to bury."

The words like stones across the surface of my mind; I don't really hear them, though I'm nodding, sinking fast into his gaze. "You want a ride?" he asks again, and I get up, brush off my skirt, my whole body coming suddenly alive.

"I know who you are," he says, and something catches inside my chest.

I tell him, "I thought so."

He moves closer, slowly, hesitantly. "From how he de-scribed you. Like gold, he said once." He nods at my hair. "Not California-blonde. The kind that catches the light, that sort of glows from the inside—" Stops, sighs, a quiver in his voice and this sun-squinted moment spinning out between us like a thread. "Funny," he says. "This isn't how I pictured you at all," and he reaches out, tentative, and I lean in. Won-der what he sees. Let him touch it—his fingers, if I close my eyes, feel familiar.

part two

late reflections

Middle of the night, a month before she left, streets silent and a late-summer chill breezing through my open window. I had woken from a strange dream, something not quite frightening, but almost—I remembered the low sigh of boats coming in, a wandering feeling, lost—and I called to her from my bed, wanting water. No response. I tried again: nothing, not even the sound of my father rolling over in his sleep. Waiting, I watched the ceiling, the bluish corners, that strange way things aren't clear in the dark unless you don't look at them directly.

"Mom?"

Still no answer.

I figured their door was closed and locked, as it sometimes was in those bad-dreaming middles of the night, and for a while I tried to fall asleep. But my tongue kept sticking, thick and dry, to the roof of my mouth until finally—heart flapping against my rib cage like wings, so scary, yet thrilling, to walk through the darkened house, the wide, shadowy silences of nighttime—I crept down to the kitchen to get it myself.

And found her there. Lights off, but the hall light had been left on, and the room had a muted glow to it like candles without the flicker. Just stillness. She hardly looked like she was breathing as I watched her from the doorway: slumped in her chair, back rounded and pressed tight against the filmy silk of her nightgown, a tempting glass of water in her hands. The way she was turned—so the chair faced the window instead of the table—I figured she couldn't see me standing in the doorway. So for a long time, I just stared at her as she stared at the hazy reflection of herself in the glass; with the light in here and the dark out there, you couldn't see anything else. Just the glow of a ghost looking in.

"Did you have a bad dream?"

I jumped guiltily. Her voice seemed sharp against the thickened stillness of night. "I—was thirsty."

She didn't turn away from the window. "Me, too."

I walked slowly toward her, my feet sticking loudly to the humid linoleum, toes creaking, weak spot in the floor creaking—I felt like an explosion that had staggered into her calm, but she didn't seem to mind, or notice. I dragged one of the kitchen chairs over to hers, lined up the aluminum legs and sat down. "Did *you* have a bad dream?"

She laughed a little. I didn't see what was funny, but at least she seemed happy, and I waited for her to say something, or laugh again, or offer me a sip of her water. I didn't want to ask for it now; there was something intent and searching in her gaze, and I watched her reflection in the windowpane, trying to figure out what she was looking for.

The silence pooled around us, flowed in from all sides, quivered only by the occasional nighttime murmur of the house. *Settling,* she used to tell me when I'd wake her, terrified burglars or murderers or (worse) kidnappers were trying to get in downstairs. *It's just the foundation settling, go back to sleep,* but that always frightened me in a different way. I'd lie awake, watching the angle where my wall met the floor and certain each creak was pushing our foundation deeper and deeper into the lawn. One day, I imagined, we'd find ourselves buried alive.

"When I was young," she said suddenly, hollow-voiced, to her reflection, "they said I looked just like my mother."

I tried to imagine my grandma's face, gone for a year now, and could remember only bits and pieces like something taken apart: the loose skin, hard lips with deep creases, hair as thin and pale as corn silk. They said she was beautiful once, but I couldn't believe she ever looked anything like my mother.

"It used to be if I looked at myself long enough, I'd start to see her." She turned her head slightly, then back again, eyes never straying from her image in the window. "It doesn't work anymore."

"You're prettier," I said.

"She didn't think so."

"I think so. Dad thinks so, too."

As if on cue, a car came down our street, headlights brightening. I could feel her tense next to me, listening, leaning closer, and then the rush of it past our house, surge of engine and lights—briefly, an image beyond her reflection—fading slowly to silence and darkness as it disappeared into the black. She sunk again into her chair.

"Dad's gone," she said. "It doesn't matter what he thinks anymore."

I stared at her, how her face was starting to crumple in the corners. "He'll come back," I whispered, tugging at her sleeve because I could hear it in her voice now, that she was in one of her worse moods, her lock-herself-down-in-the-basement moods. The ones where sometimes she would stop in the middle of a sentence and not start again, as if forgetting I was there, and I knew all that mattered right now was to keep her talking and see if maybe the sadness would pull back, burn away to clearness, like morning fog across the lake. "We can stay up," I told her. "We can all have breakfast together. It'll be fun. He'll come back soon, Mom."

But she just shook her head and smiled sadly: "Oh, Case." As if I had so much left to learn. "They don't come back once they leave. You need to remember that." She paused, the smile fading to blankness, tilted her head again, and clinked ice cubes against the glass as she stretched to get a different view. "That's when you have to *do* something."

"Do what, Mom?"

"Just don't. Don't get yourself in this position. Because you won't know until you've lost it." She paused. "What it means. Love. What you mean anymore."

I frowned, vaguely insulted. "I know what love means," I told her.

She just shook her head, eyes still fixed on her own reflection. "Nothing," she said. "I look nothing like my mother. Can you believe it? She's gone. It's just me now." A slow smile pulling across her face: "I could be anyone."

And the way she said it, the excitement and the familiarity, relieved me; here was the mother I was used to. I touched her leg, the silky fabric, the warmth and fleshy give of it. She looked down. "Why are you awake?" she said, as if just now noticing I was here. "You don't have to wait up."

I stared, struck silent, so warm and flustered beneath her full-on gaze. "I had a bad dream," someone said, and it was me.

She looked back at the window. "Me, too," she murmured. "We can wait up for him together." Laughing, suddenly, but she didn't seem happy this time. "We can wait together. To wake up from this."

"Mom?" I tugged at her glass of water, still thirsty but mostly looking for something, anything, to make her stop talking that way. "Can I?" And she handed it to me, full and sweating beads down its side, so slippery in my hands that I think I heard it before I even realized I'd dropped it: the angry smash of breaking glass, splash of water against my ankles and the too-loud silence of afterwards. I felt her hands grab my shoulders, pulling me close to her as we stared down at the glittering field of shards, suddenly and dangerously beautiful, spread out around our bare feet.

"Don't move," she said urgently. Her hands on my shoulders squeezed until they hurt. "Don't move, okay?"

"Okay," I whispered, mesmerized by the glass. In the dark room, you couldn't see how far it had spread. You could only see the light catch in sparks and flashes, the way it does on ripples in the water. "What should we do, Mom?"

She didn't say anything for a long time, and after a while I looked up at her. She just shook her head, her face somewhere far away. "Don't move," she said again.

"Should we wait for Dad?"

She laughed a little to herself, snapping out of whatever

had grabbed hold of her. "There you go," she said. "*That's* what love means." But she didn't explain what she meant, and before I could say anything, she caught my eye and smiled, rubbing my shoulders a little more loosely with her hands. "It's okay," she said. "We're okay here, aren't we, Case? Me and you."

I nodded, relief filling me up, swelling against my lungs like a balloon. "You and me, Mom."

"Like a tango. Like a last dance. Just the two of us." And she nudged my cheek softly, and I smiled, pulled away but not too far. I could still sense the spilling warmth of her legs next to mine, the summery heat of her like a magnetic field pulling me in—I closed my eyes and tried to hold on to the feeling. After a moment, she took my hand into her lap and held it there, and I could feel sleep pressing closer now, fought it, pushed it back, not even thirsty anymore, not wanting anything but to stay here with her, in the dusky glow of another room, and listen for the sound of my father coming to save us.

"I understand what it means, Mom," I told her, quietly, before sleep seeped in. "Falling in love. I'm old enough to know some of these things."

But she just sighed, a sad sigh with a smile underneath it. "Casey, Casey." Pressing our hands together, palm to palm, like pressing against a mirror. She met my eyes in the reflection of the window and we stayed there, doubled in the glass, all of it shattered around our feet and our reflection, together, played out a thousand times where I couldn't see it—*Casey, Casey.*

"You're never old enough," she said, "to know what falling in love means."

what falling in love means

There was this time in winter driving with one of them, what was his name, the one with a brown leather jacket and a blue El Camino, knees in his jeans worn bald and pale and almost ready to rip—that's right, he did have that kind of almost energy. Almost too much stubble, but not; almost driving too fast, but not yet. Up and up the hills through Duluth, overpasses invisibly slick with black ice, that kind of early-morning or late-night cold, and which was it? One blending into the next without her noticing, not until a colorless sunrise began to whitewash the horizon over the lake and she thought with a kind of startled self-awareness: I've spent the night. We've spent the night. *And on like that, without direction. Flinging themselves through the empty intersections. Up the rise of Highway 53 and down a little, then back up,* I know a place where you can see everything *he'd said (and she knew the place, she'd been there before with someone else, but don't tell him that, it will ruin everything), so she'd said* Show me *but he couldn't remember exactly where it was, no way to tell him without telling him too much, so they spent a while going back*

and forth. She didn't mind. She liked this part. She liked the
climb, liked even more the going-down moments when she
could see, in brief glimpses past the guardrail, as the lattice of
bare-branched trees and darkened houses came momentarily
apart, the whole sleeping city beneath them and beyond that,
the thick gray solid of frozen water. She liked knowing he was
lost and she knew where she was and where they were going—

Until that part when he looked at her and she looked at
him and something unsaid passed between them. The heat
turned up so high and blasting with a hiss like heavy breath
out of the vents and she reached for his hand, didn't mean to
but it was there in his eyes Take my hand, take it, touch me
so she did without thinking and his skin was so warm, hard to
remember how cold it was and then they were flying—the inevitable silence of it, almost peaceful, but suddenly the spin of
the world outside the windshield, so close to the rail was it getting closer? and this dizzy feeling as it came into her view,
briefly: that faraway frozen lake, the only thing beyond her
that seemed to be steadied, sure, staying in place, and she felt
herself lifting off the seat, the painful stab of the belt across
her chest and slamming back into the dusty upholstery—
silence. Loud this time, the silence, and not peaceful at all.
Then the release of a breath they'd held together, then her
heart coming back into its own beat:

Almost. Almost. Almost over the edge.

doorways

And a sharp turn: down, down, down through the Hollywood hills toward a place so big you could lose yourself, everything spreading outward, up, around. Fast enough to forget, to hide inside the brighter span of this busy, skyless world—pink hair and palm trees and the angry red clots of traffic jams, blue-and-yellow-striped umbrellas in the sun, an intricately tangled spiderweb of color. I feel buzzed, stormy, electric and crackling at the edges—afraid and amazed and so very much *alive* in this neon rush of city.

"Too fast?" Kevin asks, yells over the swell of wind and Rolling Stones—noticing, I imagine, my hands white-knuckled on the console, held breath and closed eyes.

"Never," I yell back.

"I forget where you're staying. It's down on Cahuenga?"

But can't we just keep driving forever? No destination except not to end up where I started, flying fast and forward, never back, and I yell it before I can convince myself not to—"Just take me wherever you're going."

Easy to say things like that, suddenly, things I'd never say. I'm a tourist in this, unknown and unattached. *You can be anything*, she'd say, and I can be: forward, desperate, here goes. He smiles. "I was planning on it," he says. "You don't want to change first?"

"Not really." Smoothing my hands down the rippling black skirt. "I'm okay like this."

He doesn't say anything, just glances at my skirt and switches lanes. The kind of driver who doesn't use a signal or check a blind spot. "Anything you want to do? Anything," he says, looks over and holds my eyes and it seems to mean something, *anything, anywhere*—the thrill of it, knowing we're moving so fast without anyone watching the road.

"Just take me somewhere," I tell him. "Anywhere but back." And he smiles again, and we go, fast and smooth through these streets I don't know, someone beside me to take me there, and down.

We end up in Venice, where he says he works—*Nicest office space in town, you'll see*, before he stops talking for a long stretch of city. We pass canals, the kind I saw once in a book on the real Venice, only these canals don't seem to lead anywhere but to parking lots, everything greenless and crowded with chrome. We're braking now through the neighborhoods and I feel it coming to a stop, the frenetic rush of sun and people decelerating to lazy streets, a building heat, and, distraction slowed, the surreal emptiness of dreaming. The world has faded to gauzier colors, diffusing in the thin air— pale pinks of boxy houses, that subconscious film of fog and smog over everything that isn't right in front of me. Even the foliage has lost its substance, skinny wrists of palm trees rising thin and leafless into peaked blue.

I think of home, its thickness and density: the coarseness of stone and bark, the rich, dark smell of soil, of pine, and a wider landscape rolling forcefully along the horizon. Dex told me once he felt *real* there, that he'd found in Minnesota a stability he'd never had before—and I can feel, for the first time, why he might have wanted that beneath his feet.

So what were you doing there, anyway?

"Hey." Kevin turns down the radio. "You okay?"

I glance over. "You never told me," I say after a moment. "What you do."

He hesitates, looking back at the road. "I'm a writer," he says, no elaboration. "You?"

"I'm an actress."

I'm not sure why I lie about it, but I like the feeling, the safety in this falseness. He doesn't seem surprised, which surprises me. "You're in the right place, I guess."

"Right place. Wrong reasons." I gauge his response. "Aren't they always?"

Sad eyes and a brief smile. "Not always."

We're there. We work our way, slow, tense, through the crowds along the side streets near the boardwalk. He parks in a spot marked Reserved next to a restaurant with dark, dirty windows; *Carmencita's Big Fajitas* it says in a sign above the glass, and I realize, suddenly and sharply, how hungry I am. How long it's been since I ate that turkey sandwich on the plane. I can almost taste the peppery flavor of grilled steak, creamy guacamole and hot cheese spilling over the sides—"Give me a hand?" Kevin says, and I swallow the emptiness, stepping out of the car onto a sidewalk gritty with straying sand.

He leads me around the corner to a set of small metal stairs, which stoop toward a small metal door: the basement, it seems, of the empty restaurant. "Lunch?" I ask, half joking, half hopelessly hoping, as he goes down the stairs ahead of me.

"Not exactly." He fiddles with the knob. "I can get you something once we're on the boardwalk."

"I thought you were showing me your office."

He doesn't answer. I watch his back, entranced, the familiar messiness of his hair and the way it sticks out a little, glistening in the sun. There's this curlicue shadow on his neck beckoning like a coiled finger—hypnotizing, pulling me in, as I listen to the clicking sounds of metal against metal.

It takes a long moment of fumbling silence for me to realize he's picking the lock. "What are you *doing*?" I whisper, but even I can hear it in my voice: the thrill of it, the stir, the pleasure of danger, albeit for the questionable prize of stolen fajitas.

"Don't worry," he tells me, voice casually loud, "this place is deserted. I'm not doing anything illegal. Well, mostly not. I just use it as my storage space when I'm not selling." The door springs open suddenly and he turns, winks, tosses me a paper clip twisted like a loose knot. "Can't be a rich kid in Hollywood without a little mischief. Dex should have told you that."

"What exactly?" *That he was rich, that he was mischief, that he could break in where he shouldn't go...*

"Told you about *me*. The trouble he'd get me out of— you know the deal, big brother watching my back all the time." He pauses, face turned slightly away. Then he flashes me a quick smile, a smile that makes us both forget. "Hang on, okay?" And before I can stop him, he ducks inside the black mouth of the empty doorway.

I realize then this is the part they don't show in *Bonnie and Clyde*–type movies: what it's like to direct the action on the outside. Empty hands, that uncertain cast of your eyes—*Just relax*, she'd tell me, *you're a natural. You can be anyone*, and I smile at a passing family dressed in matching Universal Studios T-shirts. They smile back—a good start. I lean against the railing, putting on this role like dark shades: arms crossed, amusement mild and vague as Mona Lisa, an occasional clearing of the throat to cover up mysterious rustlings inside. *Push your sleeves up to the elbows*, the director might say; *that sweater looks suspiciously warm for this weather*. And there it is, sinking in like sun, the *calm* of it, confidence of the getaway girl. That covert romanticism. Any minute now he'll bound up these steps, hop into the convertible without opening the door, pull you in beside him and you'll peel off, smiling beneath his arm, his hand steady at the wheel as rock and roll flares like triumphant gunshots in the background—

"Hey, little lady," I hear from the doorway. "Ain't you gonna come down?"

And when I turn my head, jarred back into my own skin, it's John Wayne looking up at me: a life-size cardboard cutout and behind that, Dex's voice. Kevin's. He pokes his head into view, smiling. I shake my head, can't help but laugh. "What the hell are you doing down there?"

"They used to make cowboys stand in doorways like this," he says. "In the movies."

"Doorways like what?"

"Short ones. So they'd look taller." He rests his chin on John Wayne's shoulder, looks up at me expectantly as he squints a cowboy scowl, and I feel everything heavy and anxious lifting away into this laughter. A new game of pretend — different masks, but the same lightness. "So does it work?" he says.

"Come on," and my voice is loud, clear, no longer afraid of who might hear. "Get out of there."

"No, really, how does he look?"

I take a deep breath. I take in the broad shoulders, the gold-glossy hair, white teeth, that look in his face that says *Yes. You're safe. Yes, I've got you covered.* "Like he knows what he's doing," I whisper.

"What?"

I smile and shake my head. "Tall."

Nodding with approval, Kevin leans the cardboard against the railing and gestures for me to come down. "You said you'd give me a hand, right?" And I make my way obediently toward him, stop just outside the darkened basement where he's waiting at the threshold. I follow his gaze through the shadows to a far wall where I can see them lined up: Tom Cruise, Luke Skywalker, Cameron Diaz, a barely clad gladiator, piles and piles of flat, frozen celebrities stacked against each other in the dark.

"I thought you were a writer."

He shrugs. "Gotta make a living somehow. I sell them," he says, nodding at the cutouts. "On the boardwalk, to tourists."

"And people *buy* them?"

"You'd be amazed what people go for around here. Anything to get closer to a star." He turns and looks down at me, and I think it might be working, think he does look taller in this hunched-over space. "And this is probably as close as they're going to get."

"Pessimist," I tell him. I smile. I stop smiling.

He swallows. Blinks.

I look away.

"This isn't right," he says.

"Probably not."

Stepping back, he disappears a little into shadow, leaves me on the threshold. "They used to make women stand in *taller* doorways," he says from the dark. "So they'd look short."

"And how do I look?"

It hangs there for a moment between us, unanswered, ruffling the fringe of an awkward silence. And suddenly, without warning, my stomach growls so loudly it breaks even the thickest moment into gentler pieces; we both grin at the same time, laugh with the same embarrassed relief. "Guess we better hurry." He turns toward the audience of cardboard. "Want to help me out here?"

He sets up shop while I buy us overpriced Mexican from a nearby stand: fat bean burritos, churros that sparkle with cinnamon in the sun. We eat unashamedly fast on lawn chairs while the stars stare straight ahead over our shoulders. I wonder if it's always this same square of sidewalk he claims as his own; this time, in any case, we're facing the long stretch of bustling boardwalk, sandwiched between a tarot-card reader and someone selling, according to her hand-painted advertisement, the "World's Greatest Wine-o Jokes." Strange enough, made even stranger by the tall, glamorous-looking brunette nodding off to sleep behind the sign.

"Try not to make eye contact," Kevin whispers when he notices me staring. He crumples up his burrito wrapper and leans back in his chair. "She'll sell you anything from pot to her own jewelry."

"That desperate?"

"She tried to sell me a dime bag last week. Along with her ChapStick."

I take in, for a moment, the long legs, groomed waves, the buttery gleam of her skin. "I don't get it. She looks like she just stepped out of a commercial."

He shrugs. "Wannabe stars who don't make it. Better than going the other route."

"What's the other route?"

He gives me a funny look, as if he can't believe how naïve I am. "We'll go walking tonight," he says. "Over on Sunset by the sleazy motels."

I feel my face getting warm and I lean back to match his pose, cross my arms in front of me. The joke teller starts to drool a little in her sleep. "What did Dex do?"

"You tell me."

"I mean out here. Before he left." I glance over, then quickly away from the look that tells me I've said something wrong again. "He didn't like to talk much about L.A.," I add quietly.

I feel his eyes linger on me for a long, silent moment, invasive as fingers at the nape of my neck, brushing my hair back for a closer look. "Worked mostly with our dad," he says finally. "On the sets and everything, meeting writers, producers. Kind of lined up to take over the family business." I glance at him, and he sees something in my face that makes him frown a little. "You know our dad's a screenwriter, right?"

I could lie. I could act the part. But I'm too curious to do it now, and I shake my head, brace myself for more.

"TV drama," Kevin tells me. "Courtroom soaps, cop shows, that kind of thing. He produces occasionally. Won an Emmy once."

"And Dex…" I pause, trying to imagine this man I knew as a dock worker, this echo of my father, dirty hands and scruffy cheeks, thick-armed and dark with the residue of raw ore and sunlight, working in television. All the solid and the heat of him washed out: gray suit, pastel tie, insubstantial as an italicized credit scrolling over the screen without anyone noticing.

"And Dex what?" he pushes.

"Why was he in Two Harbors?"

He blinks, as if it's slowly dawning on him just how little I know about the man who brought us together. "He was shooting a pilot," he tells me. "One of those North Shore, quirky-character dramas. It was set in a town up there—Duluth, maybe? I can't remember now. Anyway, the pilot folded, but he said he liked Minnesota. Needed a change of pace. And, well…"

"Well what?"

Kevin smiles, but it seems empty. "Well, he met you, didn't he? What better reason to stay?"

I shake my head, can't force a smile back. "I just don't get why he lied to me, then. Why he didn't tell me who he really was."

"That's not so strange. Haven't you ever wanted to be someone else for a while?"

He doesn't know me that well yet. But if he did, he'd know there's no way I can argue with that question.

"I guess I'm just surprised. I thought he hated that kind of thing. The whole superficial Hollywood thing." I look back at him quickly. "No offense."

"None taken." And he smiles as if I've missed something obvious. "Of course he hated Hollywood. Why else would he move to some place like Duluth? *No offense.*"

I smile back. "Fair enough."

"Anyway," he adds, "everyone hates Hollywood in the end. If you stay here long enough. It messes things up, messes families up. I figured you'd know that by now."

A plunge in my stomach, chaos of thought—*How does he know, how can he know if Dex never knew, how did Dex find out if I never told him—*

"Guess not." He looks down at his folded hands, tangled, white-knuckled, like something knotted too tight. "Sorry. I thought he would have told you. About our mom."

"Oh." I feel something both relax and sicken, remember the images I'd tried to forget: a limp hand, a bottle of pills, the always-unsolved mystery of a suicide. "He told me a little."

"Did he tell you how?"

"A little."

"Really fucked up my dad. Depression and stuff, ever since. We used to be really close to him when we were younger, but after Mom died..." He squeezes his hands to-gether, then lets go, as if releasing the tension of whatever it was he was going to say. "Figured he would've told you that, too."

He gives me an intense look as if gauging how much I know; I wonder if he can tell I'm gauging it myself and not liking what I come up with. There's a low buzz between my ears, and I shake my head to clear it, close my eyes. But it just gets louder, building, a quivering drone like I'm about to faint until I realize it's coming from above, and *whoosh*—a plane passes over us, brief climax of sound trailing off along the coast, and fading before the meaning really registers. I watch it shrink against the blue, realize Kevin is listening, too, catch his eye and look quickly away. He does the same.

"Anyway." He clears his throat.

"Yeah."

"Well." He smiles, nodding at the sleeping joke teller. "I could sure use an icebreaker. Wonder if last week's offer still stands."

I shouldn't laugh, but I do, anything to crack the thickness of this moment and let in a little air. It works for now, and he lets me sink into the comfort of mindless silence, watch her as she sleeps and he makes a few sales: James Bond, Charlie Chaplin, James Bond again. I watch everyone passing by without noticing her, the kind of girl who came out here to get noticed. I watch a Rollerblader down the block play "The Star-Spangled Banner" on an electric guitar for quarters in an upturned hat; I watch the guy next to him, decked out in a maroon bathrobe and gold turban, play a keyboard on the ground with his toes. I watch the shadows stretch toward late afternoon, thinning and darkening.

It makes me wonder where I'd end up if I came out here to get noticed. If I came out to start a new life.

Where I'd be now.

"I was thinking," I tell him, turning, and stop. My voice seems especially loud, the words carrying extra weight. "I was thinking, if it's okay, I might stay out here a couple extra days." He gives me a long look, and I don't know how to read it. "It's an open-ended ticket, right?"

Nodding, squinting in the sunlight, or maybe smiling and trying not to. "Want to see the sights?"

"I guess." I squint back and wonder if I'm going to say it or not. He waits, watches me expectantly. "Actually, my mom lives out here," I blurt, and he raises his eyebrows. "I'd like to see her."

"That's cool." A beat. "She lives...?" I can hear the question in his intonation: *She lives where?*

"In the area," I tell him casually. "Can't really remember right now."

"You don't remember where your mother lives?"

I try to ignore his skeptical look. "We haven't—we don't really talk much."

He stares at me, a look that reminds me of Dex: taking it in, seeing something I can't see, and I know I'm not fooling him anymore with a false cool, fake calm. "How long?" he says, and I look away, watch the crowds move past, and twist my burrito wrapper into a nervous origami of coiled ropes. After a while, he gives up. "Sorry," he says.

"You didn't know."

"But I know where you're coming from. Which reminds me"—Kevin glances at his watch—"I'm supposed to be at my dad's house in an hour. Before the post-funeral gala ends." He stands up and starts pulling the cardboard into clusters. "I'd better take off. Let you do your thing."

"But we just got here," I tell him, and I suddenly realize how much I'm loving these crowds, the sleeping vendors, the too-bright sun and, mostly, the ability to talk to someone, look into someone's eyes and see them looking back. "How far away does he live?"

"Ten miles, I guess. Maybe fifteen."

"You need a whole *hour*?"

He shakes his head. "You haven't driven in L.A., have you?"

I look up at him and he seems so tall again from this angle, so much older than he is — folding up his chair, breaking down his sign, and all I want is to keep riding along, keep moving moving moving before I have to stop and figure out what to do, what all this means —

Please.

Please don't leave me alone today.

I stand abruptly and glance down the boardwalk as if taking in the crowds one last time. I wait for what seems like an appropriately long moment of reflection. Then I fold up my chair and meet his eyes. "I guess I'll head back, then," I tell him. "To the hotel, I mean, if you don't mind dropping me off. It was nice meeting you." I wonder if he can sense the held breath behind my voice, the bluff I'm waiting for him to call; I just smile and hope like hell I'm playing this one right.

Kevin doesn't answer. He studies my face, slowly and seriously, as if waiting for a cue or trying to figure something out, his own face as closed and dark as something boarded up. "I've got to be honest," he says finally, a mysterious smile spreading across his face. "A West Hollywood party is the last thing I feel like going to right now." He tilts his head toward the direction we came from. "Want to grab a drink somewhere?"

There is a warm feeling rising inside me, flushed and weightless, like light. I just nod and smile back. "Sounds like a plan," I tell him, picking up a stack of celebrities and hugging them against my side. "You lead." And he does, and it feels so nice to follow someone with direction, long strides, a destination. I stay close, almost touching, so I don't lose him in the crowd. I stay safe inside his shadow.

We drive without talking. The sun at sharper angles now and gold in the air where there used to be white, darker shadows spilling across our laps like wine. Along the sidewalks, the city is waking up in a new way: shorter skirts, louder voices, outdoor cafés blurred and buzzing with people as we cruise slowly by. They all face the street as if waiting for someone to arrive, to recognize them.

At some point, he looks over at me and purses his lips, half smiling, half considering, like he's noticing things he hasn't noticed before. A little wrinkle in his forehead as he takes me in, and I don't know what he's seeing. But I know, as the traffic clears briefly and he looks back at the road, as we pick up sudden speed, flying light and breathless through the city streets, that I haven't felt this in a long time. The feeling like I'm going somewhere.

He says he's taking me to a bar called Bar ("Really, that's what it's called"), a few blocks down from his apartment on Hollywood Boulevard. We park at his building first so he can change his clothes, and he leads me to an elevator with lush red carpet and mirrors for walls, dizzying, a ricocheted reflection of myself all around me. I watch him press the letter "P," which I know from movies means the penthouse, and glance up at him, impressed. He notices but pretends not to.

And inside: an apartment of tall white walls and pale wood floors. A few pieces of plush furniture, and beyond that, emptiness as wide and stretched as a held breath. Across the living room, filmy curtains sway in a breeze off the balcony; a potted plant rustles, quietly reshuffling its waxy leaves. But otherwise the room is all stillness and space, the kind of uncluttered simplicity you might see in a catalog spread or just before moving day.

I can't decide how it makes me feel—unusually calm or unusually small.

"I know it's a little bland," he says quickly, sensing my uncertain response. "But you get used to it after a while."

"It's nice," I tell him. "Definitely a modern look."

He nods. "That was Dex's call. Not really what I'd go for, but he played the older-brother card on that one. He always had that kind of minimalist style, you know?"

I blink, the realization catching me off guard—that Dex used to live here, that this is where he stood when he came home from work with carefully messy hair and smooth cheeks, tailored suit jacket slung over one shoulder. This is his glass side table, his sofa, his sense of style. And remembering the jumbled clutter of his thrift-store apartment in Two Harbors—the postcard wallpaper and cheap souvenirs, a tourist's life, how easily I was fooled—this elegant minimalism suddenly seems wonderfully and cruelly honest.

"Anyway," Kevin says, "make yourself at—" He stops, and we both look awkwardly away from each other. "There are drinks in the kitchen if you want. I'll—just be a minute."

He takes long strides across the gleaming wood and disappears into one of the two bedrooms flanking the balcony. I find my attention pulled, my body pulled, instantly toward the other.

Because I know it's there, behind that closed white door: the stilled, secret heart of his other life, the one without me. His neat, naked, goddamn minimalist answers.

I can't bring myself to look.

Instead, I trace the surfaces, the textures and exteriors, the appearances: a careful distance. I run my fingers along the flinty granite face of the kitchen counter. Touch the ivory knobs of drawers and cupboards, smooth and round and lusterless, each its own cool egg of release. I press my hand against the firmness of the wall, the next wall, grazing a path from kitchen to hallway and hallway to living room, everything the same pale solidity of bone.

Imagining how these walls would feel against my back, in the dark.

Or the overstuffed white couch, deep and soft as an embrace—I close my eyes, and open them, and keep moving.

I find myself, finally, in front of a bookcase and a noticeably undusted display of framed photographs. A miniature gallery of family history; my gaze wanders slowly along the shelf, face refracted in the glass like something shattered. Dex and Kevin smile back at me from most of them, with ski hats and parkas, with golf clubs, with tropical tans against the backdrop of a turquoise sea. A mountain, a canyon, a village with storefronts in an alphabet I can't read. I pick them up, one by one, and hold them and try to imagine what came after the flash. What Dex said next, what he was laughing at, where they were going, and when, and why. But the pictures won't animate. They won't fill that familiar screen inside my head. Frozen in time, it's the only way I can see him: smiling, silent, and forever withholding, like a pearl beneath his tongue, the truth I never knew was there, waiting to be told.

I find it behind the others without meaning to. A trace, a clue, the evidence I knew was coming but would never really be ready for. There are three of them in the silver-framed photograph: Dex on the right in a pale yellow polo shirt (when did he wear polo shirts?), the curve of his shoulder concealed by the fuzzy swell of the photographer's thumb. An older man on the left (his father?), wearing dark shades, a dark suit. And between them, smiling with the brightness of a flashbulb and the calm-eyed confidence of adoration, pink dress and pink lips and the pink flush of both their arms around her, I see, staring back at me—myself.

Or something close. Her hair is a little different, a little longer, and parted on the wrong side. Same color, though, as mine, and the same blue eyes, too, same smallness of height, same slight angle of the chin. Same crook of the arm loose and strong around her waist: I know what it's like to be there, in that cleft, that cranny, pressed up against that man.

I know that look in her eyes.

I know it because it's the look I've given myself in bathroom mirrors, door locked, the concentrated silence of putting on a character and seeing how it comes out. This girl in the photograph is like that, like a character you can play but never really sustain. She is self-assurance squared. She is a girl who would let them love her, who would smile into the camera like that and beg for it, *Love me*, who would make them helpless with it, and who would never be so stupid as to love them back.

It must be why she looks so familiar.

This is the girl I've always wanted to be.

"Let's hit it," he says from behind me, and I glance over my shoulder. He has changed into a tight black T-shirt made of a glossy material that seems to deepen as the light moves across it, and dark jeans, soft and sandblasted. He smiles at me and I try to smile back, but it feels as stiff and frozen as the smiles I'm holding in my hands. "What are you looking at?"

I hold it up and gauge his reaction from across the room: curiosity or confusion as he moves in for a closer look, then some kind of realization, then the realization that he should hide his realization. He looks up at me, doesn't say anything. I can't help thinking he'd make a terrible actor.

"She kind of looks like me," I tell him lightly.

"You think so?" He takes the silver frame from my hands and returns it to the empty space on the shelf.

"Who is she?" I ask him, and he shrugs.

"Family friend. No one special." He takes a step toward the door. "You ready to go?"

And I can tell he's lying about something. Face down-turned, he rubs his nose roughly, pulls out his wallet and looks with focused concentration through its depths, puts it away and finally looks up at me expectantly. I can tell; I know the signs. I just don't know what they mean and I have to ask him, can't help it—"His girlfriend?"

Kevin hesitates, considering. "Why would you think that?"

Which tells me enough. I glance back at the photograph, meet her eyes that suddenly seem less like mine and more like my mother's: fearless, forward-looking, a little too proud. Eyes that would not dwell on something as stupid as a photograph, as meaningless and impermanent as another woman.

"Forget it," I tell him, turning away. Push her from my mind the way I know she'd push me from hers. "Let's get out of here," I smile, and he leads me back down to the bustling streets, where twilight has rushed the city into a sudden and glittering darkness.

The outside of the bar is unmarked, and except for the wide column of a bouncer standing beside the door (nodding conspiratorially at Kevin as we walk past him), I would guess we were going to someone's apartment. The inside, on the other hand, is like nothing I've seen at home—red walls that warp into rounded corners and curved hallways, tall-yet-tiny tables staggered throughout a long, dim room, and an orangey light coming, seemingly, up out of the floor. The lighting is more disorienting than anything. It makes shadows that bend the wrong way, gives everyone a kind of ghostly, flashlight-beneath-the-face look that seems both comical and spooky.

I think, disappointed, that this is not the sort of place the movies portray, not what I expected from a Hollywood bar. I'd hoped for flashing lights, a throng of thrashing, drunken bodies and music like screaming, something wild and vaguely appalling to jolt me out of the lingering heaviness of this morning. I want to be shocked, the small-town girl yanked violently out of her shell—I'm ready for that. But everyone is just sitting around, murmuring quietly and sipping at bright-colored drinks in long-stemmed glasses. Even the music is muted, somber, a quiet and nonsensical blend of flutes and running water and dissatisfied moans. It's like the end of a party. It's depressing.

"It's new," he says. "This time next week, there'll be a line two blocks down the sidewalk, guaranteed. What do you think?"

I smile with my lips. I don't say anything.

He gets us a table the size of a dinner plate and orders a Crown and Seven. I don't know what that is—it sounds distantly related to a nursery rhyme I can't remember—but I blank so thoroughly on the name of a drink, anything glamorous enough for Hollywood, that I order it, too, and hope for something sweet.

"Same old crowd," Kevin announces after the waiter saunters, unhurried, away from our table. He leans back in his chair, looks around the room: thin-faced blondes in slinky black tops, short, built men in tight black T-shirts like Kevin's, and everywhere the gleam of shining tanned skin, of wan white smiles. I realize, as I slide my sweater off and adjust the thin black straps of my tank top, how easily my funeral attire blends me into this, the same old crowd.

"Is that a good thing or a bad thing?" I ask him.

"What do you think?"

"Why do you keep answering my questions with questions?"

Kevin clears his throat and looks away, but I catch the hint of a smile teasing the corner of his mouth. "I don't know what I think," he says as he takes in the crowd, the red room

rippling back into a kind of intestinal tunnel. "Aren't we supposed to like places like this?"

"Places like what?"

"New places."

"New places with the same old crowd doesn't make
them very new."

"You seem to know what *you* think." He waves away the
apology he sees building up behind my lips. "It's okay," he
adds, "I'm not surprised. This wasn't Dex's scene, either. Part
of why he left."

I want to disregard this comment, this sudden change of
subject, sidestep it casually and gracefully as a puddle on the
sidewalk. But I can't hold back my interest any more than I
can hide it. "What *was* Dex's scene?" I ask him, only it's too
late now—the waiter returns, leaning between us to set our
drinks down on the table, and in that moment of invasion,
a thin, hard torso interrupting our gaze, my question spins
out of orbit and leaves behind it a wake of uncomfortable
silence.

We both reach instinctively for a glass.

"To the rest of your trip," he says loudly at the same time
I say quietly, "To Dex."

He stares at me. "To Dex," he agrees, lets his eyes linger,
then looks away. We do not clink our glasses. We take long,
full-mouthed pulls on the same beats, and I try not to grimace; my nursery-rhyme drink tastes very strong and very
brown, and I take another gulp, hoping to finish it quickly
so I can get something else.

"So." I smile, raise my eyebrows against the awkward silence. "A writer, huh?"

"Sounds better than a cardboard salesman."

"Following in dad's footsteps?"

"I wish." Kevin looks away.

"What kind of writer?"

He doesn't look back at me for a long moment, and when he does, it's with a kind of amused expression. "I'm not *really* a writer, Casey."

"Oh." I pause. I take a casual sip of my drink as if unfazed by this news — and truth be told, I don't really have to fake it. Not much is catching me by surprise anymore.

"Sounds pretty good, though, doesn't it?" Kevin adds. "If my dad had his way, I'd be the next George Clooney, but acting's the last thing in the world I'd want to—" He stops abruptly, and it's only then that I remember my own occupational lie. "Sorry, I didn't mean…"

"It's okay. Since we're being honest, I'm not really an actress, either."

He stares at me, at the slow smile creeping across my face, and soon it's mirrored in his own, and then we're both laughing into our drinks, full smiles now, full swallows. The lights dim a little further, the way they do sometimes as the evening goes on, and the room flushes with a deeper red. It's hard to read his face now. The sharper edges of him are growing faint, smudged, as if drawn in pencil and passed from hand to hand.

"So what are you, then?" he asks, and I shake my head.

"You tell me."

"Well, I know you're in school," he says, not missing a beat, and I can't help but like that. "Only I don't know what for. I'd guess…history?" I shake my head again, and he frowns. "Too simple," he says, "I should have known that. One of those interdisciplinary majors, I bet. French-

Canadian comparative oceanography. With a minor in geographical-geological studies. Am I close?" and I'm laughing as he finishes his drink and glances around for our waiter. "Your turn."

I consider: the flat pink panes of his face, two-dimensional in this deepened light, his thin hands, intense eyes. "I could have seen you as a poet," I tell him honestly. "Or maybe an artist. Studio art. Abstract sculpture was your specialty. They always said you were good with wood."

"The praise every man dreams of." He grins as the waiter materializes and slides another drink across our table. "Sounds like a pretty nice life to me."

"It was. Until you got kicked out of school for your affair with the nude model."

"Hey, that's not a bad life, either," he laughs. "Think I could trade up? This one's not doing me much good."

His laughter fades to an awkward smile, and we look away and sip modestly from our glasses; the game suddenly seems as stale as an aftertaste, a two-dimensional role. We sip some more. We wait. The worst kind of silence has fallen, that abrupt and inevitable kind you're most afraid of on a first date, not knowing enough about the other person to be able to fill it, and I look down into my drink, mind fumbling a little, confused. *Why am I thinking about first dates?*

"So," I blurt out, sudden as a gunshot. "How come you told me you were a writer?"

Kevin runs his finger along the rim of his glass. "It's not just you." He looks up. "I mean, it's not like I wanted to lie to you or anything. It's what I'd actually like to be, or at least something like it. A screenwriter. Or a filmmaker. Or, you know, good with wood. Just something creative, you know?

The kind of person who *makes* something. Like my dad, like—"

He runs out of steam, looking away, and I can hear Dex's name in the awkwardness of his silence. "Have you told him?" I ask.

"My dad? Yeah, right. Once he gets something in his head, it's there for good. And for some reason, he saw Dex as the power-play producer and me as the actor. So that's always the way it was." He jingles his ice cubes with hollow-sounding merriment. "I'll give in eventually. It'll make Dad happy, and that's all that matters. Anyway, I'll have to get my act together one of these days."

"So to speak."

"When he figures out auditioning isn't exactly my day job."

"He doesn't know what you do?"

Kevin laughs, but it's not a real laugh this time. "Are you kidding? *Venice*? He'd kill me." He shakes his head as if conceding: *What the hell else am I going to do?* "It's fine to go against the grain for a while, for the sake of going against the grain. It's almost expected when your father's in the business. But his connections are the only way I'll make it anywhere, and I suppose he'll stop paying my rent eventually. It's just easier in the end." He pauses, frowning. "What's with the look?"

"What look?"

"You're thinking something." Silence. "You think I'm selling out."

I open my mouth to protest, but find myself closing it and shrugging toward honesty. "I'm thinking, why let your dad decide your life for you?"

"Easy for you to say."

"What's that supposed to mean?"

"You don't know what he's been through," Kevin says quickly. "How it was when my mom died, and now this. Why shouldn't I try to make him happy?" His forehead is creased along the center, a furrow in the smooth facade we've built up to this point. "I'm not the only one to put family first," he adds. "Dex did, too."

"So why did he leave L.A.?" I shoot back.

He lets a beat go by, and another. Just looking, unblinking, sorting through something behind his eyes as he looks into mine, and slowly the crease begins to flatten, the mask fitting back into place. He smiles calmly. "And what about the actress bit? What are *you* really?"

So close to something real, and still so far away. "A director," I tell him distractedly, trying to memorize the conversation we've just had, to pull together its crumbs of truth and pack them into something whole. But already they are scattering across this table, already he is leaning forward with a growing interest, and it's so much easier to just let the words flow out of me, to look down and relax back into the comfort of small talk. "At least that's the plan," I tell him, rubbing the ring from my glass into the tabletop. "I'm in a theater program back home. Stage direction. But this is really where I want to be." I look up. "I mean, in film."

"I knew what you meant."

"I'd love to make something for one of the festivals. That's my next project, to enter in one of the short categories. Something where I can direct my own story."

"What kind of story?"

His voice quiet now, mine quiet. I can't help but smile—*What else is there?* "A love story."

"You mean a chick flick." He smiles back, but shakes his head. "I overestimated you."

"This from the heir to a cop show."

"Hey," he says quickly, smile fading fast. "That's just his day job, okay?" The sudden sharpness jars our conversation into stopping; that stony defensiveness is back in his face, and I'm the one who has to look away now. Consider the right words, my own defense.

"They don't make you think too hard," I tell him, my hands folding into each other protectively. "Love stories. They don't make you search for the happy ending." And I look up, and maybe he doesn't know my story—I sure as hell don't know his—but I can see in his eyes he understands this more than he lets on. "That's what I want to make."

He nods. He seems to consider this for a moment, and it's only when I release my breath that I realize how long I've been holding it in. How much I care, suddenly, about what he thinks. A waiter whisks away his empty glass, doesn't even ask if he wants another, and then it's just us, the humming ghost-light of the room, this vague tenseness, a single drink. Kevin sighs, starts to say something, and stops again, uncertainty creeping back into his voice. "He would have liked that, you know. To hear you say that. He liked them."

My own hand over my own hand: the semblance of comfort in my lap, but lonely, no one to hold but myself. "Liked what?" I ask.

"Happy endings. A love story." And I hear it in his voice, what I feel in my fingers. I look up and he's closer, looking deeply back, a look that feels like guilt and want and ache and uncertainty all pulled in and spilling out, *needing*—"He believed in them," and I find myself pulled forward without thinking, so close it feels familiar. Like looking up from his shoulder in the dark, waiting for his hand over mine...

"Personally," he adds, eyes on my mouth, "*I'd* make a mystery."

He sits back.

I blink. I wait until I realize there's nothing to wait for and clear my throat, everything stuttered and sudden in the aftermath of that look. He raises his eyebrows, and I can't think of a single thing to say. "I'm going to find the ladies' room," I tell him finally, loudly.

"Okay."

"I'll be right back."

"Okay." Smiling now, infuriatingly calm; I smile back, quick and empty pull of the lips, and hurry clumsily down a curving hallway.

Okay, you're okay. Like an echo in my head, a drumbeat of forced confidence.

Okay.

Okay.

The bathroom is like the main room, wavy-walled and dim-lit, the only differences in the color (aquamarine, a dramatic contrast to the red and orange my eyes have grown accustomed to) and the manic action of the women who were so sedate outside with the men. In here, they bustle, yank on straying straps, shake out their hair in dramatic and violent flings of the neck. They crowd around a long mirror, pale and drawn in the underwater lights, applying mascara and shimmery glosses in short, frantic strokes. I see a stick-thin brunette shaking pills out of a plastic bag, hurry to a toilet before I can see any more. And I stand there, motionless in my blue womb of a stall—don't have to go, of course, but I had to get away—and listen to the quick yet mute flutterings of the women making themselves beautiful. Trying to imagine what it's like to be one of them before I realize: I knew that, once. How to do that. To find my calm behind a mask, to direct my own story.

And I can't remember where I went wrong.

Slowly and eventually, I make my way back through the throbbing red of the bar. After the cold, dead-body blue of the bathroom, these lights seems warmer, like a sunset, and I find myself suddenly appreciating the thickened crowd, these empty but comforting smiles, all the lives and conversations I'm passing by, a welcome distraction from my own....

"So at that point I knew I was fucked either way. I mean, if he'd just had a goddamn clue about immigration laws—"

I smile at the tall, dark-haired man who clears a brief path for me through the bodies.

"Can't believe it's been three years, has it really been—because you look—"

I smile at the tall, blonde girl with the breasts of a twenty-year-old and the face of a forty-year-old. She doesn't smile back.

"—and at that point I was like, if I'm gonna do that for money, you'd better make it a *lot* more...."

I smile and smile as if it will save my life, as if looking calm will make me calm. I smile because it's what my mother would do, and I make my way slowly back to the front of the room to emerge finally, triumphant, from the push and stagger of the crowd—and find an unfamiliar face where Kevin's used to be.

"Hey, baby, you all right?" The short, bald-headed man

with creamy brown skin and Spanish eyes stands up, looks me up and down.

"I'm fine," I tell him, not smiling anymore.

"Because you seem lost." He comes closer. "And you know, maybe I could help you find what you're looking for—"

"I can find it myself." I back away, but there's nowhere to turn, nowhere to go. The crowd has overflowed to fill the rest of the room, and all these faces are suddenly the same face, none of them looking back and all of them this identical, magazine-perfect kind of beautiful—chiseled, narrow-nosed, firm-chinned, firm-chested. I feel dazed, a trembling uncertainty filling me up and threatening to spill over the top.

Help me. Come back to me.

And that's when I spot Kevin across the room. He's standing at the bar talking to someone I can see only in brief glimpses, their faces flashing through the shifting bodies between us. Slow-motion and stammered with the movement of the crowd, the scene unfolds a frame at a time: his downturned face; her glowing blonde hair; a shimmering silver dress and the arch of her neck as he leans in to whisper into her ear. As she turns her face toward mine. Eyes that I know, that I've seen gloating back at me—and I blink, the recognition like a shove from behind, picturing the photograph in his apartment and yet remembering her from somewhere else—

The girl in the pink dress, beneath Dex's polo-shirted arm.

The actress in the movie, the one who leaves the director. The one he watched while he kissed me in the theater.

Same girl. Same face.

Why didn't I see it before?

I move closer through this loosely spun moment, time unraveling like a thread, and wonder if that's really her, if they're really the same person. What it means that Kevin is kissing the cheek of someone who belongs onscreen. What it means that she used to be with Dex...

It can't be her.

Am I seeing so many blondes that I can't tell the difference anymore?

This isn't a movie.

But it feels like one, a twist that doesn't make sense but seems so right—why Dex looked at me like he did when we met, as I pulled the ticket from his fingers. Why he wanted to watch it twice, eyes on the screen as his hand went up my leg. *Do you think she loved him?* he asked me in the dark, and I was blind enough to think the question was hypothetical; that when he looked at her, he was thinking of me, not the other way around—

And it slams into me from the right, the weight of this realization, "Sorry, sorry," someone is saying, pulling me up off the floor. "So sorry, you okay?" and by the time I regain my balance, it's just Kevin and the bartender through the crowd. I'm close enough now that he sees me and waves, holding up his drink like a toast. I make my way unsteadily toward him, searching for that silver dress, the mirror of her held up to me. But it's too late now; she's gone, enveloped by the throng of people, the warm red lights. A ghost, a memory.

"She made yours weaker," he says as I approach him. I stare at him. "What do you mean?"

He holds up the glass again, laughing at me. "Your drink. She made it kind of weak. Guess that's probably a good thing."

I take it from his hand, glance over his shoulder and think I see her—but it's only a mirror behind the bar, a wild-eyed blonde girl looking back, cheeks flushed and confused, and I shake my head, trying to clear something. "Who was that?" I ask him.

"Who was who?"

I shoot him a glare, tired of the games. "The girl you were talking to."

"The bartender?"

"The girl from the *photograph*." He frowns. "The one Dex dated?" I remind him. "The family friend, no one special? She was here, Kevin, I *saw* her. I've seen her before—"

"Casey..." He glances around the room, then takes the glass from my hand and sits me down on a stool, staring at me until I have to look away. "All I did," he says slowly, "was order you a drink. I talked to Pamela over there, but I don't know who else you think—" Pausing, he glances over my shoulder, and I follow his gaze past my own reflection to the bartender: young, blonde, glittery black halter top and a silver name-tag, *Pamela*. I blink, study her face through the sunset light, consider my own face in the glass of the mirror and try to remember the face I saw, fading out now like a closing shot—

Is this what crazy feels like? Is this what she felt, what she left behind?

"Are you okay?" he asks me quietly, and I snap my head up, take my glass from his hands. He seems suddenly reluctant to give it back to me.

"Fine," I tell him quickly. "I'm fine. I just thought—"

But it's easier not to think right now. Because I don't like to think of what it means if I saw her. Or what it means if I didn't.

"Never mind." I smile, take a grateful sip, the sweet brown flavor reassuringly familiar. "Aren't you getting a drink?"

Kevin hesitates. "I think maybe I should stop at two. If I'm going to drive you back to the hotel, I mean."

I stare at him for a long moment, and then it sinks in, a final blow: Once we leave this sunset light, once we walk back out that door, it's the same night for me as last night, as the one before and all the ones before that. It's another night of more questions, of fewer answers. It's my empty hotel room. It's my empty bed, the achingly anonymous floral comforter I left in a disheveled pile this morning, the shed skin of a life I can't climb back into—and all I want is to keep pretending, just one night of pretending it doesn't have to be that way, the words falling out of my mouth before I can stop them: "You don't have, like, a futon or something…" I swallow, mouth dry. "Do you?"

He stares at me, then looks quickly away toward the bar, and I feel something drop like a broken elevator through my chest, shame creeping its way into my burning cheeks: *How could you say that, he's paying for your room, does he think you're coming on to him, are you coming on to him, what does he think of you now?* But I realize after a moment he's only signaling the bartender for another round, and when he turns back to me, his eyes are bright, satisfied, winged with smiling wrinkles at the corners.

"It took you a while," he tells me quietly. "But I hoped you'd ask."

Two hours, three Crowns, and a very Long Island later, I stumble down the steps behind him and into the bright and jarring thrust of a night come terrifyingly alive. All around me, Hollywood breathes, seethes people of every shape and size and dejected appearance, a frenzied chaos of light and dark faces, strange languages, and violent explosions of curs-ing. I feel something threatening to scatter, a flutter of panic humming in my chest (*What was I thinking, where am I going?*) until Kevin nudges me, his arm slipping protectively around my shoulders—"Just keep close, okay?"

The thing that's been unknotting inside me comes back together. I smile and shrug as if it doesn't matter, but his arm feels nice there, we both know it, and we make our way like that, pulled tight to each other, through the crowded streets.

As he guides me unsteadily to his apartment, I realize we've been walking over the stars all evening. They're lined up in the sidewalk, gold-framed around a name and a pic-ture of a camera, a radio, a microphone, the same sidewalk stars I saw once in a Hollywood special my mother had taped. And I feel a twinge of excitement as I read those names—Cary Grant, Audrey Hepburn, Elizabeth Taylor—the surreal feeling that I'm being filmed, I've crossed a line, I'm in that world inside my TV with my mother watching over my shoulder, her arm draped around me—and maybe it's just the alcohol that makes everything seem perfect and magical and suddenly destined, but I can't help it, I know, I'm *certain* in this moment that I'm out here for a reason if

I can only find it, whatever or whomever it is I'm looking for—

Kevin pulls me closer as we're walking, so close I can smell his breath, the same flavor as the taste in my mouth.

"Don't read the stars," he whispers. "You look like a tourist."

He lets his arm fall off my shoulders, takes my hand in that protective way of his, and guides me forward and into the rest of this night—an ending I can't predict, but one that does not, for the first time in a long time, mean lonely.

I sneak a glance at the stars whenever I know he's not looking. There are blank spaces sometimes, golden and empty, waiting to be filled in.

Back in his front hallway, we linger uncertainly where we didn't before, because what do we do with this awkward end of the night, swollen and pulsing between us like a heartbeat. I focus my attention on the paintings behind us, abstract echoes of each other lined up along the walls. I didn't notice them this afternoon: splashes of pink and gray on white, swirled with blue in complex, churning patterns. The kind of paintings you don't want to see when you're drunk because they will both confuse you and move you—I want, suddenly, inexplicably, to cry.

"My mom made those," Kevin says. I hear him coming up behind me, then beside me, and I'm suddenly aware of a shifting balance in my stomach.

"I didn't know she was an artist."

"She was pretty good, huh?"

I nod, my eyes still lost in the loops and swirls. "What was she like?" I ask.

He considers the paintings for a moment and taps one softly in the corner to straighten it. "She was very…alive," he says. "A little wild, a little lonely. Everything that comes with being an artist." He touches the frame again, rubbing his thumb along the edge. "I don't know how to explain it. She was like her paintings, I guess."

"Beautiful, then."

He nods. "But hard to understand."

"Do you miss her?"

Kevin stares at the painting for a long time. Then something tightens in his expression, mouth tapering to a taut, thin line. He pulls his hand away. "I miss the way my family was then," he says. "How happy she made my dad. I don't miss her."

His voice seems too heated for it to be that simple, but I don't say anything. I step back and lean against the door frame to the rest of the apartment. "They pull you in," I tell him, nodding at the paintings. "They feel like flying. Or drowning."

He gives me a long look, and I don't know how to interpret this either. Slowly, hesitantly, he comes closer, unties the sweater I've been wearing around my waist and hangs it on a hook beside the door. When he turns back, I reach behind me, hold on tight to the molding, feet braced against the threshold, something to anchor the spinning darkness. He's so close I can feel his breath, hot and damp on my face, and I think maybe I should turn away—I know this look, this precursor to a kiss, but what do I want here, *what do I want to happen*, I know what those half-closed eyes mean, heavy-lidded, looking down beneath dark, curling lashes and the feel, suddenly, of his hand against my face. I know what's coming. I don't know what to do, but I know, I remember, those same eyes above me in the dark, the feeling of those lips—

"Can I ask you something?"

He blinks. It takes me a while to realize I'm the one who has spoken. "Sure," he says. His voice is husky, words thick with the musk of whisky and the smell of him, of them, the same smell, same voice.

I reach up and press his hand against my skin, close my eyes. "How can we—" I start, and stop. "What do we—"

The silence of the room. The expectation tinged with guilt. Any minute, he's going to walk in, I can feel it.

"What is it?" Kevin whispers, and I open my eyes.

"What did he say about me?" I mumble and pull his hand away.

Kevin steps back, face closing like a door.

"When he came back here," I add. "Did he—I mean, was he—"

"Leaving you?"

The words blunt, heavy and inevitable as something dropped, a sinking stone. I stare at him, his face changing in the gathered distance, not so much like Dex anymore. I nod a little and the room tilts, wobbles, spins with pinpricks of white like a quavering snow globe.

He doesn't say anything. Silence blunt as his words. I nod at this, too.

"I deserve that," I tell him.

"What?"

"Not knowing. It's what I deserve. The worst thing."

He comes a little closer, and the thickening silence is a

flush in my mouth, a hot, heavy taste. "It's not the worst thing."

"Then what is?"

He doesn't say. He looks away, and I can see there's something he's not telling me, and the world won't stop its crazy dance of seasick lights, surges of thought like electric pulses through my brain—

My hands squeeze against the door frame. He reaches out, puts his hands against my shoulders, and I close my eyes, and I open them. "Whoa," I say, and laugh a little. "I don't think I've drunk this much in a while."

"Why don't we—"

"No, I'm fine now." I smile at him. The world is calm again, my balance steady and certain in his arms, and in this pale gray dimness coming in from the skylight, pink-tinged with the neon of a still-throbbing night outside, I think he looks like someone I've known forever—that familiar, that safe. "You have his eyes," I blurt.

He takes a step back and leans against the door frame, both of us on the threshold now. "I know."

"His mouth, too. Smile, I mean. I probably know you as well as him."

He tilts his head, or maybe that's me.

"I didn't know he was in L.A. until they told me," I confess. "Where he was. Why." A pause. The world rocks forward, unsteady again. "Kevin, why was he on that plane to Minnesota?"

"Let's just go inside."

"Did he tell you?"

"Casey—"

"Why?"

"You don't—"

"Why was he on that plane?"

"Because of *you*, okay?" The words bursting out angry and sudden, louder than I expected. He looks down at me, the same confusion in his face, same quivering uncertainty that's twisting wildly in my stomach. "Is that really what you want to hear? That he was coming back to you, that he loved you? That *you're* the reason?"

I stare at him for a long, silent moment.

And I laugh. The kind of laughter that blurs your vision, that seems like crying but feels lighter. Laughter that is relief, that is the awkward answer to guilt. That is, above all else, horribly and unspeakably happy.

Yes, I realize. *Yes, that's what I want to hear.*

And that must be the worst thing.

"I'm sorry," he says and tries to take my hand to lead me into the living room, but I hang on to the wall persistently. A struggle. A confrontation with our hands: *Let go,* but I'm not ready yet, I'm not ready yet and he doesn't notice, looking away, *let go, let go.* "I didn't mean that," he's saying. "These things just happen. You're not the reason, that's not true," and the world drops its grip as he pries my fingers from the door frame. As I fall into his arms, he finally meets my eyes: a collision of regret as we steady each other, the hold coming loose, the balance, and the truth rushing up with a spasm in my stomach—

"You're wrong," I tell him. "Falling in love—that's always the reason."

I manage to make it to the toilet before it all comes back to haunt me.

the rest of her life

Sunday morning. That holy kind of hush to it, sun wrapped under clouds, air heavy and hazy as something half-spoken: a strained silence, a hesitation. Alone on the porch, she looks out across the disheveled lawn, patchy with crabgrass and clumps of white clover, past the sidewalks cracked with dandelion, pushed through from beneath into the gray light of morning, and tries to imagine tomorrow.

The rest of her life, she thinks. The beginning of something. Why doesn't it feel that way, like a beginning?

His car coming into view at the end of the road: it rises up to glint dully in the morning light at the top of the hill, and that, she thinks, is what this feels like. Not like a beginning. More like a moment hovered and spun over some kind of summit, a moment of looking both forward and backward and seeing, in every direction, a downward angle, a settling toward gravity. A descent into the dirt and dust kicked up by the very thought of going anywhere at all.

It's not what she used to imagine when she pictured her wedding day. What she saw, despite her mother's warnings about men, about dependence, about all your eggs in some-one else's basket: rockets launching. Stars shooting. A built-up sudden flight through lightness and freedom, her life yanked forward and up, pulled wildly along in the thrust of someone new, and her whole past trailing faded and forgotten in the wake of something brighter—

Not this moment of clumsy incompletion. This sense that there are two halves to her now, and nothing whole.

He pulls the convertible, old but gleaming with wax and shine, into her driveway. He is grinning and clean-shaven, hair ruffled from the car ride, and she smiles back because that's how she should feel, that's what she should do. That's what a bride would do, even if it's just a courthouse ceremony, even if her mother will sleep through it and wake, hours later, hung over with no one to complain to. She smiles because it's what he expects, and because, despite everything, he still makes her want to smile.

I like your dress, *he says, getting out of the car to open her door.*

She rises. It was my mom's, *she tells him, and although this isn't true, it makes her feel better to imagine it was.*

You look beautiful. *He runs a hand through his hair, what he does when he's nervous, a habit that will sink, as if fatigued, to a pulling at his beard later in life.* Beautiful, *he says again, awkwardly now, and she looks down modestly, wondering why she can't feel his words and looking up after enough time has passed for her to know the feeling isn't going to come.*

You look ready, *she says.*

And you?

She walks toward the car despite this sense that she should run upstairs, heart thumping, to tell her mother something. What it is, she's not sure: *I love you,* or *I'm sorry,* or maybe just *This is it, this is the day something changes.* Or *good-bye. That's all, just good-bye.* As if it might make a difference in how she feels.

Mrs. Maywood, *he calls her, opening her door, but she just smiles and kisses him and shakes her head. Not yet his wife: three hours to go.*

Not yet a mother: seven months left until I'm part of the scene.

But she's no longer a daughter, either, not with these bursting suitcases, not with a new house five blocks away and a borrowed ring in her jacket pocket. As she slides into the front seat, her packed-up life tossed behind her onto the worn vinyl, she feels that hovering feeling again, that downward glance in all directions. The rest of her life, she thinks, the be-ginning of something, this is it, this is it, but it doesn't work, doesn't ease this sense of almost, not quite. *This moment of wondering what her role is when all she feels is in-between, wondering who she is and where she's going as the road opens up into a future obscured by the rise of the hill—a future they always told her would be bigger than this, because with that face of yours, that presence, that something, your future will be stardom, stars and rockets, will be as strong and green and surprising as dandelions through concrete. You'll go far, they said. Past these gravel roads, these dead-end streets. Past a life spent looking beside you at this man behind the wheel, this man who won you over with his quiet way of looking back, his eyes like the ocean you've never seen, his broad shoulders, his steely strength like your father's—a man who promised you all that he had, a man who couldn't promise you enough, yet here you are beside him...*

And as you crest that hill, as the moment begins its sink into the rest of your life, you look at that man and you realize it, a feeling as stunned and blue-blurred and sightless as the spotlight thrown suddenly off you, the dark fall of a curtain:

I do. I do. I love this man.

And the trailing thought like an afterglow:

How did I let this happen?

the morning after

I wake to the pulse of a soured night in my mouth, belly-flopped on the overstuffed couch with a plastic wastebasket beside my face. All around me, the tall walls of the living room gleam bare and white, shadows curving in the corners: the sickeningly pristine interior of a toilet bowl. It's enough to make the feeling come back, and I close my eyes, slip into the middle-world between sleep and queasy sunlight.

Like an angel, Dex says. Against the shadow of my eyelids, he's perched on the near end of the sofa, running his hands over the tangles in my hair. That is my role today: something chaste but fallen, wings tattered on the way down, a grubby scuff of mangled purity in the midst of all this white. Bruised.

A penitent angel, he adds.

I smile into the pillow. *False advertising.*

Look at me, and in my half-dream, I raise my heavy head, squint up into his face, the blinding brightness of skylight. He's smiling back and I feel reality relax to this, a dream that hovers so magically close to real, just hold it in your head as long as you can and let it play out, see where it goes—*You look*, he says, *you are*—

"Are you okay?"

I jolt awake, head pounding in the sudden light, and look up to see Kevin's face in place of Dex's. He smiles down at me, but the smile is forced, awkward, as if he's not sure what to do with this train wreck of a girl sleeping on his sofa.

"I'm fine," I tell him as convincingly as I can.

"You were talking in your sleep."

"Really?" I sit up and regret it immediately; my stomach kicks, hot and angry, with the movement. "What was I saying?"

"Something about your mother."

And I remember in a jarring rush the second reason I came to L.A. The search I need to begin today.

"I have to run out for a while," Kevin says. "See my dad and everything." His voice is strangely pitched, a little stiff, as if he's rehearsed these lines before. "But I'll meet you here this afternoon?"

"Sure."

"You're going over to your mom's place, right?" He doesn't wait for me to answer, just hands me a wad of twenties. "For cabs."

I stare at the offering. It seems somehow inappropriate in the context of this scene: the awkwardness of the morning after, my rumpled clothes and rocking hangover, money being passed over the sheets. I clear my throat. "You really don't have to—"

"So you can get around." He drops the money into my lap. "Or in case you want to go back to the hotel. To change, I mean." He stands up, puts his hands in his pockets, and backs slowly away. "See you later, okay? This afternoon? There's a key on the counter. You can take it with you."

I stare at the bills unfolding slowly against my black skirt. "Sure," I mumble, and I hear the door close sharply, and then it's just me and the silence, the money in my lap, the rest of the day waiting like a promise, like a threat.

I get up slowly, tripping over the trash can, and find my way to the bathroom where I wash my face and rinse out my mouth. Look up to see a drawn white ghost staring back at me from the mirror. Her eyelashes are damp and matted together. Her hair is an explosion of knots. But her face, pale and clear in the silvery frame of the mirror, looks resolute, more calm than my rolling stomach will let me feel. She reminds me of my mother, of the dream I woke up from — a steely-eyed girl ready to face whatever comes next. And she reminds me, just as suddenly, of someone else, the rest of last night coming back to me in a flood of images....

When I get to the bookshelf, the photograph of the girl isn't there anymore. Just an empty space where the silver frame used to be, a pale outline of dust that tells me I didn't imagine it. That tells me Kevin must have moved it, that tells me something strange is going on here, but that doesn't tell me what I need to know: whether or not she's who I think she is, the actress walking hip-swayed and cool-eyed across the screen.

I stare at the empty spot on the shelf, that dark ghost of unanswered questions. A missing identity.

It doesn't take me long to find her.

Or at least find evidence of who I think she must be. She stares back at me from the shower shelf in the form of a pink razor and a bottle of herbal, flowery shampoo. A tampon in the medicine cabinet, an out-of-place tube of lavender hand cream. She haunts Dex's sparse bedroom in small, innocent echoes — two ticket stubs to the ballet, a woman's watch (broken clasp, an hour behind) lying dusty and limp on the edge of his desk. Beside the unmade bed, three fragile roses have dried in a blue glass vase. I think, and try not to think, of what their pursed purple lips could speak of, what they have witnessed between these sheets.

She is tucked, finally and most conclusively, into his bottom dresser drawer. Red halter top cut low in the front, swirling floral skirt with a red lace hem. The clothes smell faintly of a woman's perfume, musky and sweet, as if they were put away before being washed, and I wonder what this means, where they were before he picked them up and folded them between his rough hands. I wonder if he smelled them, and what he thought about as he brought them to his face. Closed his eyes.

The V of the halter top dives deep into the shadow between my breasts. The skirt, brushing the inside of my leg, feels like fingers, soft and teasing. In front of his mirror, I try her on like a role: arch of an eyebrow, half-smile nesting in one corner of my mouth. It all fits me better than I thought it would.

And for a moment, in another woman's skin, I lie back against his wrinkled blankets, their quiet histories, the folds and shadows and mysteries of this second life. I bury my hands under the mounds of cotton and wonder what my mother will think seeing me like this. A *natural*. *You always were good at playing the other woman.* And I stretch my arms into those secret depths, my body across this bed.

fade out

So let's get down to it, then.

He nods: Fine with me. *Sits back in his director's chair, crosses his arms and looks up at her, legs spread a little. She notices.* You know the lines?

Memorized them.

He stares at her, waits. You know the lines?

Cut to: her slow smile. I don't need the lines, *she says.* It's an audition. That's how it works.

She smooths a hand down her hair, breasts, hip, down. Takes a step closer to him, eyes down too, and she hesitates, forgetting what comes next. It's a black-and-white film, but they shot her in color somehow, just her and no one else, and she seems to glow from the inside—red dress, gold hair, eyes like something deep. He notices.

I don't need the lines, *she says again. Between his knees; I know this role, how to play this angle, and it feels like me up there on the screen.* I'm what you want. Aren't I?

Great. You're doing great.

And cut from his face to hers, full-screen—

I'm what you want, *she whispers.* I'm what you're looking for.

I pay for the cab with the money Kevin left me, but I don't go back to my hotel to change. I wear, instead, the filmy red halter top, the silky skirt that isn't mine, and impractically lacy underwear that I buy from a lingerie store down the block. Clean, damp hair smelling of another girl's flowery shampoo, mouth stained with the plum-colored lipstick I found in a drawer all those years ago: I look nothing like myself, and it's thinking this that lets me picture my mother's reaction when she sees me. A quiet gasp, smile blossoming slow as a rose in the middle of her face, a face that won't have changed much in eight years except for that flash of something unfamiliar in her eyes: surprise, recognition. A swelling respect, something as close to pride as I can let myself imagine, and before I know it we're coasting through the city, past streets named after romantic places, a world of older movies—*Santa Monica, La Mirada, Sunset Boulevard.* The dreamy images in those names, like dusk over villas someplace far away, mirages brighter than this town of split sidewalks and blue gray air. Names like love stories, that make me forget the heavy residue of my hangover, and I feel myself smiling into the rush of wind through the open window, the lightness of these newfound fantasies filling me with hope until he slams his brakes—end of the line in front of that memorized address, and only then do I remember to be afraid.

1117 Sunset, Hollywood CA, 90038. Though don't feel you have to write back.

"You sure you meant one-one-one-seven?" the cabbie asks. We stare in mutual surprise at the building I've been waiting eight years to find—crumbling, brown, gated, wedged between a motel boasting hourly rates and a boarded-up Denny's. An unlit neon sign slopes downward above the darkened glass door: *Dukes 'n' Daisies*, it reads, and underneath, *Hot! Hot! Hot!*

Not the sort of place my father's prediction had implied.

But there's the number in peeling, stick-on metallic script. The only clue I have, the only thing I can trust, and I hand over the money that isn't mine. Open the door and take a step. "This is it," I tell him. "Thanks a lot." I force one last smile, he pulls away, and then it's just me and the door staring each other down, the eerie white sunlight of a midday standoff. The darkened glass: my own reflection. It's like I'm already there on the other side, looking out at what's done, what's gone.

It's done, *he says.*

Don't say that. It can't be. *She leans against him in the doorway and looks up, pulls his tie, pulls him closer.* I'm sure I could convince you. Just give me another read, one more audition...

Babe, Stella already cast the part. It's done, nothing I can do. *He's trapped, caving in, nowhere to look but in her eyes.* Really, there's nothing...

Bullshit. You're a director, *she whispers.* Direct.

He touches her hair, the side of her face, and I can almost feel him touching me; I know that look in the doorway, that threshold balance. She takes his hand. Puts her hand into his, makes him guide her, down.

Direct me, *she says.*

You're convincing, I'll give you that. *He closes his eyes and breathes deep.* Believable. Stella's call, though.

Your call, *and they slide into the room. Against the closed door, locked:* It's up to you, *she tells him.* You've known all along how this has to end.

It's closed.

I don't notice the sign until I'm about to go in—I've been here awhile, worked myself up to it, ready to find the truth, the twist, and all of a sudden I see a twist I didn't expect: *Closed on Sundays.*

And I feel, more than anything, utterly relieved.

This is not the kind of place I hoped to find. Just the ring of it, *Sunset, Hollywood,* and I expected a house with a balcony and a view—at the very least, an apartment building with a built-in doorman and well-kept facade, and who wouldn't? *Sunset Boulevard, One-one-one-seven,* the graceful architecture of those numbers—so pure and thin, the reason, perhaps, that I've always pictured slender Colonial-style columns out front, or maybe the lean arabesques of palm trees all in a row. Cool, white, clean: nothing *hot hot hot* about it.

Nevertheless, I can't leave. Despite the disappointment, I still crave this threshold, its pinnacle of hope, a thousand possibilities beyond my square of sidewalk. I move closer and touch the shaded glass through the iron ribs of a barred gate. I pull on the handle (hard; locked), wait there for a moment and try not to think, because whenever I start, I can only picture my mother in tight blue daisy dukes. Standing there for I don't know how long, losing the feeling of time as it slides by faster, I almost expect a familiar face to come into view from out of the shadows, meet my gaze in the glass—

But it's still just my own reflection, and when a cop starts giving me funny looks from across the street, I walk away.

Think: *I can wait one day. What's one more day?*

But that's not the way it feels.

One day is nothing. Nothing, nothing.

Yes. That's the way it feels.

And like I'm lost—it feels that way, too, wandering down a sidewalk eerily empty for so many cars rushing by. Like I'm losing it, something, time, a chance, the light won't change and the cars fly past and everything is building toward this screaming impatience that's going to rip out of me soon and what if I can't stop it—

Which is when I see it down the street. A sign—a *sign*. Blast of fate in my face, the magical distraction of it, TWO HARBORS in plain black caps on the marquee, and the thought of her is flung from my head as fast as the thought of someone else slips in. I move numbly through the intersection and toward the familiar. I can almost imagine him striding next to me—this film is still the two of us, together in the bluish dark—only he keeps walking too fast. He won't slow down. And I'm losing him in a sudden crowd, dark-haired tourists all around, that glimmer of sandy hair moving farther away and I'm running, crazy with it, slow down, *come back—*

And why should I? *Face contorted in anger, she struggles against his arms, but he holds on tight, insistent.* Like fuck there's nothing you can do and you still cast her over me, so why should I come back?

Because, *he says quietly,* I love you.

Liar.

I do.

A pause, confused: an unexpected change of script. Liar, *she whispers.*

Stop acting.

She stares at him. Pushes away, puts down her script. That's not your line, *she says.*

He shakes his head and pulls her back. Don't make it about a movie. This isn't a movie. I want something real, *and he leans in close, throws her screenplay to the floor.* This is something real.

And eyes closed, I can hear her reply: *Say it again,* and he does, and she melts, gives in, holds him close and lets the happy ending take over. I keep my eyes closed. I don't want to see what I know is coming. How, looking over his shoulder in the embrace, her smile fades, the truth comes out in her empty expression, the audience knows it now: She's leaving him. She probably never loved him at all. And the director's face, blissfully clueless—no idea he'll be wandering along the dull gray coast when the movie ends, lonely on some anonymous pier looking out at the colorless sunset and never really accepting, even when the credits roll, that it's over. It's definitely but indefinitely over.

I watch it again. I wait for them to come in and make me buy another ticket, but they don't bother. A thin crowd trickles out, replaced by another group of black clothes and wan faces, the lights dim, and I slip away to the welcome mindlessness of the screen, eyes growing heavy. *It's intense,* the director warns her when they meet. *A self-reflexive role, a part about playing a part. Think you can handle it?*

Think you can?

I don't mix business with pleasure.

So let's get down to it, then. And when I fall asleep, it's me up there, the woman in red, the slow, sure smile that wins them all over. *I'm what you're looking for,* I tell him, Dex's face fading in where the director's used to be, and for a moment, up there onscreen, I know what I'm doing. I can put on this throbbing-red control, easy as the slip of a dress. I can feel his arms around me again and I can be the one to close off, to leave him first this time. But I know even then that it must be a dream. I know even in sleep that I'm the one left behind, the director with no story to tell, and when I wake up, it's into the black-and-white of an empty the-ater—credits long passed, screen cut to gray, the stillness of an ending that came too soon for me to catch it.

And I think of you, the plane, the sudden silence: how it must have been to go down alone. This empty seat beside me, and the questions you'll never answer. Definitely, indef-initely, over.

tells

I get back to the apartment and Kevin is waiting for me. Hair rumpled as if by nervous hands, rakes of frustration, and eyes widening when I open the door—"I thought you'd left," he says, moving quickly toward me. "I didn't think you were coming back." An apprehensive relief settles across his face, and I stand there and take that in for a moment. A new plan is starting to form in my mind. "Where have you been?" he asks, and I just shake my head and close the door, playing out the silence for all it's worth. I walk slowly through the living room, sink down into the white couch, watch him, wait; he stares back, blinking a little too rapidly, and finally sits opposite me in one of the beige suede armchairs.

A face-off, though he doesn't know it yet. A new confidence is pushing through my fatigue, the hopeless feeling I've felt since walking out of the theater lifting slowly, shored up by the ammunition I realize I've had all along.

"I want you to tell me what's going on," I say calmly.

He frowns, an automatic and artificial rebuff. "I don't know what you're—"

"Starting with the girl I saw in the bar last night. The girl whose photograph you hid somewhere." I insert a pointed pause. "Or I'm out of here."

I don't know why he wants me to stay, but I know enough to call him on it, and it seems to work. Something twitches beneath his eye, an agitation he can't hide; his cards are on the table now, his hand laid bare. He looks down, leans heavily on his knees, hands folded tight and white against my words. "What do you want to know?" he says finally.

"Who she is. And what you're hiding about her."

Silence. His focus stays on the floor as if he hasn't heard me, though we both know he has and that he doesn't have to answer yet; I'm not going to leave after just one shot.

"Fine," I tell him, crossing my arms. "Victoria Fallon." He looks up. "Ring a bell?"

The start in his eyes tells me it does. "Maybe," he says uncertainly. "How do you know her name?"

"She's an actress. In a movie Dex seemed to care a lot about. Maybe too much about. I saw her name in the credits." He looks away and I lean in, doing my best to hide the heart-thump threatening to unbalance my voice. "Is she the reason he liked that movie so much?"

Is she the reason he liked me so much?

"Because he dated her, you mean." Kevin gives me a long look, as if gauging how much his words have disarmed me, and I look steadily back. "Isn't that what you're really asking?"

"It's a simple enough question."

He nods slowly, smiling a little as if something has dawned on him. "You're not asking why he cared about the movie," he says. "You're asking if he cared about her. You're asking if he cared about *you*."

I stand up to leave, but he waves me back down: "Okay, okay. I'm sorry." He sighs, seems to be struggling to find the right words as I lower myself slowly, threateningly, back onto the sofa. "I don't know much about her," he says carefully, looking down. "But it's true they dated once. She's not a very nice person, they weren't very good together, and she left him about six months ago." He looks up at me. "Happy?"

I shake my head. "So why did you lie about her?"

"I didn't."

"Why call her a family friend? Why get rid of the picture, why tell me I didn't see her when I did? Didn't I?" Silence, nervous and tensed. "What are you hiding, anyway?"

"Nothing."

"There's something—"

"Do you want to meet her?" he says suddenly. He rises with the abruptness of someone struck with a brilliant idea and the slightly frantic expression of someone looking for a way out, any way out. "Right now? Will that convince you I'm not hiding anything?"

I stand up, heart flushed with triumph, and frustration, and fear, and anticipation, but none of it in my eyes when I meet his. "No," I tell him. "It won't. But it might convince me not to leave."

We drive. Fast on the freeways, furrowed in our private silences, we drive like we're late, though really we're just killing time—I can tell. I don't mind. I don't mind the wind-rushed uncertainty of our direction, Kevin blinking nervously behind the wheel and not looking at me, not speaking.

I don't mind the aimlessness, every doubling back infused with possibility. I lean my head against the seat, look out the window and smile. Hope he can see me, in mirrors and side-glances, smiling just to make him wonder. I feel it coming back now, a certain hope I'd lost this morning, because suddenly there is a plan, a plan that is answers and confrontations, and right now in this car like a flame, a red shot through the dark, a racing heart—hair against my face, face pressed against the force of wind and all of it building up toward something lighter—a plan feels like enough.

We park the car at what appears to be a condemned warehouse except for the valet and bouncer standing guard out front. Without a word, the bouncer nods us through a heavy metal door and down a long, damp hallway with another metal door at the end. We walk the length of it silently, shoes gritting against the wet concrete. As we near the door, I can hear the heartbeat of a muffled bass growing louder, deeper, as if ready to burst—and suddenly we're in the middle of a throbbing nightclub, starry and swirling, the thrum of the music and the rhythm of the colored lights like something synchronous, pulsing, alive. Down a metal staircase, into the churning belly of the warehouse basement, we walk, it seems, through a dream that shimmers with bodies, sweat, the eerie, ultraviolet darkness of black lights against neon. "Head toward the back," Kevin shouts in my ear, and he guides me through the crowd to yet another hallway, dim and mercifully silent once he slams its unmarked door behind us.

"What the hell is this place?" I ask him. I can still feel the bass drum thudding through my feet, can still see the freaky ultraviolet eyes staring back at me from the dance floor.

He nods casually down the hallway. "My weekly poker game," he says. "Pretty laid-back group, celebrities' kids, mostly. Or people who like to leech off celebrities' kids." His eyes seem distant and composed, impenetrable.

"And which type is she?"

"I think you know enough to guess." He looks away. And before I can ask him any more, he leads me to the last door and opens it quietly.

Inside, the room is larger than I expected, square and lined along the walls with the kind of dark red leather you'd see in restaurant booths. Carpet and ceiling the same rich, charcoal color, the only lights coming from four mounted televisions, each set to a different channel, and from the hanging yellow lamp above the poker table. Beneath its muted glow, four players are finishing a hand, and no one seems to notice we've entered the room.

I scan their faces quickly: all young, all generically beautiful in that way that takes effort, and none of them familiar. I can't tell if I'm disappointed or relieved.

"She'll come," Kevin whispers in my ear.

"Jesus Christ, Erika," one of the players blurts out suddenly: a small, almost feminine-looking boy with creamy dark skin and a leopard-print shirt. He leans back in his chair and lights a cigarette. "It's not fucking heart surgery."

"Will you shut up?" says Erika, a brunette with her back to us. "I'm thinking." I see her fingering the pile of chips in front of her, counting slowly.

"Come on, baby, you know I've got it," says a third player, grinning and tapping his cards against the table. He reminds me of the Midwestern frat guys I used to know: broad shoulders, backwards baseball cap, a wide, flat, friendly face. He reaches over and brushes the brunette's hair away from her face with overdramatic tenderness. "Don't you want to see it? Don't you want to give it up to me?"

She laughs, slapping his hand away, and throws her cards facedown across the table. "Keep dreaming," she says. "And take your damn pot already."

The fourth player at the table, a pixie-looking waif of a girl with chopped white-blonde hair and pale skin, sucks disconsolately at her pink martini and doesn't say anything.

"Kev!" shouts the frat boy suddenly, squinting at us through the lamplight as he happily rakes in his chips. "What's up, man?"

The brunette has spun around in her chair to reveal a sultry, heart-shaped face, dark eyes and a wide smile, which fades the moment she sees me. "Been a long time, Kevin," she says in a low, slow voice, eyeing me critically.

"Too long," he says, resting his hand against my back. "And unfortunately, we really can't stay—"

I watch the brunette's smile fade further as jeers of protest rise up from the boys. The pixie girl just leans back and stares at one of the TV screens above my head with obvious boredom.

"No, really," Kevin is saying, almost robotically, as if reading from a script, "we just came to find Victoria. To talk to Victoria."

"Come on, man." The frat boy tosses him a chip, a pink and gold flash twirling out of the darkness; Kevin catches it in front of my face, and the boy winks at me. "You know Vicki doesn't play on Sundays."

"We see right through you, Kev," says the leopard-shirted boy.

"You came to *play*."

I can feel the change in Kevin's hand, stiff and uncertain now through the thinness of my shirt. He opens his mouth but doesn't say anything, and I see something twitch beneath his eye again and know without question, hate myself for not knowing it sooner: She's not coming. Of course she's not coming.

She was never going to be here in the first place.

"So, Kev," says the brunette, straddling her chair. "Who's your friend?"

He looks helplessly at me, and I turn away.

"Lila," I tell her, stepping away from his hand. I meet her evaluating gaze, her firm chin, and find myself smiling calmly. "Lila Maywood."

"Well, Lila Maywood," says the frat boy. "I'm James, and this is Phoenix, Monique, and Erika." He gestures around the table and ends up pointing at an empty chair beside the brunette. "You any good at poker?"

"Not that being good is a prerequisite," says the leopard shirt, Phoenix. He brings his cigarette briefly to his lips, a passionless kiss, and exhales delicately. "In fact, we'd kind of prefer it if you sucked."

"We already have enough players," Erika says firmly.

James winks at me again.

"Guys, really," says Kevin, still trying to catch my eye and failing miserably, "we really just wanted to find Victoria. I'm sure Lila doesn't want to play—"

"I'll play," I interrupt.

Erika raises a perfectly filled-in eyebrow and crosses her arms over her perfectly large breasts. "Can you afford it?" she asks.

"Kevin'll cover her," Phoenix offers. "Won't you, Kevin?"

I turn back to him and he hesitates, glancing at the piles of chips already on the table. "Do you even know how to play?" he asks me quietly. And adds, like a kind of pointed afterthought, *"Lila?"*

I could tell him the truth—that I used to hook up with a high-stakes poker player I met at the Mille Lacs casino back home. That instead of normal dates he brought me to VIP poker lounges and thought he was doing me a favor. But I just smile and shrug my shoulders casually, sit down in an empty chair with Erika on my left and the pixie girl on my right. "I'm sure I can figure it out," I tell him.

Phoenix waves someone over, and I realize for the first time that a cocktail waitress has been hovering silently in the far corner of the room behind a large set of speakers. He whispers something in her ear and she disappears, reemerging from her corner almost instantly with two large stacks of chips. She hands them to Phoenix, and he slides them, grinning mischievously at me, across the table.

"Hey, come on, guys—" Kevin protests meekly at my back, but no one pays any attention to him.

"We play dealer's choice," Erika says, shuffling the cards expertly. "Double blinds on all games. Greens are twenties, pinks are hundreds." She stops and offers me the deck and a humorless smile. "Try not to clean him out too bad."

"I'll do my best." I smile back and cut the cards.

"Texas," she announces, and deals the hand, fingers delicate and flying.

James whistles at his cards and tosses a single chip reluctantly into the middle of the table. "You're going down for this shit, Erika."

"I hate this game," pouts the pixie girl. She holds up her empty martini glass and the waitress hurries over to whisk it away. "I fold."

"Big surprise," someone mutters.

"You'll have to excuse Monique," Phoenix tells me, tossing two chips on top of James's one. "Her daddy won't buy her the new personality she wants."

"Your call, Lila," says Erika, and I glance at my cards—jack of clubs, four of spades, a lousy hand. I push two chips into the center of the table, and Erika echoes my bid. "James?"

"Forget it." He tosses his cards down. "I got enough out of you last hand."

She deals out the next round of cards, faceup in the middle of the table: seven, nine, ace. Nothing helpful. "And then there were three," says Erika, fingering her chips and glancing up at Phoenix.

He knocks on the table. "Check."

Her eyes on me now, all their eyes on me, but for some reason this face-off with her seems to matter the most. For some reason this is where I feel most like my mother: beneath the threatening confidence of her smile, its knife-blade curve, its bright red haughtiness. Its condescending expectations.

I push my full two stacks into the middle of the table. "All in."

She blinks. A loud yell bursts out of Phoenix, who throws his cards across the table and leans forward, laughing. Kevin is trying very insistently to get my attention and I shrug him off, keep my focus steady.

"And then there were two." I smile, but she's not smiling back anymore.

"We don't play no-limit poker," she says coldly.

"Shut up, Erika," James says, grinning. "I gotta see this."

She just shakes her head, runs a hand absently over her hair. She glances down at her cards, the stacks of chips in front of her, the considerably larger pile I've pushed into the middle of the table. Then she looks back at me and I watch her gaze run over my clothes, down my tight red shirt, my breasts, into my lap and slowly back up again. She looks me hard in the eye and shakes her head again, smirking a little now. "You haven't got anything."

"Speak for yourself." Not missing a beat, and pausing a moment before I nod toward her diminishing pile of chips. She looks away. Chin up, eyes down, tapping her fingers thoughtfully on the cards lying in front of her. And placing them, without comment, on top of the rest of the deck.

I hear Kevin let out a long breath behind me. Heart thumping, I pull back my two stacks along with the handful of chips scattered around them. When I see Kevin start to reach for the cards in front of me, I push them toward Erika, and she shoves them roughly into the deck before passing it to James.

Kevin pulls a chair up to the table. He tries to nudge my shoulder playfully. I ignore him, stack my new chips into their own small pile and line it up next to the other stacks, a colorful wall built up neatly in front of me. "Don't I get to see your cards?" he asks. His voice is falsely playful, light but limping, like a small, injured animal.

I look at him pitilessly. "You show me yours, I'll show you mine."

Whistles and cheers from the boys across the table. Erika's cheeks flame as dark as the walls. A voice from behind us, low and familiar: "Now there's a scene I'd like to see."

And I know, without looking, that it's her.

This is how the camera would cut it: out of the shadows, walking slowly forward as the shot zooms slowly in—with the suggestion of an impending collision, enough so the audience can feel it coming, an inevitable impact—the actress emerges. She is not in red this time, not in silver, not in glowing Technicolor. She is wearing a simple white summer dress, full in the skirt and tight in the bodice, a dress as beautiful and dull as a blank canvas. Scarlet lips and flesh-toned heels. She's grown her hair out since the filming, and it shimmers down her back in waves, rippling with light: I picture rolling yellow hills, wheat fields in the midday sun.

Skin tanned dark, a little too dark. Icy blue eyes. She stares at me for a long time before anyone says anything, and I'm not sure how to interpret her gaze. My mind is as blank as the canvas of her body. The only thing I can think, as I twist the silk between my fingers, is that I don't know what to say if she recognizes her clothes.

"Victoria…" Kevin's voice is a step too high to be as casual as he's trying to make it. "I thought you weren't coming tonight."

"Guess you were wrong." She hasn't taken her eyes off mine, and as she moves closer, the corners of her lips lift up just slightly, as if on strings; there is a mysterious connection here, an obvious recognition buzzing out between us like static. "Good thing," she adds. She walks around the table, nodding at Erika, squeezing James's extended hand hello, and finally taking a seat beside Phoenix, directly across the table from me. "You must be the new girl," she says finally, her words still low with the muted importance of a voice-over. "I've heard a lot about you."

"Really." I glance at Kevin, who is staring at Victoria like he's trying to tell her something. "Can't say that I've heard much about you."

It's not until I look back at her and see sudden color in her cheeks, the taut strings of her face fallen limp and tangled, that I realize this might sound like an insult. "I mean—"

"I'm surprised that you haven't heard more," she says quickly. She lingers on that comment, as if regaining her composure in the pointed silence that follows. "Weren't you Dex's girlfriend?"

A collectively uncomfortable murmur rises from the rest of the table. I feel them looking at me with a new kind of attention, but I don't know how to read it. "I was," I tell her calmly, surprising myself with the steadiness of my voice. "I hear we have that in common."

"I hear we have a few things in common."

"What do you mean?"

"I need a drink," Kevin announces loudly, gesturing to the cocktail waitress. She has emerged with a martini for Victoria: something clear, plain, pure and shimmering as her dress.

"I don't get it." Phoenix looks back and forth between us. "What do you have in common?"

But Victoria just shakes her head. "Kevin," she says, taking her martini from the waitress. "Don't you think you should introduce us officially?"

"I'm Lila," I tell her before he can say anything. "Lila Maywood."

She pauses, drink hovering at her red lips as she meets my eyes, unblinking. She knows I'm lying, I think, and I wonder if she's going to call me on it. But she just takes a sip and puts her glass down on the table. "Lila, the new girl," she says mildly. "Pretty name."

"Don't let her fool you," says Erika, leaning back, and the pixie girl laughs.

"Yeah, she's not new at anything."

"Quick takeover," James adds, shuffling the cards.

Victoria smiles, a kind of patronizing smirk, and I wonder if all the girls in L.A. are as mysteriously threatening, or as easily threatened, as the ones I've met tonight. "A quick takeover," she repeats, and I can't tell what we're really talking about here. If we're still talking, beneath these introductions, about Dex. "Isn't that a little optimistic?"

"One way to find out," I tell her.

She stares at me for a long, silent moment. Then she nods toward the cards. "Deal me in."

We play. "Good, old-fashioned five-card draw," announces James. "No wilds. And no limits." He winks at me, and I wink back this time. They all notice.

"You know, Lila"—Victoria rearranges the cards in her hand—"we don't usually allow actors at our table. An unfair advantage in poker." She leans forward as the bidding comes back around to her, casually tossing in another chip. "You never know when they might be lying to get ahead."

"Jesus, Vic, give her a break," says the pixie girl out of the blue, and I'm too surprised to feel appropriately grateful.

She shrugs at me and sips her drink. "I mean, do we have to get all tense and shit?"

I lay down two cards, wait for two more. "Who said I was an actor?" I ask, glancing up at Victoria.

"Fresh off the boat. I can tell." She twirls the stem of her glass between the fingers of her free hand: a slow circle, a careful swirl, like a shark. "Not a bad way in, hanging with this crowd."

I smile a little. "Sounds like you would know."

Phoenix starts laughing into his cards, but stops when Victoria shoots him a look.

"Anyway," I add, sliding a green chip into the pile, "aren't you another actress at the table?"

"I've been around longer than you have." She glances at her cards and folds, leaning back and crossing her legs with a flash of tawny skin. Beside me, Kevin clears his throat and looks away. "In case you don't know it yet, that means something in this town."

I stare at her, then down at my new cards: the straight I almost made, but not quite. I try to slow my thoughts enough to wrap them around whatever's going on here. *Pretty girls trying to bring pretty girls down*—that's what my mother would say. But I know it's not that simple. We're fighting, I realize suddenly, over someone who isn't coming back to either of us. An empty pot, a memory, the only victory left to see who folds first.

"Hey—you in, Lila?" says James, who has raised my bet.

"No, she's not in," says Kevin. He leans into me, lowers his voice. "Casey, you all right?"

And I hate him right then for being so familiar. So close a consolation prize. For being, when I turn to meet his eyes, almost exactly who I want to see. He blinks, and I look quickly away. "I'm out," I tell them, handing James my cards. He passes the deck to Victoria, who starts to shuffle.

"Stakes are getting higher in here," she says, glancing back and forth between Kevin and me. She is watching him now with a growing interest, and she looks away only when Phoenix nudges her, yawning.

"What are we playing, Vic?" he asks.

"California lowball. Triple-draw, kings wild." She glances up at me, still shuffling. "Know the game?"

"It sounds familiar."

The pixie girl frowns and crosses her arms. "I hate this one, too."

"You know what it means, don't you?" Kevin's voice fills my ear and I close my eyes, try not to be distracted. "Aim for a low hand."

"I know what it means," I tell him. "It means I want nothing." And when I open them again, she's watching me, smiling. "It means nothing wins."

"I'm sitting out this hand," the pixie announces loudly, and Victoria stops dealing, pulling the cards back in to reshuffle.

"That's shitty, Monique." James looks up from his massive pile of chips, which he's still organizing. "At least wait for your deal."

"Fuck you," she says cheerfully into her martini.

Victoria starts to slide me a card, then stops. "That makes you the big blind," she reminds me. "Unless you want out of the game?"

I give her a long look. Then I throw in my chips and wait to see what I get.

We play out the hand, drawing once, then drawing again. A silent intensity falls over the table as the pink and green pile grows upward, outward, a sudden and blooming flush, like roses. We strip our hands down to the barest bones we can make them, everyone trying to shed dead weight, to release their burdens, to come up lightest. By the time we draw our final cards, Erika has folded, followed by James, then Phoenix, and suddenly it's down to a single bet, back and forth like a volley, just me and Victoria. Emptied out, stripped clean, the final call just a matter of degree: Who, between the two of us, has let the most go?

She calls my bet and raises me five hundred dollars.

James whistles, low and long. Kevin leans forward, but for once he doesn't try to stop me. I glance at my cards, at what I've achieved: nothing. I have nothing.

And I know, without looking up at her, that I'm not going to win.

"Go ahead," she tells me quietly. "Call me on it. I'm an actor, too, aren't I? How do you know I've got it?"

Her steady gaze, cool and sure. That icy blue confidence I've sought and found, faked and perfected. *I'm what you want,* the actress whispered onscreen. *I'm what you're looking for,* and I realize that it's true—this is who I've always tried to be. This is who Dex must have seen when we met: the closest approximation to the woman he lost in L.A.

And it hits me then, how much we share, and what it means. That even if Dex did love the girl he was flying back to, I don't know anymore if that girl was really me.

"I know what you've got," I tell her, more confidently than I feel, and I toss my cards onto the mound of chips. "But you can keep it."

There is sighing, booing, cheering, relief and boredom as she pulls it in across the table. Kevin reaches beneath and squeezes my hand. I let him. Because I'm too tired to want anything else.

"I remember now why I usually go home with more on Sundays." James smiles and throws one of Victoria's stray chips at her. "Because *she's* not around."

"Yeah, what are you doing here anyway, Vic?" Erika asks. "I thought Sunday night was date night."

"Canceled," Victoria says. Quietly, and without emotion. "It seems an old friend of his came into town."

Then she looks at me, hard and meaningful, and I look at Kevin, and he's looking down, and suddenly it all crashes into place. This competition playing out beneath the cards. The other thing we have in common. Her open animosity from the first moment she saw me, and Kevin's lies about the photograph, and his hand on her silvery hip in the bar—how he leaned in and whispered into her ear, the way he'd lean in later to whisper into mine—

Finally I understand: She hasn't been competing for Dex. She's been competing for Kevin.

"It doesn't matter," she announces to the table. "I'm not worried about her."

I meet her eyes, a steely blue. "You sound pretty sure of yourself."

"Why shouldn't I be?" Victoria glances at my stack of chips. "She seems to be on her way out."

"Look, guys." Kevin rises awkwardly from the table. "We're gonna get going. We really should get going."

He puts his hand on my shoulder, then takes it off, and I can feel him hovering uncertainly at my back, waiting for me to make the next move. I stand up slowly, and her eyes rise with me, face blank and unrevealing now. "Nice to meet you, Lila," she says.

"Likewise." I smile at her. "It's been...telling."

"Any friend of the family..." But she doesn't finish.

"Listen, man," James is saying to Kevin, "I don't care, but at least settle up with Vic, won't you?"

"It's okay," she says, winking at Kevin and sliding a finger slowly down her stack of chips. "We can settle up another time. I think we know the score, don't we?"

This last pointed comment is directed at me, one final, dead-on shot. "I'll remember it," I tell her evenly. Kevin turns to leave, but I stay behind, take her in one last time: the shimmering dress, the glittering eyes, all blue and white and gold. The dazzle of her, a surface glare like sun on water—dark and deep beneath the gleam. "You're quite an actress," I tell her. "I've always thought so."

"Thank you." She smiles. "You're not half-bad yourself."

"I didn't mean it as a compliment."

She just smiles wider. "Neither did I."

He takes me into the hills. One of those cheesy lookout points where high-school boys make romantic promises none of them will keep. It's the kind of view that opens up onto a tangle of lights and a steep drop below, where his hand on your leg would feel thrilling, dangerous, where you might look up to see, or catch in brief glimpses, the whole world spreading out beyond the city, dark and breathless: a wider life just waiting to be held.

We look out, and down, and up at the lack of stars. We don't look at each other. We don't speak until I feel like I'm going to explode with it, and even then I say it quietly, carefully: "She dated Dex. And now she's dating you. That's what you've been hiding."

He doesn't say anything for a long time. He looks down as if ashamed, which he probably is, looks up, puts his hands on the wheel, then takes them off again. "I didn't know how you'd take it," he says finally.

"Then it's true?"

"You think I *want* it to be true? That he's dead, and now she's—I mean, how sick is *that*?" He takes a shaky breath and stares straight out the windshield, forehead furrowed with an invisible decision. "Yes," he says after a long moment, voice light with a kind of surprise, as if he's admitting this to himself for the first time. "Yes, it's true."

"So why did you lie to me?"

"It's complicated."

"Complicated." He nods. "And everything else you told me—about Dex, about why he was on that plane—I suppose that was complicated, too?"

"What do you think?"

"I don't *care* what I think," I yell. "I just want you to tell me the *truth*. Why the hell do there have to be all these secrets?"

"Now there's a question," he says. "Lila."

I stare at him. He doesn't seem ashamed anymore, though he still won't look back at me. "That's different."

"Why? Why do you get to keep *your* secrets?" There's an edge to his voice, a building anger, and now I'm the one who has to look away. "Because I know you have them. I know they're there. I know there are things you're not telling me, things about Dex. I know what happened the last time you saw him—"

He stops. A hush, a rush in my stomach like something dropped; I stare ahead and down, at the pinpoints of light and the darkness above them, the sudden flatness of the world, as if the sky has fallen through and shattered stars across the city.

"What did he tell you?" I ask.

"He told me you're the one who left." His words are cold now, hollow and unforgiving, and he finally turns to me, and I wish suddenly that he wouldn't. "That you got scared, and you took off. Like they always do."

I look away. I look at my reflection in the side mirror, the truth of it blurred across my face. "You don't know the whole story," I tell him quietly.

"Well, maybe you don't, either."

"Then why don't you fill me in. For once."

But he doesn't say anything. After a while, he reaches for the ignition, hesitating before he turns the key. "Who's Lila?" he asks me.

I shake my head. "She has nothing to do with this."

"She's your mother."

I don't answer.

"Isn't she?"

Silence.

"Look," he says, "don't you *get* it? Don't you see how we're alike?" And he pulls my face to his, a sudden heat and closeness, his skin and his shadows and this space between us all the same pale blue of nighttime light. "You miss him," he says, eyes dodging back and forth between mine. "I know—I do, too. And there are things you want to go back and change, things you want to make right with him, and you can't. So you start to think maybe if you can make things right with someone else, all this will *mean* something. And then you can forget." He leans in. *"That's* what I'm doing with her. Isn't that what you're doing with your mother?"

His breath in my face. The heat of his words, words that seem so right, even when I don't know what he's trying to tell me.

"Isn't that why you want to find her?" he asks quietly.

I shake my head. At his lips, his voice, his everything, look up at him and blink away. "I don't know," I tell him, breathing deep, the cool night air a relief on my face. "I don't know what you're talking about."

I can feel him watching me, eyes delving through the long and painful silence. Waiting. And then he sits back, starts the car and shifts gears, and for a full minute we don't move, don't talk, don't think. We sit there in the *almost* of that moment and let everything seep back out to emptiness. Then we drive down to Hollywood and its nighttime glitter, its impossible brightness, back into the push and glare of the city where this space and this silence, all these wider possibilities, are already a dream, fading in the light. A memory.

drifting

Independence Day. Our last day, our last fight, and our first: the afternoon Dex took me fishing even though he didn't know how, borrowed a motorboat and gunned us out into the lake in pursuit of trout that wouldn't bite. *I should have known*, he'd tell me later, sharp, trying to sting—*so cold, who knows if there's life in there at all?*

But not until later, once we got back to shore, those last few moments without knowing they were the last. Before that, we found ourselves drifting in the burnished gold of an early summer: sun seeping into our skin, our boat lullabied in the rocking waves, we sat in a slow silence edged by lapping water and our own deep breaths, contented.

We'd been dating for three months now.

Things were moving along.

Things were, in fact, approaching an indisputable perfection like some sort of elusive finish line of love, which is probably why the conversation came up and probably why I'd developed a headache halfway through the afternoon.

Maybe I could sense it coming, the rocky part before the end, the part that is always hard to maneuver.

"I give up," he said, reeling in his line. I glanced at him, startled. "Too rough," he added. "Too early, maybe. Whatever it is, they're not biting. Want to go in?"

I smiled and shook my head. "I want fireworks."

He laughed. "You've got a while to wait."

"We could boat over to Wisconsin and buy some now." But he just smiled. "Come on, didn't you play with fireworks when you were a kid?"

"Nope."

"Little ones? *Sparklers?*" I frowned. "Where the hell did you grow up, anyway?"

I didn't mean it as a real question—more a rhetorical point—but I don't think he realized that. He looked down and fiddled with his reel; I turned away and pulled awkwardly on my line, feeling out the tension.

"My mother's favorite holiday was Independence Day," I said finally. "Guess I should have explained that."

"Really?" Dex gave me a strange look.

"She used to say it was the only day we could blow things up for a good reason."

He didn't answer, just reeled in the rest of his line and lay his rod along the floorboards of the boat. He leaned toward me, and I could feel his eyes sinking deep into my skin—or maybe it was the sun, or maybe the heat of saying too much and realizing it too late. Whatever it was, it made me feel itchy, edgy. I rubbed my knee and kept the other hand steady on my pole.

"You say things like that a lot," he said finally.

"Like what?"

"Things your mom said. Weird things your mom said."

I shook my head and laughed, but it sounded empty. "I do not."

"Like you're trying to tell me something." He paused, seemed to be searching for the right words. I shifted uncomfortably in my seat and kept my eyes on the length of line stretching thin and silvery away from the boat. "Casey," he said after a moment, and stopped. "What would you say if I told you—" and stopped again. "Told you I understood you more than you think?"

"I'd probably say you were wrong." I looked up at him finally: the intensity in his face, things coming to a head, and I didn't know if I wanted to stop it or let it build. But I did know there was something there, in the deepness of his watery gaze, that looked familiar. "What do you mean?" I asked, quiet now, caring more than I wanted to.

He looked out at the open lake, the empty horizon yawning wide and landless before us. Hesitating: there were details, I could tell, that he didn't want to tell me. "There's this dream I keep having," he said finally. "A memory, really, of this day before my mom died. She took us to a carnival. She loved carnivals. The brighter and cheesier the better— all those stupid boardwalk games, and the funhouse, the fast rides. She was the kind of person who made everything an event, and carnivals were her favorite."

I pictured a beautiful, sandy-haired woman coming over the top of a Ferris wheel, laughter fading in the rush of wind as she swooped around in endless circles.

"I keep thinking of the last time we went," he said. "All of us together. She wanted my dad to take her on the roller coaster. It made her feel more alive, she said, and she wanted him to feel that, too. She thought about things like that."

The sandy-haired woman leaned against an older, thicker version of Dex. He smiled, pulled her close as they climbed higher and higher—and as they neared the top, suddenly it was my father's face smiling down at my mother's. It was his laughter I heard, as unfamiliar and forgotten as hers. And I realized that while I missed my mother, I missed my father—the way he used to be around her, his laughter and lightness—just as much.

"I think I know what you mean," I told him. He nodded, and for a moment we didn't say anything. We watched two speedboats pass each other in the distance, bouncing uncertainly in each other's wakes. "So what happened?"

"Nothing, really. They went on the ride, and I waited at the bottom of a hill to take a picture. She was big on taking pictures, too. In case you forget the good stuff, she said." He smiled. "I guess I keep remembering how happy they looked as they passed me. Laughing and waving, hanging on to each other, like they could forget everything else. It was like a movie. Like it was too perfect to be real." His smile faded. "Anyway, the picture didn't come out. And two days later, she killed herself."

I stared at him, then looked away. The pole in my hand suddenly felt awkward and heavy, simple and stupid. I put it down on the floor of the boat and reached for him, folded my fingers into his.

"We never found out what really happened," he said, looking down at our hands. "The police had to call it something, so they called it a suicide. But who knows if she did it on purpose? There wasn't a note, there wasn't any reason."

He shrugged. "I had no way of knowing. Dad had no way of knowing."

"I'm so sorry, Dex," I said quietly. "I can't—I don't really know—"

"You don't have to say anything. That's not my point." He turned to me with an intent look. "My point is, I get what it's like for you. Not knowing what happened, or where things went wrong, or what she was thinking when she left. If any of the good stuff was even *real*." He squeezed my hand. "I know what it's like to want an explanation. I used to think that's all I wanted."

"But not now?"

Dex shook his head. Then he pulled me into his lap, smiling a little to lighten it. "It doesn't matter if that was real," he said. "Why am I trying to figure that out? *This* is real. This is all I want."

We let our eyes sink into each other for a moment, his half-smile lingering and the echo of those words like a kiss waiting to happen. Then he held me close, his breath against my neck, and for a long, swaying moment, a rocking back-and-forth moment before I caught myself, steadied myself, I closed my eyes and pretended it, too. That maybe this was all I wanted.

He said quietly into my skin, "Tell me you love me."

I opened my eyes. Turned to face him, but I couldn't hold his gaze for long this time, so I turned away and moved back to my own seat. I picked up my pole and reeled in; he sat still beside me and watched as I tried to untangle a clot of seaweed from my hook.

"Please tell me," he said again, almost whispering now.

I stopped pulling at the seaweed and stared at my hands.

I don't know why I didn't say it. I don't know why I couldn't pretend myself, for a moment, into the kind of girl who could say those words and not be afraid of them: such small words, short words, easy to drop as spare change. But it was opening my mouth that made me feel suddenly off-balance, seasick, as if there were a kind of vacillation involved, and I didn't like this feeling of uncertainty creeping up over my answer, the tug inside my chest as I waited for something to come out—

Closed, open and closed again, like a fish. I looked out at the missing land on the horizon, the thin line between the emptiness of water and the emptiness of sky. "You really want me to say it?"

"I want you to mean it."

Because I can say it, Dex, I can pretend it, I can, I'm good at pretending . . .

He pushed the seaweed clump off my lap and grabbed my hands. I felt the breathless world converge to this, to his hands over mine. "Listen"—he leaned forward, leaned down and looked up past the frayed blonde curtain of my hair—"don't close off here, don't slip away. I want you. I want *you*, I want you to tell me the truth. Right here, right now, what you're thinking." He swallowed visibly. "Because this could be something good, me and you. The *you* underneath all of it, whatever it is you can't let go. . . ."

The air thinning with every word. The crushing weight of them against my chest, my lungs.

"Because I love you," he said.

Just like that, like it was that easy. I stared at him, a smile pulling at the corners of my mouth. I remembered the actress's response onscreen, the safety in a scripted role.

"Liar," I whispered.

He closed his eyes, head down. "Don't do that. Don't. This isn't—"

But he stopped himself from repeating the full line: *This isn't a movie. This is something real.*

"*Stop acting,*" I reminded him. "Isn't that your line? Or is it mine?"

"I don't need the lines," he said coolly, looking up. "There, happy? *I don't need the lines.* I did once, but I don't anymore. This is really me right now and you have no idea what I mean, you'll never know—"

"Dex, don't start that." But he kept going, voice rising, and it hurt, the words like stones flung one after another and I felt my own voice rising against it, "Don't tell me what I know, Dex, stop it, what do you know—"

"I understand, Case, and I don't want to *fake* it anymore, okay? That's what I'm trying to tell you, I know—"

"You *don't* know," I shouted, and he stopped, startled. "You don't, you can't, you don't know what I feel. What if this isn't faking? What if it's *me*? Did you think of that? What if I don't love you back, what if it's not just a line?"

Silence. A breath. Another breath against the stillness, and in standing up to the unsteady rocking of the boat, I came dangerously close to falling over the side; he grabbed me, steadied me, sat me back down and held me loosely and my body was doing this funny twitching thing and I hoped he didn't notice but he probably did, and we rocked like that until the silence seemed worse than the shouting.

"It's going somewhere," he said finally, his breath warm in my ear. "We're going somewhere. That's what you're really afraid of," and I pulled away, faster than I really meant to.

"I'm not afraid," I told him, the air between us coming back into sharpness. "But I need some space."

"How much?"

I let it hang there for a moment and watched his expression, the transformation. How suddenly he was the one who felt afraid, and I liked that, how it kept him off-balance. It balanced out my own lack of balance, like two wrongs making one of us right again. "I don't know," I said. "A lot, I think. More than this," and I could see it click in his eyes, that feeling of a misstep, the slam of your heart as you try to catch yourself before going down. He looked away, shoulders hunched. Looked at our feet, lined up straight and mirrored as a face-off.

"Say it," he said without looking up. "Say what you're thinking. For once."

I took a deep breath. I waited. It wouldn't go away, this angry rocking in my stomach, and I stared at his lowered head, hair ruffling gold in the sun, and I knew. Knew that I loved him—couldn't help it, when the hell had that happened?—and I hated him for doing that, wanted, needed so much to hurt him right then, and I found the line back to myself, the only way out of this: "I can't."

He looked up. He waited.

"I don't love you," I told him.

The words like plunging, sinking deep through the aching, the icy blue, to numbness. "Fine," he said, nodding, looking away.

"But it doesn't mean—"

"Stop." He shook his head. "Just stop." Thin press of his mouth as he reeled in the rest of my line, and everything else I wanted to say knotting up behind my tongue—I nodded, looked toward home, tried to swallow something down. The horizon blurred with a stinging heat as he gunned the motor into the silence. We made our way like that, growl of it shaking the seats, back to Agate Bay, and he dropped me off and he didn't kiss me good-bye and later I watched the fireworks alone. Their shattered brightness, bursting hearts, the beautiful and terrible fall from light to dark above the lake. There were people all around me, and they cheered and ahhed and held each other, and no one seemed to think it was sad. One by one by one, same fading fate to black: I watched them silently until they were gone and the sky was only stars, still, dull, and cold.

what being in love means

On his day off, they went to the lake, and a freight happened to be pulling into port just then. It slid smoothly into the shadowy pocket of water between the ore docks, and his fingers slipped smoothly between hers. They were sitting across the bay, feet dangling off the breakwater; they'd been walking along it, toward the lighthouse, but stopped in the middle to watch the boat come into the harbor.

It's so big, she said, *even though it seemed shrunken now, cowering beside the massive coppery stretches of the docks.* I never really look at them.

They're bigger up close, *he said. He sounded proud, in awe.* You have no idea how it feels, looking down into the hull before it's full. This enormous empty space. Like it takes a minute to understand the size of it.

So how can it float?

It's the way they're made. They can carry a lot, *and for a while they watched the one in port. Slowly, it was filling up. The silvery black stream of taconite looked, at a distance, like heavy tar smothering the hull.*

It can't be that simple once it's full, *she said*. It's full of iron. You'd think it would sink.

That's true, *he said*. *He weighed it, for a moment, in his mind. Then he said*, It has to do with displacement, I think. When it moves through the water, it makes a wake along the sides that pushes the boat up.

So why doesn't it sink now? While everything's going in?

He shrugged. Too shallow, I guess. *He sounded unsure.*

So once it sets out, it can't stop for too long?

I don't know.

Or it'll sink, then.

He said, I don't know. *He smiled. He kissed her in that hollow spot behind the jaw, trying to tickle with his lips. She felt like pushing him away.* I didn't know you cared so much about what I do.

Will it sink, Dex?

But he held her close, still smiling, and he said, Don't worry. They make sure it's always moving, so it's safe, *and that made sense to her.*

second chances

When I wake up, he's not there. Almost like he never was, bed cool and sheets spread flat across his side: an apparition, a ghost I've slept with. An emptiness. I lie there for a long time and stare at the bedroom ceiling, its unevenness, shapes in the shadows like clouds.

It's day outside, but heavy, gray. A storm coming. The murmur of traffic reminds me of a lullaby, humming and lilting in its stop and go.

Will you sleep with me? Kevin had asked. *Just beside me. Just so we don't have to sleep alone,* and against my better judgment, I gave in—because I was too tired to fight it, or maybe because I was too lonely. The reasons didn't seem to matter anymore. Face peaceful and tucked inward, he looked more like Dex than ever. It didn't make sense that I kept expecting to hear the click of the door, to see, through the darkened room, his face coming slowly into view.

I close my eyes. *Wake up,* you'd whisper, and your breath would tickle, phantom fingers on my skin. *Wake up, Case, wake up.*

"Wake *up*, Kevin." And I open my eyes with a start, realize that the murmurs of traffic have not been traffic at all. That there are voices in the next room too quiet to recognize as voices until they swell with volume, and I sit up, stare at the closed door, the words seeping underneath. "—living in a fantasy world. Your brother—"

"Dad, listen—"

"What would he say—think of you if he knew—"

"But it's not like—"

"—how can you—saw you with her—think she actually *meant* something?"

The guilt-ridden images flooding back to me as I listen: Victoria's hands at Kevin's waist beside the bar, and Kevin's hands at my own waist, my back against the door frame and the pulsing ache of Dex's voice in my ear. His eyes in mine on that hill above the city, and Victoria's eyes meeting his across the poker table.

Are they talking about Victoria? Or are they talking about me?

"—can't bring back what's gone, Kevin, and she seems like an easy way to do it, I know. I know you miss—"

Is that what I'm doing here? In this apartment I can't leave, in this bed that isn't mine—am I trying to bring you back?

"—but she's not the way to—I don't know, *resurrect*—not healthy—"

"That's not what I'm trying—"

My feet bare and cold against the floor, voices louder as I near them, across the room to the closed bedroom door: I put my hand against it, steadying.

"You have to let go, Kev," he says through the wall. "You have to—"

"Dad, I know."

"She means nothing. Nothing. Understand me?"

"I *know* that—"

I walk into the room to keep from hearing any more.

When I was young, one of my mother's favorite movies was *The Great Gatsby*. I can see now that it was the era she loved: that shameless opulence, such power given to status and beauty, the lush and deceptive surfaces of a world she saw as more controllable than her own. But at the time, I just figured she was in love with Robert Redford. He had this look about him that I recognized from old photographs of my father, the same look he'd have in later years when I'd catch him staring distantly out our kitchen window. A kind of half-hearted longing, contentment tinged with a mysterious sadness, as if remembering the way things used to be, or could have been.

The man standing beside Kevin in the living room reminds me of that look, of Gatsby. It might just be that he's dressed the part: creamy button-down shirt with thin blue stripes, pale slacks, tanned skin creased with wrinkles and that distinguished, Robert Redford sort of austerity. The balcony doors are open behind him, and with the skyline at his back, a slight breeze ruffling his smooth blond hair, Dex's father might as well have just stepped out of a movie or a magazine, a spread where they carry polo sticks and toss white sweaters casually over their shoulders. But it's also the way he looks at me from across the room. This sad, solemn look like he can see in me the memory of what he's lost, that severed link to Dex that I'm seeing, reflected, in him.

"I didn't mean to wake you," he says, quiet now, slow-moving and slow-speaking as if through water. I can't tell what he's thinking, too much of it washing over me at once — the residue of his angry voice, my own confusion, and this softening uncertainty in his expression as he takes me in. I'm suddenly aware of my bare feet, my limp red clothes, the shadow of a sleepless night in my eyes. I feel like an awkward gash in the midst of this clean, white, sunlit world, and I find myself wondering what he thinks of me. If it was me or Victoria that they were discussing. And why he's staring across the room with an increasingly mysterious intensity.

"You didn't wake me," I tell him automatically. "And I didn't mean to interrupt anything." I glance at Kevin, who is standing behind the wide white couch and staring at his father, tensed, expectant, almost fearful. I can't help but wonder why he's not more concerned with what I'm thinking right now, what I've overheard.

She means nothing.

Nothing.

"Anyway," I add, "I'm sure you two have a lot to talk about—"

"Don't go," the man says, and I look back at the eyes that haven't moved from mine. His are darker than I noticed before, deep and green, mysterious as shadows through trees. "I'm Jack Stone," he says, walking slowly toward me. "Kevin's father. We haven't met."

"Casey Maywood." He leans against the door frame, closer than I'd like, his face unchanging, unreadable. I clear my throat and glance nervously at Kevin, who is still watching his father with an inexplicable fascination. "I'm sorry I didn't meet you the other day," I tell him, looking up.

"Not as sorry as I am."

"At the funeral, I mean."

"You were there?"

"Of course," I pause, uncertain. "Isn't that why you wanted me to come?"

He just blinks as if the words haven't registered, a strange smile hovering behind the familiar jawline, and suddenly I'm fed up. With him, with Kevin, with wondering, constantly wondering, what's really going on. I want, abruptly and intensely, to get out of this blinding sunlight of scrutiny and back away, walk out that door at the far end of the room and give up on whatever it is that's keeping me here until he says, without segue or explanation, "You must be an actress."

A *sudden memory. A black-and-white flashback of my mother's face, those lessons learned in the basement*: Remember who you are, *she whispers.* Remember you can play them, too.

And I smile. Because it's what they don't expect, what I don't expect, and it's enough for me to feel this new character coming on like a rush, a sweet and familiar drug. *You must be an actress.* "How'd you know?" I ask him. Watching Kevin for a response as I say it.

"Just something about you. It's like Kevin was saying," and Kevin, hearing this, finally snaps out of his trance and looks at me. I keep my face blank and let him wonder what I'm thinking. "That wholesome look," his father adds quietly. "You've got a face for the business."

"They've told me that."

"Though it takes more than a pretty face. Did they tell you that, too?"

I shoot him a raised eyebrow, a smile that could mean anything. "I know what it takes."

"Oh, really?" His eyes skim down over the rest of me and I don't mind that, weird as it should feel—I can play the kind of girl who doesn't mind that. I can stay cool. I wonder if Kevin is realizing how little he knows about this girl standing in his bedroom doorway, this girl who could be anyone, and I take a step closer because that's what she would do. She would not be ashamed. She would be aware of her audience, her control of the room, the effect of her performance on the man above her and the man watching helplessly from behind the sofa—*Not so wholesome now, am I?*

That's what this girl would be thinking. She would not be thinking of Dex.

He smiles softly, looking down at me. His body is bowed over me now, almost touching, the moment both sudden and endless: a spinning top thrust full and fast into a motion-less blur. Neither of us blinking, neither of us looking away. After a moment, he nods, though I haven't said anything, and his smile widens as if pleased to see something come across my face. "That's what I thought," he says.

And then he steps away, expression sliding instantly, as if into character, back toward a businesslike solemnity. "Maybe you'll rub off on Kevin here," he adds, and I'm shaken by the abrupt sunlight in my eyes, the unsteady space in front of me. "We've just been discussing…" He stares pointedly at Kevin. "His acting career."

Silence. As if frozen on the screen, the moment too warped and heavy to roll forward without a clumsy pause. I glance at Kevin, looking for a cue, a way to respond to this lie we all know is a lie. But he's watching his father right now, something unsaid passing between them, a message I can see I'm not supposed to understand.

"It's hard sometimes"—Jack Stone crosses his arms—"to watch your children make mistakes you've taught them to avoid."

"Dad," Kevin says quickly, "maybe we should—"

"For example," he adds loudly, "when I know a certain project is wrong for Kevin, a pointless waste of time…" He smiles, but it's a smile that seems more like condescension, and Kevin doesn't smile back. "What do I do? Let him head down some dead-end path?" A pause, a quieter voice: "Let him make the same mistakes his brother did?"

"Sure," I shoot back, a surge of defensiveness flooding through my chest. "He can make his own decisions, can't he?"

"Not in this town," Jack says, still staring at Kevin. "There's not a lot of forgiveness to go around here. No *second chances*. So what do I do?" He turns back to me, moves closer as if to intimidate, but I won't look down, I won't back away, I am not someone else's mistake, and after a moment, I see his cool front begin to falter. A weakening support, the whole thing threatening to come crashing to the ground—

I tell him quietly, "I think there are always second chances."

"You don't really think that." He puts his hands on my shoulders as if to say something important, something fatherly and significant, a life lesson end to this discussion. But when he opens his mouth, nothing comes. He shakes his head slightly as if confused. "Do you?" he says finally.

And I realize then that through the gaps of this businesslike facade he's put on for me, for Kevin, for some unknowable reason, I can see another man. A man who doesn't look like Gatsby anymore, like any romantic character. A man who looks like an old, tired father who doesn't know what to do with this mess he's been left. A man who has lost a wife and a son in the span of a few years. No bells and whistles—just straight-up, simple grief. It's a look I've seen before, in the mirror of my father's face looking down into mine, and even if I don't understand what's being said in this room, I understand what I'm hearing in the silences. That same old echo: *So what do I do?*

"Let go," I whisper.

He blinks, as if surprised by what I've said. Eyes stumbling for a slow, puzzled moment between mine. Then he wakes up. His hands fly off my shoulders as if burned, and without a word, he turns and walks toward the front door.

Kevin springs to life at his back. "Dad, wait—"

"About that project, Kevin," he calls over his shoulder, "that audition you mentioned..." He pauses, turning at the door to size up his son from across the room. "I don't want to hear any more about it," he says coldly. "This is done. Finished. Are we clear?"

Kevin looks down, nods without a word. Jack turns away, but before he can leave, my own voice springs out of my mouth like a hand through water, last grasp at a rescue line—"Mr. Stone?"

I can tell he doesn't want to look at me. But when he does, it's with a softer gaze, a reluctant forgiveness, and I feel relief like a balloon in my chest, the weight against my shoulders lessening. Because regardless of all that I still don't understand, at least it isn't blame staring back at me.

"I'm sorry," I tell him quietly.

He shakes his head. "For what?"

For making Dex come back, I think.

"For your loss," I say.

He just stares at me. Starts, inexplicably, to laugh under his breath. Then he opens the door. "I meant what I said," he tells me from the hallway. He looks me up and down one last time. "You've got what it takes. Be careful with it."

And with a gesture like the tip of a hat—or maybe just a sweep of his hair, brush of the eye, I'll never know—he's gone.

ghost of a chance

In the aftermath, the apartment collapses into silence, a kind of eerie dreamworld, the only thing holding its logic together having slipped past us and through that door. A clock ticks faintly in the background; a breeze stirs the top page of the *Hollywood Reporter* on the coffee table. Then Kevin turns and closes the balcony doors behind us, and his movement brings me back, makes me remember what I've overheard.

"You're probably wondering what that was about." His voice is tight and hesitant.

I fold my arms. "I know what it was about."

"You do?"

I pause, gauging the sudden panic in his expression, and wonder if I really do know the whole story. "Look," I tell him, "maybe your dad's right. Maybe what you're doing with Victoria isn't healthy." I pause. "Or maybe what you're doing with *me* isn't healthy. Is that it?" He just stares at me, and I raise my eyebrows, wait for a response that apparently isn't coming. "Fine," I shrug. I start to move across the room.

"No," he says quickly, "no, please don't leave. Just—" He glances at the front door as if trying to make some kind of decision. "I need to talk to him," he says finally. "I need to wrap up a couple things, but I promise I'll explain later...." And he's crossing the apartment now, suddenly and inexplicably animated, grabbing his shoes and wallet and looking around wildly for his keys. "You'll probably want to go somewhere, but meet me in Venice this afternoon, okay? We'll talk about it then." He opens the door and stands there looking at me as if waiting for some kind of permission. "Okay?"

I don't answer. I look back as evenly as I can. "You're going to miss him."

He wavers a little, then nods as if he's seen in my face whatever he's waiting for, and maybe he has. The door clicks shut behind him like an empty chamber, an anticlimax. I stare at the blank face of it and wonder what I'm going to do now.

Another cab, another try: Dukes 'n' Daisies, but for some reason I'm not as hopeful this time. I think it might be the weather. Hotter than yesterday, sky thick with impending rain, Los Angeles seems somehow wilted, aching to release a pervasive heaviness in the air. Along the sidewalks, palm trees droop like old, threadbare tatters of something brighter, and even the storefronts seem dark today, quieter, blurred. My reflection against the strip-club door is less sharp against the overcast sky, as if I'm fading at the edges; this black skirt and white tank top (an undershirt I borrowed from Kevin's drawer) make me all too plain in the colorless air. Like a ghost, I think. I could pass through the door like light. Float up the stairs and through another closed door: gray, metal, blank as a chalkboard before I know what I'm going to learn today. I could find myself in the middle of an empty room, beside an empty stage, lights only half lit and the darkened eye of a disco ball spinning with the lethargy of a hangover. No music, no nudity, no swirling gauze of smoke along the ceiling. No sign of anyone, including my mother.

"You looking for something?"

She emerges out of the shadows beyond the stage: a girl my age, dark red hair in a teased ponytail and a long crease of cleavage rising out of her low-cut shirt. Hot pink daisy dukes and thin, tan thighs; a name tag, *Tiffani*. She chews loud gum and looks down at me with a frown, vaguely annoyed or confused or both. "We don't open till one, you know."

"I'm—" Trying to get over my disappointment, glancing quickly around the room for anyone else. But the only other person I see is an older woman behind the bar filling a condiment container with olives and cherries. "I'm looking for someone."

"If you're looking for Alan," she says with an icy inflection, "he'll be back at six. He interviews all the new girls. You might want to wear something else," she adds, glancing down at my chest.

"I don't want a job," I tell her. "I just want to look around."

"In that case." She smiles, comes a little closer, and cocks a hand on her hip. "Look all you want."

I blink, glance away, not quite sure what she means but pretty sure I don't like the tone. "Sorry to be a pain," she adds, closer still, and still smiling, "but turnover's a bitch around here, and I need the rent. You know?" She winks and snaps her gum. "Maybe not."

"I'm looking for my—for Lila Maywood," I tell her, blushing, though I don't know what makes me feel more embarrassed: my search for a stripper, her needling eyes, or the fact that I don't know where my mother is. "She gave me this address once. I think maybe she works here." Hesitating, conceding to the possibility: "Or worked here a while ago."

Tiffani shrugs and leans against the hostess stand. I wonder if it's how she greets the men as they walk in: legs spread, chest out, shoulders back to give them the best view. "Pretty name," she says. "But I've never known a Lila. And I've been here since I was sixteen."

I can't help the surprise. "Is that legal?"

"Anyway." She lowers her voice. "Sorry I can't help you."

"Then maybe Alan remembers her?"

Tiffani offers a cynical smirk and shakes her head. "Alan isn't the type of guy to remember names, if you know what I mean. But maybe..." She glances over her shoulder, calls to the woman behind the counter: "Hey, Liv. You know anyone named Lila?"

"Who's asking?" The woman squints against the bar lights, walks closer. "I already told—oh."

Staring at me, blinking with surprise. Her hair is the same fake red as Tiffani's, as if they all use the same kind of dye, though her shirt is a little less tight, her shorts a little less short, her thighs a little less thin. She's got a name tag too: *Olivia*, worn in the middle of her blouse like a brooch. She stops in front of me and folds her arms. "Boy, aren't you the spitting image."

Tiffani shrugs—*There you go*—and wanders slowly away to wipe down glasses at the bar.

And I remember the name.

This woman named Olivia is my best friend now, she's kind of an actress too.

We watch each other for a long moment, considering. "You adopted or something?"

I try to smile a little through my confusion. "No. Why?"

"Well, you gotta be her daughter. Am I right?"

I nod.

"She never told me she had a daughter. Figure if you're looking for her, maybe she gave you up."

"Oh."

My voice sounds as small as I feel, and she notices, steps forward and speaks a little faster. "Not that that means anything, sugar. She didn't tell me a lot of things." It should cut the hurt a little, but it doesn't. I stare at her, without words, without questions, my mind blank as her voice picks up speed: "I got a girl about your age. Left, though, for New York. About the time Lila moved in, actually."

"She lived with you?"

"Well, of course she did. She was my daughter."

"No, I mean my mother. Lila."

"Oh. Yeah, she lived with me on and off for a while. A few years ago. You know, back before she got married."

A held breath...

"Oh." She pauses. "You don't know."

And there it is, the confirmation: the release, and the emptiness afterward like something punched out. "You sure she's married? *Remarried?*"

Olivia crosses her arms. "About as sure as I was she didn't have a daughter."

"You know where I can find her, though, right?"

She hesitates, and in the dim light on this side of the stage, I can't read her face, and I'm glad. "Sugar," she says, "maybe we should sit down..."

what she told me

A woman on a bus: end of the night, beginning of the ride. It's late, or early, depending on direction, trees gliding silently in the lessening dark and mile markers counting down, a ticking bomb of destination. She's headed west, running from sunrise and another life, and for a while, dawn struggles, slowed by the chase: a new day, red at the rim and fragile as a dream, rises up through the bluing dark and hovers, perpetually, on the brink of morning.

She closes her eyes against the wait; but in the dark of her mind, uglier memories come back. The panics, yes, but mostly the numbness, the cavernous emptiness packed neatly into capsules—that sense of the shell, of nothing underneath, floating and fuzzing far out of consciousness and do you know how that feels, did he know, how it feels to lose yourself with every swallow of a pill—she opens her eyes. Heart skipping a little and thoughts crisscrossing without destination, but she doesn't mind the wandering, the lack of focus. At least without the drugs there is the feeling she's all here, her body and her mind tied tight together, never losing that grip and *occasionally those brighter moments of cresting, high and higher above the slow-moving world. She can be anything, she can be anyone, and she feels it most then, the hot rushing heave of alive.*

Sometimes people stare. On the outside, none of this is apparent; she makes sure of that. On the outside, she is smooth hair and smooth skin, creamy, golden, glowing with something that doesn't often pass through these towns in Minnesota, Iowa, Missouri. She feels the lingering glances of the passengers behind her and knows they are admiring. It's why she believes she is doing the right thing.

Eventually, a rest stop somewhere in the blank middle of a blank state. She gets out to stretch, watch the sun breach pink and swollen as something just born, or wounded, and she realizes this is the first time in a long time she hasn't seen the sunrise through a window. The first time she's felt this space all around her, the wideness of the world, her own possibilities unfolding into light like a curtain pulling back, and she turns to face the future in front of her, strung up on the western horizon beneath the white smile of a low-hanging moon—

She boards the bus. A destination that means a role, a role that means herself. And back there, behind, beneath the rim of that glow rising up, her daughter is waking to something else.

"He was trying to help her."

She looks up: "What?"

"My dad. With the drugs. They said she was sick."

"Don't have to tell me."

"But she didn't believe it? That he was trying to help?"

"What do you think?"

"I think…" A pause, quiet. "I think maybe he was right."

"You can say it," she says. "She was crazy. Beautiful and charming and flat-out, nuts-and-bolts crazy, but who isn't? Can't make it out here unless you're a little bit crazy, and I'd say she made it eventually."

In Hollywood, they want her naked.

It's not what she imagined. In her mind, she saw lights around mirrors, pink powder and a soft, upward glow against her face as someone else brushed her hair. She saw red carpets and camera bursts and always, always the gleam of other faces looking up at her, that awe in their eyes like they could still see the crown glittering atop the gold.

Instead, there are want ads, closed doors at agencies, and too many people laughing at the attempts. You? Chrissakes, how old are you? *Casting calls for movies like* Forever Hung *and* The XXX Files. *Photographers who promise fame for money:* I can take ten years off you like that, just let me see a little more….

It's not what she imagined. It's not what she promised, indirectly, by leaving, not what she knows she's capable of. There are characters inside her, any role you could ask for, and all she needs is the cue, the moment, the chance, why won't anyone give her the chance—

In the meantime, she shares an apartment with a woman named Electra who has two cats and a cocaine problem. She was a model until a botched plastic surgery forced early retirement. Now she has a caved-in nose and too much time, nothing to do but buy drugs and shoes with the settlement and nag

*her older roommate for stories, distractions, fictional escapes
from this life that lacks a lens.*

Except she's running out of them. Escapes.

And hope.

And money.

"Which is when she met me."

"Here?"

"Seven years ago, probably. She was looking for a job up
there, but Alan said no way, only girls on stage. He let me
take her in as a waitress, kind of a favor. It was lonely. It *is*
lonely."

"I know."

"How?"

A pause. "Don't you mean Hollywood?"

"I mean when no one looks anymore."

"Oh."

"I used to be the one onstage, you know. They all looked
at me once."

"And my mother?"

"Would've given her tits to be onstage. But they looked
at her anyway."

*She takes the job because there is money and because there
are men. There are rich men, and there are men who act like
rich men; she doesn't have a preference. Both tip well, and both
give her the same glances: quick and appreciative during the
music, long and hopeful between sets when there's nothing
else to look at.*

She thinks, I haven't lost it. Not quite what she expected out of this, her first job, her first independent responsibility in the real world. But it's enough to remind her of who she is and what she knows how to do.

The only preference she has is for bad marriages. She's good at finding them. You can tell by the eyes (blue-rimmed, glazed over more than most), the mouth (smiling, but never cheering, the respectful type), the wedding band (a little too small, cutting into the flesh—been there awhile, time to take it off). These are men who have run out of expectations, and they appreciate anything they can get. Brush of the hip, an extra button unbuttoned: more than they hoped for. A walk to the bus stop, arm in arm: like a dream. The exchange of soft words, soft hands, high-school groping with the difference of time, thicker padding, an awkwardness that comes from body, not mind: It is nothing, she thinks, like riding a bike. But it is enough.

"I don't believe it."

"You don't have to."

"My mother wasn't like that."

"Sugar, no one starts out like that."

"Maybe—I don't know, maybe—could it have been, like, revenge or something?"

"I don't follow."

"She thought my dad was having an affair."

"So?"

"And eventually he did."

"So?"

"So maybe she found out. Maybe it was her way to get back at him. It's why she left, isn't it?"

"An affair?" Laughing. "Honey, it was never an affair."

"What do you mean?"

"Lila left home because she was an actress. She wanted to be *seen*. Nowhere better to be seen than Hollywood, but you gotta take what you can get."

"I don't understand," and she reaches out. Pats my fingers, gently, like a mother; I pull away.

"Men weren't Lila's revenge, sugar. Men were the only audience she had."

It becomes a hobby, a new performance every time: the woman she becomes when they take her in, when she lets them think they've saved her.

The divorcés want distraction. The near-divorcés want a reason. She provides both, suggests the promise of a Hollywood fairy tale: Cinderella, Pretty Woman, true love in a strip club, though they don't know she's played this role before, that it never means a happy ending.

The brokenhearted want someone else—a surrogate, a memory reincarnated—and as an actress this is her specialty, though she never stays for long. To leave them behind seems doubly cruel, their lovers gone two at a time with one step out the door.

She's not evil, after all. Just restless.

There are rich ones, sometimes—old and unattractive, perhaps, but with large, empty houses and bottomless wallets, and these men are especially hard to walk away from. They promise spending money, new jobs, the old dream, another chance; they promise things she knows won't last, though for a while, she'll pretend otherwise. Use their monogrammed towels, sleep in their tailored sheets, let them think of her as their unlikely prize, their investment, high-return. But never for too long. Always it's back to Olivia and the apartment they share now, always it's back to Dukes and the other men, it's moving away from the basement she knows is waiting if she looks back, if she remembers...

chance at the ghost

"If she remembers what?"

Olivia shrugs. "You tell me. All I know is, she never wanted to talk about home."

"Never wanted to talk about me, you mean."

"Hey, don't take it personal." She tilts her head, nudges me a napkin as if I'm about to cry, and I wonder if I am. We're sitting at the bar now sipping Cokes and eating maraschino cherries, and I feel my stomach start to turn, empty of everything but sweet, heavy red. "It's not that simple sometimes," Olivia adds, "mothers and daughters. Sometimes mothers aren't done being the daughters, if you get my drift." I shake my head. She sighs and taps her long pink fingernail on the side of her glass. "What I mean is, maybe it wasn't about you. Your mother didn't exactly act like a *mother*, and maybe forgetting about you was the only way she could—you know."

I don't know what exactly she's referencing, but I don't ask her to clarify.

"Makes me think maybe it's good Nancy left," Olivia is

saying. She looks up, as if to remind me: "My daughter, in New York. Gives me a little more freedom, you know? I could pick up anytime. Just *go*. I could pick up and do all kinds of things." She fidgets nervously with a cherry stem. "Just like your mom," she adds.

I clear my throat. I don't want to know any more, but I need it, a helpless addiction to information. "So where is she?" I ask quietly.

"Last I knew, she was in Vegas. But that was a good… oh, I don't know…three, three and a half years back? Probably moved on a long time ago." She looks up, sees something threatening to crumble in my face, and looks away, talking fast. "Older guy came in one time. Late sixties, roly-poly, not really her type. But she was acting kind of funny those last days—skipping work, nervous all the time, wouldn't tell me where she was living. Like she was hiding something. Like she needed a *change*. So when she found out he managed a show in Vegas—the works, showgirls, stages, said she'd have a good shot out there—well, that was it." She finishes her drink, rubs the lipstick mark off the glass, and doesn't look up. "Got married in his hotel," she says. Her voice is quieter now—nostalgic or sad or jealous, I can't tell which. "I couldn't get off work to see. But that's what I hear."

And I feel it come down to this—end of the line, last chance at the mystery. "Do you remember the name of the hotel?" I ask her.

Olivia sighs, smiles, and shakes her head. "Honey, even if I did, she wouldn't be there. Not one to settle down, keep connections—you should know that. She lived with me for years, and you think I heard from her since she left?"

That thickness rising up again, sweet and syrupy, hot and anxious—*I need something here,* and I want to tell her that, *something to take away from this, a next step, a place to go,* but I can't figure out how to say it, and she's giving me this look like I should have expected what's coming. "There are some people in this world," she says, patting my hand, "when they leave—they don't want to be found." Her voice quiet, her eyes twitching away as she looks deep into mine and sees someone familiar. "Trust me," she says.

I look down, then up, anything to distract me from this feeling—along the walls, around the bottles and the beer signs, across framed pictures of sneering women, signatures across their breasts—

And stop. Stare. Wonder if I'm crying, blurry-eyed, or if I'm just seeing things, blink hard because it can't be, that can't be her photograph over the bar: Victoria Fallon, half-naked with an illegible signature across her body, and I blink again and she's still there and could this be it? Could I be going crazy, honestly crazy? Do you know it if you're going crazy, do you know enough to question the connections you make, the coincidences you find? Or is this a sign, my hereditary connection to fate, is there a reason I'm staring at the sly smile of the girl who was me and became someone real....

"Is that—" I pause, point at the frame, the world sinking into an illogical dreaminess (*wake up—wake up—you're still asleep*). "Is that girl's name Victoria?"

Olivia frowns, squints to get a better look. "I don't think so," she says after a moment. "I only knew her as Baby. One of the headline acts a while back. She left a year or two ago."

Her face changing, coming alive the way things will if you look at them long enough: and the longer I look, the more I begin to wonder if I'm imagining things, if I'm seeing similarities that aren't there—

"She's an actress, though, isn't she?"

"Probably trying," says Olivia. "Who isn't?" She walks around the bar to straighten the picture, which is crooked only once she touches it. Then she turns and gives me a long, puzzled look. "You know her, sugar?"

But I'm walking away by then, backing away, don't know if I know her, don't know if I want to know if I know her because I'm afraid, suddenly, of what I might find out about her—about myself—

"You look," she says before I turn and run, "like you've seen a ghost..."

stripped

I end up in Venice, its streets slow and humid with the thickness of a deep sleep. Tourists wander under hazy skies, aimless, blinking uncertainly without their sunglasses like something just born. They suck at straws and buy things to make them feel better. I'm out of money, and I don't think it would work for me anyway.

It's gray. It's calm, the barbiturate of bad weather. It's what I need to numb myself, pull far enough away from my own mind to stop thinking about what I've learned, what I want to forget, and that's when I see Erika, an uncomfortably familiar face undercutting the reassuring anonymity of the crowd. She's sitting at one of the stations along the sidewalk: two folding chairs, a painted advertisement, purple lettering and the swollen moon of a crystal ball—*Palm Reading, your Future for Five $$*. For a moment, I'm not positive it's her. The humility of that chair, the bored slump of her shoulders—none of it harmonizes with the polished, high-stakes poker player I met last night, and I try to hide my face while looking, edging closer. But before I can turn away, she pulls off her blue-tinted sunglasses and catches my eye, lips parting with a kind of stunned surprise, and waits.

I smile a little, a hopeful truce. She doesn't return it. We take a moment to absorb each other: her baby-blue sundress, strapless, legs crossed and immaculately shaped down to the platform flip-flops, and my white cotton bareness, plain and dull as a sky full of clouds. "Lila," she says finally, putting her glasses back on and looking up at me with a pale blue gaze. "I didn't expect to see you again."

I cross my arms. I can do this. I can do it without sunglasses to hide behind. "I didn't know you worked here, too."

"It's how I met Kevin. The palm reader and the celebrity artist." She smiles, lips only. "He wanted a future and I wanted a pretty face. We traded."

"Have you seen him today?"

She doesn't answer. The breeze lifts the fringe of her hair a little; she leans forward, opening her hands to reach for mine. I look down at the smooth bowl of her skin, waiting for me to reach back.

"I'll do it for free," she says.

"It's not really my thing," I tell her, though thinking back over the past two days, I'm not positive I'm telling the truth; destiny suddenly seems like a temptingly sane explanation for the coincidences I've stumbled across.

She smiles again, wider, and shakes her head. "You think *I* believe in this flaky fate shit? Come on, I'm just curious."

"About what?"

"Let's see." She gestures to the chair beside her. "Unless you're afraid to know."

I sit down, crossing my legs away from her. She takes my hand in hers, which are cool, soft and creamy like clean sheets. I watch her turn it over and back, running her fingers along my fingers, tracing the lines inside like a street map: lost, uncertain.

"You should moisturize," she says.

"I hope people don't pay you five bucks to hear that."

She doesn't answer or look up, just keeps on tracing like she's zeroing in on somewhere to go. I can't help staring at the downward curve of her face, the unwavering line of her pink lips. Her long dark hair bows inward at the ends, as if guarding the narrow swoop of her jaw, a perfectly groomed and impenetrable shell, and that's when I feel it coming back, the envy and the empathy I felt as we stared each other down over the cards: this is someone my mother would have been proud of. And someone she would have hated.

"Here's your lifeline," she says, drawing a long, mani- cured nail over the arc of a wrinkle in my palm. "It shows how long you'll live, and how you live your life."

"It's long," I tell her, watching her finger run all the way to my wrist.

"But shallow. I would have guessed." She raises her eyes and stares at me through the blue glass. "You let other people control your life."

I don't look away. But I relax my palm, deepening the creases, and hope she doesn't notice. "I thought you didn't believe in this fate shit."

"Do you?"

"No."

"Well, then it shouldn't bother you, should it? What I say."

I take a deep breath and keep it in, vow not to blink first. All my blood is rushing, it seems, to the skin on my hands where her hands are holding me. She looks down, traces her fingernail softly through my palm. It tingles.

"This is your head line." She points to a long, thin knife-slash in my skin. "Your mind. It's strong through here, and straight, see? You're levelheaded. Not very emotional, although it's scattered on the ends."

"I don't see that," I tell her, and I don't, though I'm not looking very hard.

"Wispy. See how it feathers off the side? Falling apart?"

My mind fraying at the ends: a string unraveling from two poles to the center. I shake my head, don't think about it for too long. "What's this one?"

"The heart line," she says. "It's how you love. Or if that's too scary, how you let people love you."

"It's not scary."

We both stare at it, the answer of it, a smooth curve like a question mark.

"It's short," she observes, "but deep." She presses her finger into the pleat of skin. "Here's a broken heart. And here." But all I can see are her nail marks bowed like crescent moons inside my hand, and I'm about to call her out on it when she takes her own hand and holds it up to mine. "Like this," she says. She points to a tiny space interrupting the length of her own wrinkle. "That's a broken heart."

I look at the mirror of our hands. Beside each other they look like a gesture, an offering of air. Nothingness we hold together. "Who was it?" I ask her.

"I haven't gotten to it yet." Her voice quieter now, and hardening. "My heartline's like yours, see? Deep. You might not believe me, but it is—it's deep."

I look, and it's true. Our hands, the maps we hold in

them, so different except for that sharp wedge of a line and the broken hearts I can't see. "Is deep a good thing?"

"Depends on the guy, I guess." Her grip a little harder now. "Like anything." There is a low note in her voice, and she leans in, leans forward, and I can see too much of her skin, the gray in-between of shadow down her dress, too much of her at once—I try to look away, but she won't let me. "I know what you want," she says quietly, conspiratorially. "We all know what you want."

I pull my hand away from hers. "What are you talking about?"

"Girls like us," she says. "We're all playing the same game, aren't we? And believe me, you're not the first to try it with that family. Just look at Victoria." She pauses. "Just look at me."

I shake my head. "Girls like us?"

Erika stands up and folds the sign, tilting it inward to blankness: unreadable.

"What do you mean, girls like us?"

"Oh, come on." She pulls her chair into her chest and folds that, too. "Look at me, and look at you. What do you see?"

"I don't know," I tell her, voice fraying a little. "I don't *know* what I see."

"A fake," she says coolly, stopping her folding. "A performance. Isn't that what we're good at? Aren't we all just actors looking for the same break?"

And it sounds so familiar—*Remember you're actresses.* The same old mantra: *Remember who you are.* "I guess so," I tell her quietly, though I'm wondering, for the first time, why I ever wanted it that way.

"Waiting for the right part," she says, looking down at me, "making the right connections, keeping up the right front. I can see you doing it, too. And I knew how to do that, I *had* that, and I let myself fall for him anyway. And everything was fine until you came along—"

I stare at her, the heat in her cheeks and the sinking in her eyes as she looks away. "You mean Kevin?"

"Who do you think I mean?" she snaps.

"But isn't he dating Victoria?"

Erika gives me a funny look. "What are you talking about?"

"I thought—" I hesitate, realizing this is probably something Kevin has kept quiet. "Never mind."

She bends over her sign to latch it closed. "I thought it was there with him," she says quietly, almost to herself. "You know? Something real, something…" She stops, helpless. "Deep."

Then she shakes her head and pulls her folded setup into a pile. "Not that I expect you to understand."

I stare at her. I stand and slowly fold up my own chair. I don't know what to say except nothing; all I want is for her to pull back, walk away and take her confession with her, dropped in my lap like someone's crying baby. Impossible to soothe, to quiet—what to say to this stranger, myself?

"Erika," I try, "I'm not doing anything with Kevin." She makes a scoffing noise and pulls the chair out of my hands. "You've got it all wrong."

"Right."

"No, really," I tell her. "We're not together. I used to date his brother. Honestly. My name isn't even Lila."

She looks up, meets my eyes one last time: cool, impassive.

The glasses cast pale blue shadows on her face. They make her look tired.

I tell her, "I'm not who you think I am."

She just nods. "Maybe I'm not, either," she says, and she walks away, refuses my help, carries it all alone. I watch her disappear into the crowd. I stand in the space she's left behind, look down at the lines she traced and find myself wondering if that's it—the future, fate, the rest of my life. If the end could really be there, tucked inside my own hands: small and simple as a fold, invisible as a broken heart.

He finds me on the beach. Far from the water, but close enough to the boardwalk that I figured he'd find me if he were looking; we sit, sinking a little in the sand, watch families build castles that lean and crumble. He doesn't say anything for a long time, as if he knows that's the right thing to do on a beach, on a sad and cloudy day. After a while, he takes my hand. But it's not the same skip of the heart anymore, same closeness of approximation. It's not, I realize, enough.

"It won't last," I mumble, pulling away.

He looks over at me. "What won't?"

"What they're building." I nod at the family closest to us: a mother, a father, a little boy, all working on the same giant sand-castle along the shore. They laugh, chatter, dig their fingers into mud and pile tiers upon tiers of bucketed sand onto a smooth foundation.

"Why not?" he says.

I let silence fill the space between us, thickening like fog. "I only saw the ocean once before," I tell him quietly. "In Florida. I was really young. We went to Disney World, but I don't remember that part. I only remember the ocean."

He listens, waits. "You and your mom."

"And Dad. All three of us. We built a sand-castle together; that's the part I remember, that it was this perfect sand-castle. It was bigger than I was. But we built it by the water. We were used to lakes, didn't think about the tide, and before we got to finish it, the waves came in and sucked it down."

I watch them make a paper-napkin flag for the highest tower. They're proud, I can tell. They're content; they're finished.

"It won't last."

Kevin takes my hand again, holds it tight so I can't pull away. "You didn't find her, did you?"

I watch the little boy, imagine I can hear his bubbling laugh even this far across the sand. I don't answer.

"Did you?"

He keeps wandering into the waves, out deeper each time before they notice and pull him back, laughing. I want to tell them it's not funny. I want to tell them to hang on tight; you never know when it's going to pull you under, and down.

"Casey," he says, and I blink, meet his eyes. "What happened today?"

"Nothing." I smile a little, shake my head. "Absolutely nothing."

"You didn't see her?"

The wind pushes back Kevin's hair, ruffles the collar of his navy blue shirt; I think I can hear something like thunder, and the air is getting colder. "I saw Erika," I tell him pointedly. "I talked to her for a while."

His eyes shift, skitter along the shore.

"What are you doing?" I ask.

"I don't know what you're talking about."

"She's in love with you."

"She is not."

"But you want her to be." He squints against the clouds. "Don't you? And Victoria. And me." I stop, let it sink in. The sand-castle family is packing up, going home, like they know what's coming, what's about to hit.

I tell him, quietly, "I know what you're doing."

I know how to do this, too.

"And it's not going to keep your mind off him forever."

"Casey…" He sighs. He looks like he wants to say something else, but he doesn't, and we lean back and watch the waves, their predictable rhythm varied only in strength. There are some that recede too soon, barely reach the shore; there are some that roll in slow and steady, that retreat just as reluctantly; and there are some, the ones worth the wait, that hit at just the right angle, bursting up with foam and muscle, over rocks, over sand, over a softening foundation with the strength to wipe it all away—

"They found part of the wing today."

I stare at him, momentarily forgetting Erika, Victoria, the waves, these constant successions. "I didn't know they were still looking."

"They weren't. It was a little south of here. Washed up onshore in the middle of some private beach."

"Just like that."

"It wasn't very much."

But enough to remind us. We both look instinctively out at the ocean, imagining the silver debris beneath, its rise out of the gray. I can't help but visualize it on this shore: a wing, an engine, maybe (*stop thinking, stop thinking*) a body, coasting into that sand-castle like a late landing, can't stop the descent in my head—

I look away, let my breath leak out slowly. "I don't want to know any more," I whisper.

He squeezes my hand. "Sorry. I shouldn't have brought it up."

"No, I mean—" And I catch his gaze, try to say it without having to say it because after all that's happened, I'm still afraid of good-byes— "I mean I've had enough. Of trying to figure everything out, because you know what? The more I know, the worse I feel." I look down, start to pull my hand away from his. "I think…I think maybe I should…"

He hears the rest in the silence, hangs on tight to my fingers. "Don't go yet," he says. "Please. Don't go."

"Why?"

"I'll help you look for her."

I shake my head, too tired to understand. "*Why?*" I ask him. "Why do you care? Why do you want me to find her?"

"Because I didn't get this chance, okay?" He stops, searches my face, and looks away. He stands up, and I stand up with him, think he's going to leave, but he doesn't. He just waits there and watches the water swell and tries to find an explanation. His body is close, his arm against mine. The smell of sea, impending rain, the smell of him, of them, everything rising up to that same old feeling: *not quite.*

"I didn't say good-bye to Dex," he says finally, and in the quickening wind his voice sounds far away. "I didn't say good-bye to my mom. I want you to find her because something good needs to come out of all this. I *need* it."

And that's when I understand. That we're both waiting for the same thing—same happy ending, same good-bye, same conclusion to the movie that doesn't end, never ends. That we're still wandering when the credits roll; that in our own empty harbors of not knowing, never knowing, there's nothing to leave behind. There's no way to let go.

Nothing to do but walk out of the theater.

I nudge his hand. "You'll drive me back?"

"The hotel?" I nod. He hesitates. "But you won't leave."

And I smile, tell him the truth: "I can't." He's satisfied. I don't tell him, don't want to deal with the good-bye of telling him, that I can't leave because I'm already gone. That I came to find answers out here, find something, someone, *myself* inside the shell of someone else, and all I found was nothing.

end of the lines

In my hotel, I become the woman in red. Unsuspecting, he drops me off with a casual good-bye and the promise of a knock on the door tomorrow. "I have this benefit thing to go to tonight," he says. "But tomorrow morning—ten A.M. sharp, right?" I nod, and he smiles. "You can tell me everything then," and there's a funny feeling as I watch him pull away, brake lights dull and pink as crying eyes, looking backwards. A feeling like I've stumbled into something I can't control: I'm not directing this anymore. It's something that happens, a passive event, natural and thoughtless as breath, as sleep.

A split shot between them: her face, turning around, and his, blindly confident. No clue she's going upstairs to pack, no idea what's waiting for him when he comes to this room tomorrow.

"Dad?"

"Casey? Is that you?"

"Daddy, I'm so sorry. I'm so sorry, I never—"

"Hey, it's okay, honey."

"Never—meant to—I meant to call, I did—"

"Casey, it's okay, calm down. Okay? Case? Hello? Are you there?"

Which is what he'll be wondering. As he leans against the door, hands flat against its blank face—I know how that feels, to wait for that answer, but this woman in red, she knows how it is not to need one. It isn't me leaning against the wood this time, bending beneath the silence. Knocking twice. Twice again, and cut to: the unmade bed, empty closet, light left on, forgotten, in the bathroom. The aftermath of something hurried.

"I'm coming home. Tomorrow morning, first flight out. I just—wanted you to know."

"Okay."

"Just wanted to talk to you. And tell you."

"Okay."

"Okay."

"Casey? Is something wrong?"

"I didn't find her, Dad. If that's what you mean."

His body, slumped in defeat, as the elevator doors close. She's not here. There is nothing here, nothing left. There is nowhere left to go but down.

"It's not what I mean, Case."

"But you're wondering. What I'm thinking."

"I'm wondering when you land. That's all I'm wondering. That's all that matters."

"Because I've been thinking…"

He finds his car through the haze of surprise, digs for his key. It must be here somewhere. There must be a way in, a way out of this parking lot, this maze of silent cars that aren't moving, aren't going, are never going anywhere.

"About what?"

"Remembering. How she used to say things happen for a reason."

"Yes."

"Like fate. Destiny and fortunes and all of it—it all meant something. There's a reason for everything we do."

"She was sick, Casey. I don't think we can understand—"

"I don't mean her reasons. I know her reasons now, and I don't….Anyway. I'm talking about mine, my reasons, why I was meant to come here. Because I could *feel* it, Dad, when I left. There was a reason. There was something here to find."

"Maybe there is."

He closes the door. Sits inside, and the shot is the angle of what he sees: the empty glass of the windshield. The empty sky, white with sun, blank as paper. No storm. No clouds. Something has passed without his noticing. There is nothing.

"Never mind. Can you pick me up tomorrow?"

"Of course."

"Thanks, Dad. I'll call you when I land."

"You know, Case, even if you don't find anything—even if there's no such thing as fate, or destiny, whatever else she believed in—you can make something out of this. I believe in that."

"I know you do."

"And I'm here whenever you're finished."

But when the credits roll, it's only a lonely hotel room. The flotsam of a sleepless night: half-empty cups of water, a pilled red robe limp on the floor, torn-up letters and scattered envelopes like shed skins, everything missing their insides. Meaningless.

Except one. I didn't notice it before. One of her letters, an envelope my father gave me before I left, its yellowing shell of paper—the familiar loops of her handwriting, but an unfamiliar return address, curlicued on the back and across the seal...

L. M. 8123 Mulholland, Hollywood CA.

A last chance? One last, hopeful shot as the screen goes black, last clue, last lead, one final twist of fate?

Because my bags are packed. Because the sky's still waiting, heavy and wet, to fall, to finish. Because there's nothing left to do but wait, anticipate a conclusion that isn't coming, never comes, and I've done that for eight years, and I'm tired of waiting—

It's why I find Mulholland with the last of the money Kevin gave me. Why, when the cab pulls up to the cliffside mansion I always envisioned, Colonial-style columns and all, I find myself tensed and breathless with hope. Why I put myself, one last time, in front of a door: the wild dream of it, unlikely but magical expectations, the tightening breath of a climax as I pull it in and close my eyes and knock myself back into her life.

Listen. Wait.

No answer.

I try again. It reverberates on the other side. A chuckling echo, *ha ha ha*, as if mocking the emptiness, and I can't let that go, let it go at that because when it's done this time it's done for good—so I just keep knocking. A steady rhythm, a quickening rhythm. I knock hard, harder, hard enough to feel it buzzing up my arm. I knock until it starts to ache, and then I let it all come out—I pound eight years into that door, slam my empty hand against the emptiness, and somewhere along the way I've started to cry and I'm laughing, too, because it's kind of funny if you think about it from a certain angle—crazy, but funny. Funny that it's me, I guess, that I've come this far, this is truly and wholly and bursting-open-at-the-seams *me* at the door, and the pulse of it all is still ringing in my fingers when I realize someone is turning the knob—

And step, startled, away. I feel hot, breathless, pink-cheeked and red-eyed. So much blood rushing through me, so sweatily and heart-trippingly and ravenously *here* as the door pulls open and a silent, staring face comes into the light.

disclosure

"What do you want?"

The dark-eyed woman in front of me folds her arms over her heavy breasts and looks me up and down. I swipe at my cheeks and look fearlessly back: plain black button-down and matching skirt, silver-streaked black hair and brittle toffee skin. A Spanish accent heavy with impatience: "No visitors," she says sharply. "*¿Puede leer?* Read the sign."

I glance at a small gold plaque beside the door. ALL GUESTS MUST BE ANNOUNCED.

"I'm sorry," I tell her, "but I'm looking for Lila Maywood. Does she live here?"

The woman blinks, as if surprised by the name, then frowns. "No visitors," she says again. "You must leave now."

She starts to close the door, but I step forward, put my hand against the dark, heavy oak. "Please," and my voice, low and insistent, seems to surprise her. "She's my mother," I tell this cool-eyed woman, this doorkeeper to the last chance I've got. "I just want to find my mother."

She considers, her expression softening, lingering on my

face, my hair, the plain blue dress I put on before I packed everything up. Behind me, the wind pushes and shakes the thin trunks of trees; I look back to see a sudden gust send their branches waving in the air. She opens the door.

"*Espere aquí,*" she says in a reluctant tone, leading me into a massive entryway. "Don't touch anything. I will see if he is gone."

I nod, heart thumping as I take in the gleaming ivory floor, the gold-papered walls, the glittering crystal chandelier at the top of a majestic staircase. Above me, the ceiling arches high as a held breath. A fountain in the middle of the room gurgles softly: in its wide, clear pool, mermaids made of blue-veined marble stare down at me with large, empty eyes.

I look away, something caught in my mind like a snag.

"Wait," I tell her, looking back, "whose house is this?" But she's already disappeared into the golden glow beyond the foyer, and in the corner of my eye, I see someone else turning toward me—

I spin to meet her frantic gaze as she spins to meet mine, but it's only my reflection in a large, framed painting. The disappointment of my own face. I walk over to the wall, smooth my hair in the gleam of the glass and straighten the thick straps of my conservative dress. I try to look the part of the golden daughter, the not-messed-up one, the one you'd want to come back to.

The Pretenders, it says.

Stepping away from my reflection, I look up at the painting itself, which is not a painting after all, but a large advertisement for a television show. *The Pretenders* sprawls across it in thick, white capital letters, and above the words, the cast stares back at me with matching smirks, matching guns, drawn and ready. I remember the show from a few years ago. Something about beautiful undercover detectives...

You know our dad's a screenwriter, right? Courtroom soaps, cop shows, that kind of thing.

I take in the series of framed advertisements lining the wall: *Legal Action, Special Unit, The Beat,* others I don't recognize. My eyes catch the glint of a gold statuette in a mounted glass case, the familiar arched back of a winged figure, what I recognize from TV as an Emmy award. And I know even before I look at the name on the Emmy—know without doubt or hesitation, know with the kind of certainty you have in a dream—whose house I'm in. Who wrote for all these television shows. Whose address she scribbled on the back of an envelope before mailing it to my father.

She knew Jack Stone.

Does that mean she knew Dex?

"Just hold on a second," says a voice from somewhere deep inside the house—a woman's voice, a familiar voice. My mother's voice? I can't tell yet; after eight years, I'm not sure I remember what it sounds like. Dazed, I walk past the staircase and toward the hallway where I can hear two sets of footsteps and a man's voice responding:

"You have the invitation?"

"Don't change the subject," the woman says.

He sighs, and I recognize Jack Stone's smooth, tired tenor. "What else is there to finish?"

The staccato of her high heels pauses somewhere around the corner.

"I want to know what she's doing in L.A."

I step closer to the wall and the empty space beyond.

"I want to know why you didn't tell me she was here."

And I peer around the edge, my breath caught in my throat—

"Well?"

At first glance, there's no mistaking her: golden hair twisted back with one perfect strand left loose beside her face, just the way she used to wear it. Hip cocked in aggressive confidence, forming a shimmering curve of black satin evening gown, and a hand resting against the side of her neck as if framing the face she knows will get her what she wants. But it's the face that gives the fantasy away. It's a face I can't see clearly—she's wearing a slim black masquerade mask, as is Jack—but its unforgiving mouth, its cruel jaw, the eyes glinting like something sharp tell me it's not my mother's face.

It's Victoria's.

"I told you," says Jack—they haven't noticed me yet, still peering around the corner—"I didn't know she was here. Kevin brought her. To see how I'd react to her, I suppose. Shake me up."

She folds her thin arms. "And did it work?"

"You know, I'm getting a little tired of this jealous act."

"I'm not jealous."

"Then stop acting like it."

"I'm not acting like anything," she says smoothly, regaining her composure. She steps closer to Jack, slips her hand beneath his tuxedo jacket and pulls herself slowly toward him; I feel my heart kick in surprise as she looks up at him with a smile that makes me doubt she's dating Kevin after all. "I'm supremely confident," she murmurs, lips along his neck, free hand sliding the mask off his face. "I'm completely in control. Aren't I?"

And I can't help but think of her role in *Two Harbors*, realize that's exactly the character she's playing in this furtive hallway scene. *I'm completely in control.*

"Direct me," she murmurs.

A line straight out of the film. I wonder if this is really happening, if maybe I'm sitting in an audience somewhere and watching this up onscreen. She slips her hand into his the way the actress slipped her hand into the director's, and when I hear the soft slide of clothing, the metallic click of a belt unbuckling, I close my eyes, step back into the hall.

"You're convincing," I hear him tell her. He pauses, breathes, as if taking a moment to remember his next line: "I'll give you that."

Believable, I think.

"Believable," he says.

I open my eyes and lean against the wall, stare at my bewildered reflection in the last of the framed advertisements. *Stella's call*, he'd tell her next, and she would smile into his ear, calm and confident that Stella would not get the last word. *Your call*, she'd whisper. *It's up to you* — and my heart is beating out of my chest, mind whirling with the bright golden lights and her golden hair and his hands against it, the strands between his fingers —

You've known all along how this has to end.

It's in that moment that I focus past my reflection and on this final framed poster in front of me. It's then that I see what's mounted behind the glass: the image of two people tangled in each other's arms. The curve of her empty smile, and the bittersweet, searching sadness in his eyes. The flaming pulse of her red dress, bright as a broken heart.

TWO HARBORS, the poster reads. OPENS FEBRUARY 14.

And I think, *He couldn't have written it. I would have known that. Dex would have told me that.* But as I listen to the scene play out in the next room, as I remember Dex's obsession with this movie, his questions and his silence, as I think about the mysteries of that silver-framed photograph and everything surrounding it, I start to wonder how much I really know after all.

"Casey?"

I look up and Kevin is coming down the marble staircase behind me. He's dressed in a black tuxedo and a masquerade mask, like the others, and I can't tell what he's thinking until he pulls it off and stares at me with obvious concern. "You okay?" he asks, hurrying down the stairs. I shake my head, back away from him; I can hear them coming, hear all of this coming to a head at once, and when I feel Jack's hands against my shoulders from behind, I spin around, look up into his face as Victoria rushes, speechless and fuming, to his side.

"What the hell is she doing here?" she demands, mask in hand, looking back and forth between Kevin and Jack. Neither of them answer. They just watch me, waiting, as if for a cue. His hands on my shoulders feel the same way they felt the last time I saw him: heavy and slightly hesitant, confused, as if he remembers I'm supposed to be here but can't remember why. *Let go,* I'd told him then, and he had looked at me with a kind of nostalgic sadness before blinking back to life, and it's that sadness I can see in his face right now as he looks down into mine.

"You wrote it," I whisper. "You wrote *Two Harbors.*"

He nods slowly. "You could say that. I directed it, in any case. But the story was already written, wasn't it? Not much I could change about that."

"What do you mean?"

Victoria clears her throat and nudges closer to Jack. "Let's not forget he *cast* it, too," she points out haughtily.

I ignore her, shaking my head. "You're not in the credits," I remind him. "Why aren't you in the credits? And why—" I glance at Kevin. "Why didn't anyone tell me?"

Jack's hands fall off my shoulders. He looks up at Kevin, face as hard and unforgiving as his voice. "You said this was finished."

Kevin looks pleadingly at me. "I swear," he says, "I was going to tell you…"

"Stop trying to rewrite the movie, Kevin," Victoria says. She wraps her arm around Jack's waist. "We all know how it ends."

"Shut up, Victoria."

"Victoria," Jack says quietly, "this has nothing to do with you."

"Like hell it doesn't. I know what Kevin's plans are—"

"Calm down—"

"And I know what she's doing here, and I'm not going anywhere—"

"I don't *care* about the movie!" I shout, and my voice is surprisingly sharp, clear, the wide, booming sound of authority filling up this giant space. "I'm not here about the movie. I'm looking for my mother."

"I know," Jack says.

I waver, not expecting this reply. "You do?"

"Why else would you be here?"

I move closer. "And you know who she is."

"Of course," he says. "I knew Lila well."

The words sink in. And I feel my voice catch a little, afraid of his answer, whatever answer comes out: "Is she here?"

He glances at Kevin, then back at me, as if trying to figure out why I've asked such a question. "You know she's not here," he says finally. "She hasn't been here in years. You know how the movie ends."

With the woman who chooses a role over love. Who doesn't say good-bye. Who walks away from everyone—from the director, from the chance at a family—cool eyes looking out into the distance and its endless possibilities. A look that I remember well.

And years later, Jack's expression as I first walk into Kevin's living room: that sad, searching wistfulness I mistake for a father's loss as he sees my face and remembers someone else's.

This isn't a movie, *the director whispered to her.* I want something real. This is something real.

"It's my mother." I come breathlessly back to this foyer, to this unmasked man in front of me. "And you. In the movie. You wrote it about her."

Jack glares at his son, who is watching me uncertainly, as if afraid of what I'm going to do next. "Kevin said he told you already. He said this was over."

"As it should be." Victoria gives me an icy look. "Lila's not exactly worth the trouble."

I take in her arched eyebrow, the familiar hairstyle and well-studied confidence—I remember that autographed head shot above the bar at Dukes—and I realize why I've always loved watching her up onscreen. "You knew my mother, didn't you?"

Victoria laughs. "Does that mean you agree with me?"

"From the strip club."

She stiffens a little, but her smile doesn't falter. "Who better to play her than someone who knew who she *really* was?"

"Right," I tell her, defenses flaring up. "I'm sure that's why you got the part."

She starts to shoot something back, but Jack stops her with a single look. "Victoria," he says, "I'll meet you in the car."

"But—"

"There's something here we need to finish."

She stares at him, clearly shaken, and I can't help but notice how little she looks like the actress from the movie now, and how little he looks like the director. Suddenly, she's the one fumbling, lost, helpless, fear in her eyes as she glances at me and looks quickly away. Suddenly, he's the one in control, and I can tell by his smile as he watches her turn uncertainly and walk across the room, smoothing her hair with a self-conscious gesture, that he likes it this way.

She leaves without a word, closing the door with a pointed slam. We stand there in the entryway in a neat triangle—three actors on their marks, waiting for the next scene to start.

"Did it happen that way?" I ask Jack.

"Did what happen?" he says.

"The story in the movie. The actress and the director." I take a step forward and they both take a step, too, as if I've started some kind of strange choreography, a ritual dance of evasion and shifting roles. "Did she really leave you because you wouldn't give her some part?"

"Does that surprise you?" Jack asks. "Her leaving so easily? You of all people shouldn't be surprised."

I shake my head. "I don't believe you."

"That's because you don't want to believe me."

"I mean about the movie," I tell him. "Someone named Alan Smithee wrote the screenplay. And directed it. I'm sure, I've seen it a dozen times."

"Alan Smithee," Jack interrupts, "is a pseudonym. It's the name the Directors Guild uses when a filmmaker wants to remain anonymous." He takes in my skeptical look and raises his eyebrows. "You can look it up yourself."

"Why make it, then? Why hide your name?"

"Yeah, Dad," Kevin jumps in. "Why?"

"Maybe I didn't want to deal with questions like these," he snaps.

I take a deep breath. "Where is she?"

"I don't know."

"You do," I tell him. "I know you do."

"No, I don't," he says. "I never knew. And I don't care to find out now." He looks pointedly at Kevin. "Got that?" Without waiting for an answer, he glances at his watch and strides purposefully toward the front door. "I have to go."

"You do not," says Kevin. "You're early."

"Victoria is waiting."

"So let her wait. She's a big girl." He folds his arms. "Barely."

Jack whirls around. "That's enough, Kevin."

"No, it's not," he shoots back. "I want to ask some questions for once. You've given Casey more answers than you've given me in *four years.*"

His father takes a barely controlled breath. "I have nothing to say to you right now."

"Oh, big surprise."

Jack turns toward the door.

"You know, maybe if you'd *ever* had something to say, this wouldn't have happened," Kevin shouts after him. "Maybe if you'd given us some answers, we wouldn't have had to go looking for them ourselves. Did you think of that?"

Jack steps outside.

"Maybe Dex would still be here."

He pauses on the threshold, hand against the knob. Turns slowly back toward his son, and I can see a hesitation in his face, a crack of light widening in the dark. A glimmer of compassion before the door slams shut again. "Sometimes," he says quietly, "you don't get the answers you want," and his voice is the voice of someone who's lived far too long. "Sometimes you have to make them up yourself." He glances at me and nods a little. *"That's* why I wrote it."

I don't say anything. But I tell myself to remember this, because as crazy as everything else seems, this part makes sense.

"We're finished here," Jack says, eyes still on mine. He slips his mask over his head. "I'm going to leave now. When I get back, I want you to be gone."

I blink, startled by the words—their suddenness, their coldness.

He turns away.

"Wait," I call after him. "Wait, you can't do that." But he doesn't stop. I run to the door, lean out into the night. "You can't just end it like that!"

"I already did," he says. And without looking back, he fades away into the dark.

waking the dead

I stand there for a moment looking out at the night, still and blank as a screen cut to black. Then I close the door. I take a deep breath, press my hands against the heavy wood, and turn back to Kevin, standing alone in the middle of the empty foyer. The room around him feels like a set after everyone has gone home: dim, silent, the story finished, the lights and life drained out of it. Nothing left but the facade built up to support the scene.

Then I feel the door behind me slam against my back, and I'm filled briefly with a sharp, conscious hope—that Jack's come back to finish this, to tell me the rest of it—but when I look up into Kevin's eyes, look down at his arms around me, soft and sudden, I realize I've only stumbled backwards. Weak knees, weak stomach, I take another breath, can't seem to get enough in, and I'm trying to tell Kevin that, but the words won't come out right—

"Let's get you some fresh air," he says quietly.

"In this town?" I mumble, and he laughs, but not really.

We end up on a balcony off the next room, and we stand there at the edge, and after a while my heart stops beating so hard. Below me, a sheer drop stretches out dark and limitless, cut down the middle by a curving mountain road. The city lights glitter cheerfully against the horizon, delicate and sparkling in the distance. They seem impossibly far away.

She would have stood here, I think, at this waist-high railing, and looked out at all she'd come here to find: the lights, the cameras, this wide world of possibilities reaching out into forever, and I can almost feel her still standing here. I can sense what she must have felt, an excitement as vast and dangerous as the plunge beneath my feet.

After a moment, he pulls out a package of cigarettes and offers me one. I take it. It seems like the right thing to do at this point in the story.

"You don't know where she is," I ask him, "do you?"

Kevin shakes his head and fiddles with his cigarette. "I was hoping all along that you'd know. That you'd be able to find her." He pauses, looks over at me with an apology in his voice. "It's why I brought you out here."

"But she lived in this house once."

"For a few months. Right after my mom died."

I ask him, quietly, not sure where to begin, "What was she like?"

And I think of all the things he could say. *Alive. Hopeless. Beautiful. Beautifully and hopelessly sad.* But he just shakes his head. "She was like my mom," he says simply.

"Did she really leave him over a role?"

"I don't know. I don't know the whole story."

"But you know part of it."

He nods, and we look out together into the black.

They drink coffee. Silently, sharing the morning paper at the kitchen table, the two brothers create the semblance of what mornings used to be, or as close as they can get: Starbucks, orange juice, the Hollywood Reporter. *A month ago, there would have been hot breakfast, eggs and sausage maybe, because their mother liked to cook in the mornings; shooing away the kitchen staff, humming over the frying pan, she'd bring the kitchen to life with rich smells and the low and constant sound of her voice, a familiar melody. But since they found her in the bathroom four weeks ago—since Dex found her, limp and naked and curled up like a fetus, that's how small she looked, and helpless—things like breakfast seem too fragile to reincarnate. So they sip coffee and try not to talk about things. They wait for their father, who will sit with them and do the same. It's how they get by.*

When they hear her coming down the stairs, feet padding lightly on the polished wood, they know instantly something has changed. So familiar: the slow softness of those footsteps, the graceful and feminine faintness of small bare feet against the floor. She walks into the kitchen without the slightest sign of hesitation or uncertainty, ethereal in a white satin robe that clings to her thin body, glimmers and shifts as she moves. Good morning, she says, smiling confidently at their blank faces and offering no explanation as to her presence. She glides toward the cabinets where she finds the frying pans, as if by instinct, on the first try.

Their father enters in silk pajamas. It's the first time they've seen him outside of a suit and tie since the funeral. He grins, puts his hand against the small of her back, she whispers something low and lilting into his ear, and he laughs. A real laugh, and a smile that doesn't fade politely away. It's the first time they've seen that since the funeral, too.

The brothers exchange a look. At nineteen and seventeen, they know what's going on, what this means, and the vague inappropriateness of it all. But they don't say anything, dreading the alternative: the silent kitchen, the heavy, helpless sorrow of their father's face behind the paper, as if he might be the next to go.

So they watch without questioning it. She makes fried eggs and bacon. The snap and sputter in the pan sounds like something coming back to life. They watch their father, who is still smiling, a lightness to his face and movements like a string marionette being lifted back up off the floor. The sun through the window is a spotlight on her back, and they can't help but notice how the beams catch in her hair, golden and gleaming, how it shimmers against the white satin. It was their mother's robe. It looks good on her.

Months pass. They grow accustomed to seeing her over breakfast, a comforting feminine presence made up of sounds and smells so familiar it would be eerie if they didn't appreciate it so much. She wears the Chanel perfume their mother used to wear, a sweet scent like orange trees. She hums the same songs; they never think to ask how she knows them. She looks, in the early morning, with the sun coming bright and white through the wide windows behind her, the blue sky dazzling at her back and the edges of her blonde hair lit up, ablaze, a halo of golden light, like an angel—a beautiful echo of what they've lost.

They watch her, and they watch their father watching her, and it seems this room is filled with that light, that lightness.

They catch sometimes, in dark, darting flashes like an underwater shadow, the ghost of their mother in her eyes. Moments when they glance up at her and she'll be somewhere far away, looking past their faces and this house and this life, past the bright lights of Hollywood and toward a sadness they can sense but cannot share. They don't know how to reach her in those moments, just as they didn't know, and never admitted they didn't know, how to reach that deeper place in their mother's eyes. But even this in its familiarity is comforting, and when she blinks back to life, it is again and again their mother blinking back to life, a surrogate forgiveness in her smile.

Besides those mornings, they don't see much of her, just as they never saw much of their mother in daylight hours—out auditioning, she tells them before disappearing with their father into the bedroom for the night. But she brings all of them, occasionally, to Dodger Stadium or to the promenade in Santa Monica, the night bright and alive with carnival music. They play games of chance, buy fortunes from the psychic cats, circle the Ferris wheel and the rides that spin you into a blissfully dizzy happiness. They laugh and take pictures in crowded booths, and this time in their lives is frozen forever in the miniature frames of a flimsy piece of paper: a time so empty of heavy thoughts, so wrapped up in the magic of this woman's spell, a time so close to the life they had before their mother died, that it feels things have hardly changed, and never will.

The next shot would be her bedroom. Silence and gray light, the stillness that comes in the aftermath of a rushed departure. An unmade bed, an empty dresser drawer left open, and the heavy scent of Chanel like the aftertaste of something sweet.

They don't see her for two days. They don't see their father either, and they pretend it must be a last-minute romantic getaway, but deep down, somehow, they know the truth: She's gone. Without warning or reason, without a good-bye, and this, too, is familiar—but suddenly the familiarity of this woman is no longer a comfort. It is a naked body on the bathroom floor, it is an unmade bed. It is a silence that won't stop aching for an answer.

Their father returns with a calm, cool expression and a tall, thin brunette. He replaces her soon enough with a tall, thin blonde, then a tall, thin redhead, and as the years go by and the women get more beautiful, more loving, more eager to please him, his eyes grow even more impassive. He won't say anything about Lila, how it ended or why, and it feels sometimes like she might have been a ghost, a fantasy they imagined out of desperation. A dream that came briefly to life, to bright, blazing color, before fading away in the black-and-white heaviness of morning.

At the breakfast table, there is silence again, cut occasionally by the rustling of paper. The coffee grows cold and bitter. Their father won't meet their eyes. They think they hear, sometimes, the faint echo of someone humming before they realize it's only the sound of the television in the next room.

"We always assumed Dad left Lila," he says, "the way he left all the women after her. Just shut down and gave up like he did with everyone, me and Dex included." Kevin leans over the railing, cigarette dangling from one hand and shoulders hunched, looking down. "We didn't know until the movie came out that she was the one who left him. That maybe the reason he changed after she was gone—became so distant from us, like a part of him closed off and never opened back up...." He meets my eyes. "Maybe it had more to do with Lila than we realized."

I shake my head. "I don't understand."

"You should," he says. "Doesn't it drive you crazy that you don't know *why*? That you can't go back and ask her? Why me, why did this have to happen to me, why did she leave, why did she kill herself..." He looks away, and those last words falter with the fracture of his voice. "I mean, how are you supposed to let someone go if you don't know why they're gone?"

I don't answer. We look down into the dark and the silence, cut occasionally by headlights and the smooth sound of cars on the pavement below. The smoke from our cigarettes loops and swirls. We let the ashes build before we let them fall.

"We figured that's what happened with Dad," he says finally. "He didn't know why Lila left, and we could tell by the movie that he was still wondering. That he hadn't let her go. So what if we could find her for him?"

"You mean bring them back together?" I ask. "This isn't *The Parent Trap*, Kevin."

"No, not like that. I mean, what if we could find the real reason? Give him the ending he couldn't write? What if that was all he needed to let her go—to get back to how he used to be." He looks up. "How all of us used to be."

I shake my head. "Kevin, finding out why my mother left isn't the same as finding out why your mother died."

He blinks, then turns away, brow still furrowed with an

unresolved tension. Heat, pressure, like steam below the surface—I can sense it building up. I remember Dex looking like that, in the boat that last day I saw him, and through the dawn-tinged darkness of his bedroom, that false calmness in his face and all the questions and answers boiling behind it.

Casey. Where's your mother?

What have you got buried in that head of yours?

"That's why Dex was in Two Harbors, wasn't it?" I flick my cigarette distractedly, not sure I want confirmation of this. "He was looking for her."

Kevin nods. "Partly it was to get out of L.A., get some space. When Victoria broke up with Dex and moved in with Dad—well, you can imagine how he took that. He figured Minnesota was a good escape. And maybe, in the meantime, he could track down Lila."

"So it wasn't exactly an accident we met."

"No, it was," he says. "We didn't know about you. She never told us she had a daughter. But when he saw you in town—when he figured out who you must be—"

That recognition we'd felt, that connection at first sight: instant, invisible, destined.

Or a preconceived plot, just part of the story line. The hidden motivation; the requisite complication.

"He called and told me he was going to stay there awhile. That he needed time to get it out of you; how much you knew about her, where she'd been and where she was. Time to build up trust. But after a few months..." He pauses, jaw tightening as he tosses his cigarette into the dark. "It's like he wasn't even trying to *find* her anymore. He stopped calling me, stopped answering his phone, just—gave up. On me, on Dad, on our whole plan, gave up everything for you and living this fantasy life. Like he could pretend it was *real*, this bullshit romance in the middle of nowhere." A pause, pointed. He waits, I think, so it sinks in deep when he looks straight at me with cool eyes. "Like it wouldn't end up the way it did for Dad."

It's not something I've seen in his face before: a smoldering anger, this built-up-over-time hurt churning into hate, and maybe I should try to comfort him. Maybe all we both need is comfort.

I throw my cigarette at him instead. "*Fuck* you."

"You know I'm right."

"That's not fair—"

"Like mother, like daughter."

"And what about you?" I ask. "Talk about the apple not falling far. But then, you want it that way, don't you?"

"You don't know what you're talking about."

"Oh, really?" I fold my arms. "Think calling yourself a writer makes you more like your father? Think keeping *me* around makes you more like him?"

He twitches a little, and I can tell I've hit something, and it feels good—something finally feels good. I smile, nodding, and move slowly toward him, my words quieter now. "Because I do look an awful lot like my mom."

He moves away from me. "Shut up."

"And I might not be Victoria, but I was Dex's girlfriend, too."

"Shut *up!*"

"You got me to sleep in your bed, didn't you? If *that's* not taking after Daddy, I don't know what is."

"I mean it, Casey," but there's nowhere to go now; he's

pressed himself into a corner of the balcony, rising up on his hands, leaning back into the open air. "Please stop," he says, looking down at me, so close I can feel the warmth of him spreading through my chest, the thud of his heart against my shirt. We're almost there, we're up so high, and I smile, lean in—

"You're everything he wants you to be."

He blinks.

"You're nothing," I whisper, "but an actor."

A beat. And another. A feeling like spinning, hovering, peaking, perched on the crest of something and anything can happen—until his hand slips and his body jerks backwards into empty space, both of us sensing that sheer drop beneath us, and my hands are out and pulling him toward me, against me, stilled and steady before I realize consciously that he's started to fall—and our hearts on the same rough beats, our eyes stuttering panicked into each other's, and down. "Let's just..." I take a deep breath. "Let's just go inside."

But he shakes his head, hangs on to the railing, and all I can feel now is the empty space behind him, waiting. "Not yet," he says. "I want this done," voice thick but dull, hands loosening their hold. "Don't you want this done?"

"Kevin—"

"I want to tell you everything, and then it'll be done."

"Please. I've had enough." I hold out my hand, and he stares at it, hesitating. Then he turns around, looks out into the fall, and doesn't say anything for a long time.

The air stilled. The still night. The whole story surging up to this point, and stopping.

"He was going back to tell you the truth," Kevin says finally. "You should know that."

I move closer to him, his voice so quiet, I can hardly hear the words.

"He didn't care anymore about finding Lila. He wanted you." Almost a whisper. "All he cared about was you."

His shoulders slump; mine stiffen, the weight of confirmation bearing down. "So I did put him on that plane...."

"No," he says quickly, looking up. "No, you don't understand. I had to stop him. He was going back to find you, going to tell you everything, the whole plan." Searching my face for comprehension, or maybe forgiveness: "Don't you see, that would have *ruined* it. What if he scared you away? What if he lost you, lost what you knew..."

"But you didn't stop him," I tell him, confused. "He was on the plane."

"I—I never—" He catches his breath, and he's crying a little now; I start to move closer, but he shakes his head, squeezing the railing tighter. "I don't even remember what I said," he murmurs. "I try sometimes to remember, but it's like trying to remember a dream or something. The way you only remember pieces, and time moves so fast..." He closes his eyes, then opens them again. "I know it lasted awhile. The fight. Must've been hours, which was the point—long enough that he missed his plane. I thought that would be enough, give him time to think about it and change his mind. But he didn't. He called me from the airport. Told me he was taking the red-eye back and maybe we could talk later." Something breaking, splitting his voice in two—he looks up, lets out a shattered sound that isn't a laugh, or a sigh, or a sob, but close. "See?"

And I do. I look into his eyes and see myself there, looking back.

"I hung up on him," he says. "I think sometimes I didn't and maybe I dreamt that, but I did. I did that." He laughs again, almost. "Don't you get it? I can't stop looking for her. He died because I wouldn't let him stop. Finding her—it's the point to all this, it's the reason this happened." And he leans into the night: its yawning openness, its aching emptiness, deep and dark, a sigh of release...

"If I can't find her," he whispers, "then *I'm* the reason."

And I don't know how it happens, when it happens. When he comes away from the edge, his body folding into mine, the heavyhearted stillness of a perfect anticlimax, and the memory of something he told me once, that first night I met him as he pried my hands from the steadying door frame—"You're not the reason," I tell him. "And she's not the reason. There doesn't have to be a reason," and I let his face fall into my neck, the hot sound of his sobs filling the air, slowing, sighing toward a gradual calm. We stand there like that for a long time, and in the distance, the storm is beginning to disperse without breaking. I watch the clouds slowly gather and glide, their plushness like a curtain pulling back and the storyboard of night, dark and starry, coming into view.

After a while, he pulls away, but not very far. He squeezes my hands softly, uncertainly, like a question. I look up, his face so close to mine, so close to what I want, that question in his eyes as we catch the same breath—

And I shake my head. Because I know deep down he's not what I'm missing, and he blinks, looks past me, steps awkwardly away. He turns back to the railing, considering something; I hover nearby, watching him watch the cars moving below.

"It's like the silence gets so loud," he says finally. His face is calmer now, his voice calm, clear as the night sky, quiet as the rest of the world. "Loud enough you think you'll go crazy. Like you're already going crazy. It's like—"

I move closer.

"Like all I can think of is what I didn't say."

Because I know that kind of silence. He bends into it, looking down again, leaning farther, hanging on. "He told me to let go," he says. "The last thing he said on the phone. Told me to get some help and forget about Mom, forget about Lila. Stop trying to make Dad into who he used to be. Just move on, he said. No point trying to fix the past."

I rest my hand next to his, put us both on the edge. "Do you think he was right?"

"Do you?"

We watch the cars move toward us and away. White lights to red and fading around corners: everyone seems to be going somewhere.

"I wonder sometimes what it'd be like," he says. "If I could just let go." Squeezing the railing, that dark bone of cool iron.

And I put my hand on top of his. "Me, too," I tell him.

"So what do we do?"

My palm over his, our roles reversed. I remember his hands over mine on the threshold of his apartment, the world blurring, rocking, shaken. *Let go, let go*—the inevitable fall. But I'm not so unsteady this time. This time when my hand slips away, I know what I'm doing, certain and heavy with the knowledge of what I can sense, and what he doesn't see coming. A half step backwards, and another. He looks up, meets my eyes, and I feel it spinning out between us, all the good-byes we've never said tangled up into a single thread, and loosening.

I can see it in his face. He understands, and he does not understand: There is no other way for this to end.

"Because I'm not Dex." He looks away, mouth hard, hard tone to his voice. "Is that it?"

I don't answer.

"I'm not enough."

"Kevin—"

"Because you could stay," he says quickly. "With me. We could fix this, we could figure it out." His body taut with hope, or expectation, or fear. "We could fix it together," he says, and I feel the pull of his words, the familiar seduction of not being alone. His arms out and empty, easy as an open door.

"Stay," he whispers.

I pause. I let the wind drag away the desperate echo of his voice, the thrum of my heart a nervous dance, and when I turn to face him, he's watching me, waiting. "It's like Dex said," I tell him. "You can't fix the past, right?" I shake my head, try to smile, to soften it. "I'm not what you want, Kevin. *She's* not what you want." And the improbable lightness of the thought, the heart-stop truth of it: "Finding her isn't going to change anything."

He doesn't look away. He's quiet for a long time. Then he turns back to the railing, and the loosening line of his mouth, its release, fear smoothing toward a softer resignation, makes me think he knows what I mean. For a moment, I don't move, don't speak. I stand beside him and take everything in: the endlessness beneath us, the glittering city, and beyond that, the wider and darker mystery of whatever tomorrow might be. Because I know, once I'm gone, there are things I will forget. Details slipping quick and quiet as shadows at my back, lessening, lightening as I move away, and this isn't a moment I want to lose. I want to remember this, the gathering rush of it, so close to a memory already—as if I've been here before, here at this edge of letting go—

good-byes without good-byes

We went to the water to do it, though I didn't understand why. I'd never seen my grandmother outdoors in all my life, so it made sense to leave her where she was, safe in that blue ceramic jar on our mantel. She'd been in there for over a year now; she seemed content. Scattering her in the lake struck me, in contrast, as an idea she wouldn't have liked—and secretly, I didn't like it much, either. I liked her up there on the mantel where, in my gutsy moments, I could lift the lid off and peek inside at what were supposed to be ashes but looked more like baby teeth—small, pearly somethings worn down to beads. I liked the horrible beauty of it, the chill of knowing this was what I would become someday. Like it made me that much more alive.

She picked me up from school. I should have known then. My mother never picked me up, didn't go outside at all these days, but there she was when I walked out to walk home, waving at me from across the street, so out of context it took me a moment to recognize her. Dressed in a pink dress with little red flowers, faraway smile, a blue jar in her hand and her hair billowed out in gold-glossy waves: It's a special day, *she told me as I got closer. Her eyes were bright and blinking rapidly, as if she hadn't seen the sun in a long time.* We're saying good-bye today. *She held up the jar.*

I looked skeptically at her, at my grandmother encased in blue ceramic. Why?

Don't say it like that. You should be excited. This means something; aren't you excited? Anyway, *she said brightly, taking my hand and leading me down the sidewalk,* I thought it would make things easier. It's what people do, *she said,* when it's time to move on.

And we walked. Through the few children who had stayed at school until dinnertime—I'd had a tryout that day for some play I never went back to, though I ended up getting the part—past unsure second glances and unmistakable stares of recognition until we were on a quieter street walking the long way home. Our shadows lengthening beside us and pulling away; already the sun was starting its sink, the endless days of summer contracting into themselves like something dying.

Miss Shaner said I had poise, *I told her, trying not to look at the jar in her other hand.* She said I had natural talent.

Naturally.

I think I'll get the part. It's a murder mystery. I'll be the murderess, *I added. I thought the word sounded wealthy, full of glamour and mystique.* I have to hide it, though. You can come and see. It's the star role, but no one knows it till the end, when they find out it's me.

She offered a thin smile of approval, but her face seemed different now, stiff and far away; we passed our turn, kept walking, and that's when I knew not to talk, not to ask questions. I took her hand instead. She didn't pull away for a long time, not until we reached the lake and the empty harbor, breezy, clear, and glittering restlessly in the late-day sun.

I hope you understand, she said, slowing a little as we made our way down. She looked blankly out at the water, talking to me and not quite talking to me. It's just something I need to do.

And by then I'd figured it out. When Ellie's stepdad died, he'd wanted his ashes spread over his family's farm in Aitkin, and someone in my class had talked a long time once about how he wanted to be dumped from a plane over the ocean if he never got to see it. I knew why she was carrying the blue jar. What I didn't understand was the why of the why, why after all this time, why today...

She stopped. We'd gotten down to the shore, the rocky bank opposite the docks, and for a moment, she stared at the length of the breakwater: long straight stretch, slight turn halfway down, and the rest of it leading up to the lighthouse in the distance. I'd never noticed before how much it looked, from this angle, like a giant body spread out beneath our feet—concrete blank as bones, the bent elbow of the curve, a long, thin arm floating in the water and beckoning us, challenging us, with one glowing finger, to make it to the end.

Realizing: This is the heart we're standing on. This is the hollow space you lie down in before you go to sleep.

You ready for this?

I looked up, hesitating. And then we can go?

Sure.

And you can teach me how to hide it? Because the audience can't know. That I killed someone, I mean. I need to hide it till the end.

Well, that's easy. She looked outward, away, arms cradling

the jar like a baby. The secret, *she said,* is to hide it from yourself. Bury it down deep and forget. If you can hide it from yourself...

If you can pretend it went another way?

Looking down, halo of the sun around her face. It's like it never happened.

Like lie detectors, huh?

Exactly. Might even surprise yourself in the end. *She touched my shoulder briefly: tender, awkward.* When you find out you were wrong the whole time.

That makes sense. *Nodding, squinting, the world slivering down to blinding brightness.* I guess.

Good. So let's do this, huh? *And before I could answer, she started walking down the breakwater, long legs striding fast, faster, striding with a purpose I didn't understand. That distance, as I tried to follow, already yawning between us: the pink dress, the red and the gold, everything like a sunset slipping down and deep before I had time to take it in —*

"Think you'll ever come back?" His voice from behind, my foot out the door. I turn and he's watching me there from the edge with an expression that is not hope, that is not longing or panic or desperation. That is just simply and perfectly sad.

"Maybe." I smile, shaking my head. "Someday. When I make my own story."

He nods and looks back at the skyline. "Think you'll ever find her?"

But when I picture her face, picture how it would be, there's nothing there, nothing to see. It's looking into a mirror. It's looking into a mirror and expecting something to change before you realize maybe it already has.

"I don't think," I tell him, turning away, "she's who I'm looking for anymore."

When I reach her at the end, she's leaning over the railing, looking down. She doesn't look away from the water, doesn't seem to remember I'm here with her, and it takes me a moment, breathless, sweaty, watching her empty arms heave on the same beats as mine, to realize the jar is gone. That she's dropped it over without ceremony, without me—a plunk beneath the surface. An unskipped stone, no dance or display.

I missed it? I lean against the railing beside her, catch my breath, looking down: nothing but my own reflection looking back. You didn't wait. You didn't let me see it.

She looks up, but not at me. She looks out across the lake, away from the docks, the blank stretch of horizon like the world creased to a single line: blue and gold, sun and water, mingling, for a moment, in the glitter of crossing over. At our feet, shadows lengthen, tumble off the side and fade away against the surface.

It's like the ocean, she says quietly. You can almost pretend it's the ocean, see? And you can if you look east, away from land and sunset. The wideness of water like the wideness of tomorrow, coming in already with a deeper blue. I bet she would have liked that.

You mean Grandma?

Yes.

I don't think she cares, Mom.

To be somewhere without limits. She would have liked it.

I wait for something else. I wait for something to happen. Mom? And she meets my eyes, finally. A curious look, like she's not quite sure what I'm doing here. Why didn't you let me see?

For a moment, she keeps her eyes in mine. For a moment, she takes me in, longer than she's let herself in a long time. She smiles a little, a half-smile, wistful; there's something nostalgic here I'm missing, as if she's projected herself into tomorrow already, the bus ride she'll take, just a few hours away, the slip of a photograph from her fingers as she leaves it beside my bed, and all of it is in her face right now, a memory of what hasn't happened. The bittersweet forgetfulness of leaving: I see it building up, shining in her eyes and close to spilling, a glassiness I mistake for loss. The loneliest kind of love.

I take her hand, and she lets me, and she pulls me close without warning or reason. Sometimes this is the only way to do it, *she whispers.* Good-byes without good-byes, no drawing it out. Sometimes it's easier to let go fast when you know that's what you have to do.

I feel her gaze drifting along the surface. I wonder if she's looking for what I'm looking for—a ripple of residue, clue in the waves, some sign that it happened here, that it's over and done. But all I can see is my own reflection.

Remember that, *she tells me.*

And I think of where she must be by now, picture it like a feeling: the bottom of something deep and blue, cold and quiet, where neither of us will ever see her again.

And I'm glad to be here in the light.

fade in

"You'll be here when it's over?"

That first day, his mysterious smile. Hesitant, he paused before the theater door, looking back, fumbling nervously with his ticket stub. "I'll be here," I told him. Felt our smiles bloom at the same time. And when he disappeared into the black, leaving me only the echo of his words—the cinema of memory, seed of a love story—a smile still ghosted the corners of my lips. I watched the sky stretch blue to red beyond the windows in the lobby. I watched the sun move patterns across the floor, coiled ropes of light uncoiling, a rescue line I was meant to follow.

You'll be here when it's over?

I didn't know then what he was asking. But I knew my answer, knew the lightness rising, swelling, the hum of my body like something waking up. I knew, I recognized, the feeling of a beginning: *I'll be here.* The echo of my own words. I could feel them in my chest, the beat of a promise— they were my heart, my hope. They were a happy ending before the beginning came. And maybe, in a way, they still are.

acknowledgments

Writing might be a solitary act, but the creation of this book was not. I am tremendously indebted to the following people, who brought this story to the light of day and kept me afloat in the process of writing it:

Thanks, first and foremost, to my friends and family for their love and encouragement. I am so fortunate that the dilemmas and dysfunctions that complicate the relationships in this novel were in no way inspired by personal experience. I am even more fortunate that at the end of the day, I have such supportive, fun-loving, and individually amazing people to share my life with.

My incredible agent, Alex Glass, brought to the table an energy and dedication I never could have imagined, let alone hoped for as a first-time novelist. He has supported me through every part of this process, from the creative to the professional, and I am so grateful for his advice and friendship.

Endless thanks to everyone at Harcourt for their commitment to this book, but especially to Jen Charat, my extraordinary editor, who took on this story with enthusiasm and shaped it, with her perceptive questions and dead-on instincts, into what it has become.

Thank you to those at Princeton who lent their guidance and assistance at the earliest and most crucial stages, especially Edmund White, Joyce Carol Oates, A. Scott Berg, and Hilary Rubin.

And last, but in no way least, the most heartfelt of thanks to Stephen Schwandt—for believing in this book, and in me, from the beginning.